ONCE IN A BLUEBONNET MOON

TRUE HEARTS OF TEXAS
BOOK TWO

K.S. JONES

WOLFPACK
PUBLISHING
— EST 2013 —

Once in a Bluebonnet Moon
Paperback Edition
Copyright © 2023 K.S. Jones

Wolfpack Publishing
9850 S. Maryland Parkway, Suite A-5 #323
Las Vegas, Nevada 89183

wolfpackpublishing.com

Paperback ISBN 978-1-63977-984-0
eBook ISBN 978-1-63977-983-3
LCCN 2023932566

Dedicated To

My sister, Kathleen

For a lifetime of love, trust, and friendship.

ACKNOWLEDGMENTS

With gratitude to Richard Lee Jones for tolerating my quirks and craziness while I write my beloved books; to Jenn Brown for always being my incredible first reader; Sheri Groom and Barbara Rettig for their amazing friendship and constant support; Michelle Ferrer for her ever-present guidance, advice, and friendship; Lanita (Red) Joramo for being my sanity in a year that had none; and to Debra and Daniel Gifford for sharing the real Addy and Thabo with me. Most of all, a very special acknowledgment and genuine thank you to my remarkable daughter-in-law, Jane Capstick Jones, for her expert guidance as a female pilot in today's airline industry. Any errors in accuracy or authenticity are wholly my own.

ONCE IN A BLUEBONNET MOON

CHAPTER 1

A ddy Piper stood at the wall of mailboxes in the lobby of her Uptown Dallas apartment building. The stark white envelope, addressed to her, bore the all too familiar red, white, and blue emblem. She didn't need to open it. She already knew what it said. She'd been cut. Furloughed. On the wrong side of seniority. She was a pilot without a plane.

The elevator took her to the tenth floor where her own internal autopilot guided her down the hall to her rented corner apartment. She unlocked the door and then opened it barely a crack, just enough to slide her hand into the dark apartment and click the switch for the dimmest light.

Clutching the letter, Addy pushed open the door. She walked through the softly lit living room, drawn to the floor-to-ceiling windows like a moth to flame, and stared out at the myriad of lights, energizing an already vibrant city at night.

Rumors of the upcoming furlough had spread like wildfire, but she was so close to the magic seniority number she'd hoped she would be spared. No such luck.

When her phone rang, she didn't answer. In fact, she never bothered to look at the screen to see who was calling. Instead, she went to the kitchen, pulled a bottle of chilled Pinot Grigio from the built-in wine cooler, and poured herself a glass.

DAYBREAK BURST THROUGH THE EAST-FACING WALL of windows in Addy's bedroom—a thing she loved even more than the nightscape view from her living room. An alarm clock was never needed on her days off— sunrise was always enough to wake her. *Days off.* She threw back the sheets and sat up. Her days off felt permanent now.

Addy went to her white leather sofa with a stoneware mug full of coffee and sat cross-legged, feet tucked up under her, and opened the envelope. *So formal.* After reading, she refolded the letter and then reached for her phone. She tapped the most frequently called number at the top.

"Hey, Erin," Addy said when a groggy female answered. "Did you get a letter?" She fingered the envelope, almost offended by the low-quality paper stock used to dismiss her.

"Yeah, yesterday. You?"

"Yeah." Her voice dropped. "I was wondering if you've heard any rumors about how long it might last. I don't have much in savings to tide me over."

"Me, neither," Erin said. "I've been having way too much fun spending it. Speaking of which, do you remember Jared? The guy I was dating when we passed our checkrides?"

"Maybe." Becoming first officers seemed so long ago. "Was he the older guy? Graying?"

"That's him." Erin chuckled. "But his hair is platinum, not gray. And he's not *that* much older. Anyway, I called him last night. He offered me a job flying for his tour company in who-knows-where Alaska." She hesitated. "Addy, I think I might take it. Do you want me to see if he has a place for you too?"

"Instead of waiting this out?" Addy asked. "Erin, I don't know. It's *Alaska*, for God's sake. We're city girls. There's nothing to do up there. You'll be bored to death in two weeks."

"You might be surprised what a girl can do for entertainment on long, cold days in the dark." She laughed.

Erin had always taken everything in stride—they were nothing alike in that arena.

"No, but thanks. Let me know what you decide, okay?"

Not only had she lost her job, but her best friend was leaving.

Addy sipped her cooling coffee then picked up the phone again. Her coworker Lindsey was rational, logical, and she had a good intelligent head on her shoulders.

"Hi, Addy," Lindsey answered by caller ID. "Did you get a letter too?"

"Afraid so. Any thoughts on what you'll do while we wait it out?"

"I can't wait it out, Addy. I'm a lot lower on the seniority list than you. Mom and I talked last night, and I think I'm going home to California. She said I could move in with her while I look for another job. There are lots of smaller airlines with hubs at LAX, and some of them are hiring."

Falling back on family wasn't an option for Addy. She was an only child whose parents had died in a plane crash when she was seventeen, and neither parent had siblings. She'd never known a family structure like her friends had with aunts, uncles, or cousins, and both sets of her grandparents had passed away long before her teen years.

"What about you?" Lindsey asked.

"I'm not sure." Addy scanned her apartment. Her beloved haven. "My rent is paid through the month, but my lease is up. Last week, I got a second notice reminding me to stop by the office. I should have done it then. Procrastination never pays. There's probably no way they'll renew my lease without a job now."

"I'd ask you to come stay with me in California, but Mom only has a one bedroom. I'll be sleeping on a pullout as it is."

"That's okay, Lins," Addy said. "You know me. I'm kind of a loner anyway."

The August air was already eighty degrees, and noon was still an hour away when Addy went to the leasing office. She stood outside, one hand poised on the door handle, and ran the fingers of her free hand through her blonde pixie cut, sweeping aside her long, side-parted bangs before plastering on a confident smile. She opened the heavy glass door and walked inside.

"Hey, Maya," Addy said to the college-aged girl at the reception desk. "I came in to sign my new lease."

"That's great, Addy! I'm happy you'll be staying." The girl stood. "Let me get Gary for you."

Just her luck. No-nonsense Gary.

In his three-piece navy blue suit, Gary Larsen, the property manager, came out from his office across the lobby and waved Addy to him. As she approached, he said, "Miss Piper, I'm glad to see you'll be renewing your lease. I have your papers ready."

A half dozen file folders, two silver pens, and a notebook-sized travel packet were on his glass-top desk.

"Please, have a seat." He motioned Addy to a chair as he angled around the desk to his own. "Just a few formalities."

Her gaze landed on a brightly colored travel brochure for *Breathless Montego Bay*, which Gary pushed aside, setting her personal apartment file in its place.

Noticing her focus, he said, "Jamaica. Are you still flying that route?"

"Um, no," Addy said, glancing at him.

"Well then, tell me, what other exotic places are you flying to now?"

"None," she said, then quickly, "I mean, those locations don't seem as exciting after you've seen them hundreds of times." It was true, but still, she already missed them.

"Yes, I suppose so." Gary smiled, then pulled out two preprinted documents. He slid one across the desk to Addy, then pointed to a bolded line on the agreement. "Your rent will remain the same for the next year." Then he looked at her. "Still no pets, correct?"

"Right. No pets."

"Good." He pushed the agreement aside and replaced it with a preprinted application. "Now, if you'll just initial these lines to indicate there's been no change to your employment or salary."

Addy held the pen in her hand, pressing her fingers hard against it to suppress a nervous tremor. She had four months' rent in the bank, and her credit rating was excellent. Surely, it would be enough to satisfy any concern of solvency. This had been her home for two years, and she'd never been late with the rent or caused any trouble.

"Here's the thing, Gary," Addy said, setting down the pen. "A few hundred pilots were furloughed yesterday. I was one of them."

Gary sat back in his chair. "I'm sorry to hear that. Any chance it will be short-lived?"

"I have no way of knowing." In earnest, Addy leaned forward, closing the awkward gap between them. "But I have solid credit, money in the bank, and I was pretty high up the seniority list, so I should be one of the first pilots called back."

"Yes, well, here's the *thing* on my end, Miss Piper." He straightened in his seat. "All residents are required to sign a one-year lease. No exceptions. Without a permanent job, you'll need to pay the year in advance. That, or I won't be able to approve your renewal. Our waiting list is long and filled with eager prequalified applicants just waiting for a vacancy." He bounced the end of his pen on the unsigned papers. "Are you able to pay the required year in advance? Without a job, it's the only option."

"I can pay three months today," she said. The leftover money would be minimal, but she was running out of options.

"It's twelve months, Miss Piper."

Her gaze fell to the floor. "I don't have twelve."

Gary closed the file and stood. "I'm sorry." He extended his hand. "I assume you'll be moved out by the end of September when your lease is up. It's been a pleasure having you as a resident."

Addy walked out of the office and back to her building in a daze. At the lobby elevator, she pressed the button for the tenth floor. As the doors opened, her phone rang, but calls were always dropped when the doors closed. Just as well, she thought. There wasn't a single person she wanted to talk to right now anyway.

It was almost noon, too hot for a walk around Klyde Warren Park, which always cleared her head, and too late to hit the farmer's market. The normalcy of those things felt so distant now. A lost lifetime away.

When her phone rang again several minutes later, Addy glanced at the caller ID and answered. "Hey, Janet. It's been months..."

"God, I'm glad to finally reach you. I've been calling since I heard about the furlough."

"Yeah," Addy said, head down. "You were smart to take that new job when you did. Are you still flying for that millionaire guy?"

"Yes, now Addy, listen," Janet said, her voice insistent. "Last time we talked, you were training for the Gulfstream. Are you type rated in the G550?"

"What's going on?"

"Addy, are you certified?"

"Yes, in April. But that was just a temper tantrum when I didn't get promoted to captain."

"Well, that temper tantrum may have just paid off for you."

"What do you mean?"

"Addy, I'm pregnant."

"Congratulations! Janet, I didn't know." So there was life outside an airport. "I guess it's been longer than

I thought since we've talked. Is Tom over the moon? Do you know if it's a boy or girl yet?"

Janet laughed. "Tom is thrilled. We tried for a long time before this little guy surprised us."

"So, it's a boy!" The thought of family, anyone's family, brought envied joy. "Oh, wow, now I know Tom is excited. He's finally going to get his little man."

"Addy..." Janet cleared her throat, then started again. "I have a proposition for you. For us, I mean. I'm restricted from flying now—company policy. Twenty-four weeks means no more flight hours 'til after the baby. Thabo, my boss, hired a short-term replacement three weeks ago, but she quit yesterday. She detests the captain. To be honest, he's a real asshole, a womanizer actually, and she wouldn't put up with him." She sighed. "Can't say as I blame her. Ernst is a brilliant pilot, but he likes his liquor and women too much. Anyway, Fray Enterprises needs a reliable backup for me until I can return, and if anyone can handle a man like Ernst, it's you. You're a pro at brushing off jerks. Besides, it would just be for nine months until my maternity leave is over. Are you interested? You'd need to start immediately."

Immediately. Scary word for a woman who preplanned every single step of her life.

"Janet, I'd need time to pack up my apartment and time to think this through."

"What's to think about? You're out of a job, for a while anyway. You'll get called back sooner or later, but don't you need an income in the meantime?"

"Yes." Addy glanced out the windows. "I do. I just want to stay here in North Texas." She hated to leave her apartment. "All my friends and favorite places are here. I grew up here, Janet."

"So you can move back when you're called up again."

The sun had risen to its midday high, casting a halo of light over the city she loved. The buildings glinted, refracting the light of day, taking her gaze from one high-rise to another.

"Where exactly does Fray Enterprises fly out of anyway? San Antonio?"

"Close," Janet said. "Thabo has his own airstrip about an hour northwest of there. You've been to the Hill Country, right?"

"No," Addy said and shook her head. "I always wanted to spend a week at a nice bed-and-breakfast and explore the place, but something else always came up."

"Yeah, well, *this* came up now. Get your butt down here and get this job before Thabo hires someone else. He's a spur-of-the-moment kind of man, and he's nervous about not having a copilot in place."

On Janet's advice, Addy set an interview for Thursday, but instead of booking a flight to San Antonio and then renting a car, she decided to drive the five hours it would take. Flying as a passenger felt like fraud.

Her travel bag was half packed when she spotted the box marked *Places to See in Texas* on a high shelf in the closet where she'd left it years ago. She pulled it down and carried it to the bed. Inside was a collection of brochures—all the places she'd once wanted to see— including a pamphlet for The Bluebonnet House, a historic Hill Country Bed-and-Breakfast, restored to its original 1910 grandeur. The house was Civil War blue and had four cream-colored pillars along a wide front porch. It looked a lot like her childhood home east of Dallas. A place she hadn't thought about in a long time.

She sat and opened the brochure. *It felt right*. And the B and B was just ten miles from Fray Enterprises. It was perfect. She dialed the number printed on the back beneath the photo of a blonde woman, holding a white wicker basket filled with brown eggs, standing by a man, head down, holding a chicken. Quaint in its country splendor.

Staying in a familiar, yet unfamiliar, house might help with the fish-out-of-water feeling that was suffocating her. When no one answered, she left a message saying she would be there by sunset.

Addy tossed her travel bag onto the passenger seat of her snowflake-white Miata and set her GPS for the rural address near the Kerr and Gillespie County lines.

August was off-season for just about everything in the Texas Hill Country, especially the legendary bluebonnets and other wildflowers, which wouldn't bloom again until spring. Even if Thabo Fray hired her, she'd be gone by then, so the drying purple thistles and sunflowers along the roadside would have to do.

The summer heat on such an arid day was all the encouragement Addy needed to keep the convertible's black top closed with her air conditioning set on high, blasting cold air. She hit play on an audiobook and drove.

The highway led her south through small towns with barely anything to entice a traveler, and since her sports car never seemed to run out of gas, Addy didn't stop.

Stalks of corn and milo, baled for livestock feed, dotted the crop fields, and although the land was drought-dry, most cotton stood sturdy in weedless fields. On open ranges, cattle, sheep, or goats roamed through free-growing amber grasses until scattered stands of oak, false willow, and cedar elm took over the terrain. By the time Addy reached Fredericksburg, white-tailed deer seemed to own the land, except on the ranches where herds of cattle covered the ground.

Turning onto I-10, the highway cut through dramatic limestone cliffs, carrying her Miata over rolling hills predominantly timbered with Ashe juniper, live oak, pecan, and hackberry until her GPS led her off the interstate. She followed the road to the outskirts of town where she saw it—the big American Foursquare of her memories.

A painted wood sign hung from a thick front porch beam: *The Bluebonnet House*. It was almost a mirror image of the home where she grew up. The trees were different, but the house was nearly the same color. It even had a handlaid limestone walkway like the one her father had made, and at the base of the full-width, painted porch was a bed of white spider lilies, her mother's favorite perennial.

Memories—so real—blurred her vision.

Addy steered the Miata down the gravel driveway and pulled into a parking space near an outside staircase. With the engine idling, she stared at the house. It was uncanny in its likeness to her childhood home. She blinked away unexpected tears. Eyes shut, she took a deep breath and focused, envisioning her airplane, her pilot's uniform, her Dallas apartment—pushing out the painful memories, keeping only the good ones. She was a different person now. Older. No longer a broken young girl.

She turned off the engine and then grabbed the strap of her travel bag before getting out of the car, dry-eyed.

Addy knocked on the front screen door, its wooden

frame banging louder against the doorjamb than her knuckles did on its wood. When no one answered, she knocked again, calling out, "Hello?"

When the door pulled open, her hand went unwillingly to her heart. On the other side of the screen stood Superman—the new one, not the old one. He pushed open the screen door.

"Hey," he said to her. "Come on in." He took the black leather bag from her hand.

"Are you...?" Addy shook her head. "I'm sorry." She stepped inside but couldn't stop herself from staring into his intense blue eyes. "Has anyone ever told you that you look almost exactly like the actor who plays—"

"Superman? Sherlock Holmes? Yeah." Wearing jeans and well-worn cowboy boots, he walked into a formal sitting room, stopping at a reception desk, then set her bag down on the floor. "That's why I grew all this." With splayed fingers, he waved his hand over the trimmed stubble on the bottom half of his face. "I got tired of being called Clark Kent or Sherlock."

Addy gave a discerning look to the chic, well-defined style of his short-boxed beard and mustache. His features were crisp and flawless, except for a spot of gold in one of his blue eyes. Facial hair or not, he didn't look that different. "Your hair is a lighter brown than his."

"That guy's got twenty pounds on me too." He extended his arm across the desk. "By the way, I'm Jack."

CHAPTER 2

The framed photograph next to the guestbook caught Addy's attention. It was the same as the one printed on the bed-and-breakfast brochure advertising *The Bluebonnet House, Jack and Kaitlin Brown, proprietors,* but the man named Jack who stood before her, fumbling through a drawer of loose keys, did not have the same clean-shaven face, nor was he as youthful-looking as the man in the picture. His dark brown hair was lightened by a sun-kissed tint.

"Your message said you're a pilot. Did you fly in and rent a car?"

"No, I drove down from Dallas."

A thin line of dirt was wedged under each of his fingernails, and the elbows of his long-sleeved work shirt had stains. "Bear with me," he said without looking up. He studied each key before he dropped it back into the cluttered drawer. "These are supposed to be marked, but I guess the room numbers came off."

"No problem." Addy reached for a pen. "Should I sign the guestbook?"

"Oh, yeah." Jack slid the book closer to Addy, then focused on her signature. When she laid down the pen, he pointed to her last name. "Piper, as in the *Pied Piper of Hamelin*?"

"I prefer Piper, as in *airplane.*"

He smiled. "Goes to show my reading interests these days, I guess."

"The Brothers Grimm version?"

"Is there more than one?"

"Yes. Lots." Addy reached down and picked up her bag, then nodded to the remaining keys in his hand. "Maybe your wife will have better luck finding my room key."

Jack stopped fumbling, then gave an awkward throat clearing. He nodded to the framed photograph. "That's Kaitlin and me not long after we inherited this house from my grandfather. Turning it into a bed-and-breakfast was her dream." His blue eyes landed on Addy. "She died four years ago."

"I'm sorry." Her apology escaped as a whisper. "I didn't know."

A widowed man and a single female guest—alone together in a house at the farthest edge of town—it didn't sound like a stay her reputation needed, especially when she was applying for a local job. She studied the framed business license on the wall behind him, and then she glanced around the room. It had a familiar peace about it, but still...

"Anyone else staying here this weekend?"

"No," he said.

She took a breath. Even the air in the place set her at ease. "Look, I'm sorry, but maybe I should go to a hotel instead."

"You could, but you'd end up sleeping in your car in the hotel parking lot." He looked at her with a shrug. "We're coming up on Labor Day weekend. Music Fest and the Texas Food and Wine event both start tonight and run through Monday. He nodded to a retro telephone affixed to the wall. You didn't leave a phone number, so I called around and checked the hotels for you—every available room has been booked for months."

"You don't have a cell phone with callback?"

Jack held up an iPhone. "I do, but the number you called is our old landline business phone." He reached into the drawer and grabbed the four room keys, then slid it shut. "How 'bout we just go upstairs and try them all?"

He headed back through the sitting room to the entryway and turned, nearly sprinting up the wide, dark mahogany and white staircase. Addy followed him, but when she reached the upper landing, she stopped. The handle of her travel bag slid off her fingers, landing softly on the floor at her feet.

Directly ahead was *her* childhood bedroom. An eerie tingle chilled her. She walked to its open door and glanced inside. Cross-legged on the floor in the middle of the room sat a young blonde girl, wearing purple shorts and a tan top, playing with a three-story Victorian dollhouse. She sang a low lullaby to a thimble-sized baby.

"Hi," Addy said to her quietly.

The girl looked up, then smiled. A thin gap separated her two front teeth. "Are you the lady who flies airplanes?"

"I am. My name is Addy. What's yours?"

"Juli," the girl said as she pushed herself up onto her feet. "Daddy said you were coming. I like your hair."

Addy smiled at the girl. She'd only had her new ombré-colored rough-cut pixie—light blonde with dark brown undertones—for a week. "I like yours too."

"Found it!" Jack called out from two rooms away. He walked back past her a moment later, headed for the linen closet. "Sorry, I haven't had time to put fresh sheets on the bed." He pulled out a set of sky-blue linens and started back toward the room.

Juli giggled. "We never have boarding people."

Addy stepped into the girl's room. The pale blush-pink walls had white baseboards and white window trim, and billowy white curtains draped the double windows. Wooden alphabet letters in different colors hung on the walls, and a child's table with four chairs and toys of all kinds filled the room, but there was no bed, no dresser, and no nightstand.

"Where do you sleep?" Addy asked.

"My bedroom is downstairs by Daddy. This is the playroom."

"Oh, I see." She looked at the girl. "So, why doesn't anyone stay at your bed-and-breakfast?"

From the hallway, Jack called out, "I can explain that, but first, why don't you come and check out the room to see if *you* want to stay at our bed-and-breakfast?"

"Be right there," Addy called back, then went to where she'd left her bag on the landing and picked it up before starting down the hallway.

The room had a quiet appearance with pale blue walls and wide white baseboards. It was clean and orderly, just the way Addy liked things. Overhead, a ceiling fan whirled, gently stirring the lace curtains that covered the three windows and outer glass door.

"What do you think?" Jack asked. He pointed to the balcony. "You have your own private entrance. The stairs lead right down to your car, so you never have to see us if you don't want to."

Addy set her bag down on the dark, polished wood floor. "It's nice." She turned to Jack. "So, why doesn't anyone stay here?" Quieter, she said, "It does seem odd for a woman alone to stay in a strange man's house."

"Well, first, I'm not strange. And second, this was Kaitlin's bed-and-breakfast, not really mine. I just can't seem to let go of her dream. We rent out a room now and then to friends, and friends of friends, and relatives of friends, just to cover the cost of keeping it licensed and inspected, but I don't advertise anymore. You must have an old brochure."

Addy nodded, remembering the box that had been on her closet shelf for years. "I see." She smiled. "The room is fine. Thank you." *A single father trying to keep someone else's dream alive.* "I'll just need two nights if that's okay. My interview isn't until one o'clock tomorrow, so I'll be leaving Friday."

"Yeah, sure, that will be fine." Jack handed her the room key. "This opens the balcony door too." He backed out of the room. "I'll try to keep Juli out of your hair while you're here, but I warn you, she's a talker." He glanced at Addy with a smile. "And she loves airplanes. She thinks it's cool that you fly 'em."

Alone in her rented room, Addy considered calling Janet to see if she had an extra room, but one hadn't been offered, and she hated to take advantage of friends. Instead, she took her bag to the closet, which was empty except for a dozen matching hangers, and hung up her two white blouses and two pairs of professional black slacks—size 6 and a little baggy, but there hadn't been time to shop for a better fitting pair. Her toiletries, pajamas, loafers, skinny jeans, and two T-shirts were left in the travel bag, so she slid it into the closet, closed the door, and then went out onto the balcony.

The yard below had a pecan tree with a swing, and leggy zinnias in narrow flowerbeds ran the length of the open-slat wood fence surrounding the big backyard.

At the picnic table was Juli, playing with a Barbie who had a shoebox full of colorful doll clothes. Smoke from a wood-fired grill roiled out from under the porch overhang.

Addy reached into her pocket and pulled out her cell phone. She dialed Janet.

"Hey, just wanted to let you know I'm here."

"I forgot to ask where you're staying."

"I'm at a B and B not too far from Fray Enterprises."

"I should have asked Thabo to put you up in a hotel. Blame it on pregnancy brain."

Addy glanced around the room, her heart settling on the memories of this being a guest room in her childhood home. Above a lamp table was a painting of bluebonnets where her grade school artwork would have hung as a child, and in the corner, where a tattered tan armchair had been in her own home, was a baby blue Victorian lounge. Something felt *right* here. Whether it was long-suppressed memories rising to the surface, or something else, she wasn't sure.

"Thanks, but I'll be fine." She brushed her finger-tips over the bed's white coverlet. "Hey, do you want to go out for Tex-Mex? I'm half-starved, and I have no idea where to go. Besides, I could sure use some advice on tomorrow's interview." The last thing she wanted was to disrupt homespun father-daughter time, but then Janet had a family too. "Unless you and Tom already have plans. I'd completely understand."

"I'll bring him along. It'll do him good to listen to stories about *my* work for a change. I'm always listening to him ramble on about wine and his vineyard. Let's meet at Pecos Patio Grill on Lone Oak at seven o'clock. Your GPS will get you there."

Addy went to the private bath off her room, brushing her hair and teeth and reapplying concealer to hide the freckles on her nose, when a faint knock came on her room door. She peeked her head out of the bath-room and listened to be sure. "Is someone there?"

"It's me. Juli."

Addy went to the door and opened it. "Hi, Juli."

"Hi." The girl smiled up at Addy. "Daddy said to tell you supper is ready."

"Supper?"

"He made you a steak." Juli reached out and took Addy's hand, then pulled. "Come on. I'll take you out back."

Addy let the girl lead her down the stairs, through the house, and out into the shaded backyard.

"Here she is, Daddy."

The wood picnic table was set with three summer-time melamine plates, two of which had steak, a foil-wrapped baked potato, and a plain, thick-sliced tomato. A grilled hamburger was on the third plate.

Juli released Addy's hand and ran to the plated hamburger.

Jack gave a nod toward the table. "Your steak is medium rare, but the grill is still hot if I need to put it on a little longer for you."

"Medium rare is fine," Addy said. "But I didn't expect you to cook for me."

"You're our guest."

"But it's a bed-and-*breakfast*, not a bed-and-*supper*."

"You've still got to eat, right?" Jack high-stepped over the picnic table's bench seat and motioned to the other plate. "I had to cook for us anyway."

She had plans with Janet and Tom, but the aroma of a perfect char pulled her to the table anyway. "That's very nice of you." Being rude wasn't her nature, but neither was having other people make decisions for her. "But I have plans to meet friends at seven."

Jack looked at his watch. "Great. You've got almost an hour. Sit and eat."

She should have said *dinner plans*, but she hadn't.

Addy sat by Juli at the picnic table and then sliced through the foil on her potato. "I smell rosemary."

"There's a sprig under your potato. It grows wild around here." He pointed to his grill. "I usually throw some on the fire for flavor when I smoke pork or turkey, but steaks cook too fast for it, so I like to put it in with whatever vegetable I'm cooking."

Addy buttered her potato, and then cut into her ribeye and took a bite. "Oh, my gosh."

"Good?" he asked.

She put a finger to her mouth while chewing, then said, "Amazing."

Jack glanced at his daughter. "Juli, how's your burger?"

"It's good, Daddy." She giggled when a dollop of ketchup dropped off her burger onto the table.

"Men have a knack for grilling," Addy said. "I can't master it."

"I'm better at everything outdoors. Cooking meals in the kitchen isn't my thing." He used a paper towel to clean the spilled ketchup off the table.

"I love to cook, just not on the grill," she told him. There was no need to mention that she had no one but herself to cook for anyway. "I took pasta lessons last month," Addy admitted but then laughed. "I need lots more practice." Talking about herself wasn't something she usually enjoyed, but she felt different in this place.

Juli's bold blue eyes widened. "Like spaghetti? Daddy makes that too."

Jack laughed. "But Daddy buys the pasta noodles from the store. Miss Addy makes them from scratch."

This talk had a comforting feel. Addy glanced up, looking at the girth of the well-kept home. "Did you say this house belonged to your grandfather?"

"Yeah. I stayed here lots of summers and worked for him as a kid. I started when I was ten."

"Wow. Ten. That's pretty young. What kind of work did he have a ten-year-old doing for him?" Addy stopped, landing him a look. "I'm sorry. I don't mean to pry."

"No, it's all good." Jack smiled at her. "We're seed producers. I used to help with the fields and the harvesting."

"You *grow* seeds?"

"Just for flowers," Juli said, swinging her legs beneath the picnic table bench. "Daddy's a flower farmer."

"That's right." Jack nodded to his six-year-old. "We

have a wildflower farm." Then to Addy, he said, "Texas Seeds, spelled T-X-U-S."

"I've seen that name before! On packs of blue-bonnet seeds."

"Bluebonnets are our biggest sellers."

"I'm impressed," Addy said. "I always thought T-X-U-S stood for Texas, United States. It never occurred to me that TXUS sounds like *Texas*. I guess I've never said it out loud."

"You're right on both counts. When Gramps started selling his seeds back in the '80s, Grammy came up with the name. They wanted to market it as an all-American company and a Texas business. Texans love to support local commerce, and she loved the state and wanted it to be part of the name. That's how TXUS Seeds came to be."

"How do you manage to operate both a bed-and-breakfast and a seed company?"

"The B and B was solely my wife's business." Jack nodded to the 1910 home. "Kaitlin loved this place. And what else could a newly married couple do with a six-bedroom house? I inherited it less than a month before our wedding."

Juli stood. "Daddy, I ate almost all of my burger. Can I go watch TV now?"

"Sure, but remember to rinse your plate and put it in the dishwasher."

"I will," the girl said. She picked up her dish and headed for the back door.

Addy glanced at the time on her cell phone. Six thirty-five. "I need to get going, or I'll be late meeting my friends." She stood. "Thank you for dinner."

"My pleasure." Jack picked up his plate and then hers. "It was nice to have an adult conversation."

Addy didn't particularly want to go. Not because she was inexplicably drawn to this man, though she was, or because his little girl nourished her starving spirit, but because she felt the soul of her own seventeen-year-old self returning. And it felt pure and whole again.

CHAPTER 3

The vibrantly painted Pecos Patio Grill teemed with chatty customers who all seemed to know one another when Addy arrived at a quarter past seven. She angled through the crowd, finding the cashier, and when a break came in the woman's long line, Addy said, "I'm meeting friends. Can I just take a look around for them?"

"Sure, darlin'." The dark-haired woman pointed over Addy's head. "Be sure to check out on the patio. I seated some folks near the railing about twenty minutes ago who were waitin' for a lady friend."

Addy thanked the woman and then found herself sidestepping this way and then that way, trying to make her way through the crowded margarita bar. She pushed open the half-glass door to the patio deck, which was brightly decorated with fiesta-style lanterns, serape-colored tablecloths, and paper flowers. It took a moment for her gaze to settle on the corner table with Janet and Tom.

When their eyes met, Janet stood with a wave. Her

long brown hair was tied into a messy knot, and she wore an Army-green maternity dress, showing her pregnancy.

"I was beginning to worry," she told Addy tableside, then hugged her before fingering Addy's long side-swept bangs. "I like the new hair!"

"Sorry to be late," Addy told them. "I couldn't find a parking space. I had to park across the street and walk over." When Tom stood, hand extended, Addy shook. "It's good to see you again, Tom. Congrats on being a future dad." She looked back at Janet. "Shoulder length was way too much trouble." She turned, modeling her new hairstyle. "Short is so much easier." Then, "But look at you! You are absolutely glowing."

Janet patted her pregnant swell. "You mean *growing*, don't you?"

Both laughed. "How far along are you?" Addy asked.

Janet pointed to her rounded belly. "This is what six and a half months looks like."

The Guadalupe River, a ribbon of deep green at least one hundred feet wide, flowed far below the full wood deck, and on the opposite shore, bald cypress grew. The late August sun chased shadows from the water, leaving the barely visible flow to amble quietly by in the dusk of day.

Once seated, Addy asked for sweet tea from the waitress but passed on ordering food. "I didn't know the B and B was grilling steaks for dinner. I didn't want to hurt his feelings by turning him down."

"Him?" Janet asked.

"Yes, *him*," Addy said. "The guy is a doll, but he has a daughter."

"Does he have a wife too?"

"Widower."

Janet sat back in her seat with folded arms. "Interesting."

"Oh, c'mon, Janet. I'm married to my airplane." She sounded like a man-hating rebel, and she knew it, but nothing was further from the truth. Men just weren't drawn to her. Her feminine wiles didn't ride on feelings of playfulness, emotion, or fun. She was used to being pushed aside for more enticing females. Mainly, she blamed her lack of social skills. She just couldn't connect. Addy reached for a tortilla chip and dipped it into salsa before eating it. "So, tell me about this millionaire who needs a pilot."

"Billionaire," Janet corrected. "The man wasn't born into poverty, but he didn't grow up mega-wealthy either." She sipped her ice water. "He's not ashamed to say that he earned his first billion by the age of thirty, and believe me, he's amassed much more since. Thabo is a highly intelligent man in an unobtrusive sort of way. You'd never see it if you didn't know what to look for."

"So, how did he earn these billions?"

"If you ask him, he'll tell you he owns eldercare homes."

Addy sat back in her seat. Skeptical, she said, "I doubt someone can amass billions by owning a few houses for the elderly." She leaned forward again. "This isn't a cover for running drugs or something, is it?"

Janet howled with laughter.

"I'm serious, Janet." She should have checked the man's credentials.

Janet reached across the table and squeezed Addy's hand. "Listen, when you meet Thabo Fray, you'll see why I laugh. You couldn't meet a more normal guy."

"So, what's the story?" A knot was quickly forming in Addy's stomach.

"First, you're probably right. Thabo's assisted-living homes undoubtedly make him less than a million a year, but eldercare is only a tiny part of Fray Enterprises. It just happens to be where his heart is. It's personal to him, and it's what he's most proud of. It has to do with his grandfather. Thabo's real wealth comes from oil."

Addy relaxed. "Don't tell me he owns a bunch of West Texas oil wells."

Janet laughed again, glancing at Tom, who was head down focused on his phone. "No," she assured Addy. "Fray Enterprises produces about one-third of the world's coconut oil. Health supplements, cooking oils, body oils, essential oils—the whole shebang. But eldercare is still big business. He owns more than two hundred private eldercare homes across the United States."

"Kind of a weird business combination, isn't it?"

"Like I said, eldercare is personal to him." Janet dropped a slice of lemon into her water then used her finger to tap it down into her glass. "Thabo is a quiet man, very thoughtful, but he's dead serious about the care his elderly residents receive. The whole thing has something to do with what happened to his grandparents. I try not to get involved with his personal life, so I just hear bits and pieces, but if he gets a complaint that sounds legit, he'll have you in the air within hours."

"Right." Tom looked up, bitterly twisting the word. "Even if you're in the middle of a gala wine tasting event you've had planned for a year."

Janet shifted her eyes to Addy, then leaned forward. "The Hill Country is rumored to be the new

Napa, and Tom is desperate to be in on the wine boon. Competition with his family, you know?"

Tom turned to his wife. "Desperate is a bit harsh, don't you think?" Then to Addy, he said, "A young vineyard on twenty acres between Fredericksburg and Stonewall came my way last year. I bought it, that's all."

"And he hasn't been able to think of anything else since," Janet said. She reached out and gave a pat to her husband's hand. "Tom, darling, it wasn't as if Thabo set out to ruin your wine event. The Destin nursing home caught fire—it wasn't his fault."

A big man, Tom crossed his arms, leaning back in his chair. "But it's always something, isn't it?"

With a sigh, Janet turned to Addy. "Don't mind Tom. He just needs a vacation, which is why we're leaving for four weeks tomorrow to tour the California wineries in Napa and visit his family in Sonoma before the baby is born. I've never been to their winery, and I can't wait to see what our little boy will inherit one day."

Stress wrinkled Addy's brow. "You didn't mention that you had a vacation planned."

Janet leaned forward. "Listen, you'll be fine. The biggest problem you'll have is with the pilot, Ernst. The man can skirt a hurricane without so much as a bump, but sometimes, when he's on the ground and bored, he's a little too drawn to women and whiskey. To put it plainly, he's a high-and-mighty British snob and a spoiled playboy. I've been able to keep him on point, but until he learns that you mean business, you might find yourself stuck somewhere for a day while he pulls himself out of a stupor. That's the reason the major airlines won't hire him."

Addy stiffened. "Janet, I'm not keen about flying with a drunkard."

"No one is," Janet said. "But he won't fly if he's had a nip. The minute he takes a drink, Ernst sets a twelve-hour timer on his watch, and then he hits the start button after his last drink. Like clockwork, he calls Thabo. It's an arrangement they've had for years, and he sticks to it. I don't know why Thabo puts up with him, but he does. And you won't have any say in the matter, so just accept the oddity of it, and you'll be fine."

On the way back to the B and B, Addy thought about how she might rectify the problem of being first officer to a carousing captain. Of course, none of that would matter unless she was offered the job. It would only be for nine months, she reminded herself.

Parked beneath the motion sensor light, set high at the corner eave of the B and B, Addy climbed the outside stairs to her rented room. She used her balcony key and opened the door to a dark room, having forgotten to leave a light on for herself. Her hand skimmed the wall, finding the switch. When she flipped it on, the bedside lamp lit the room. The light was soft against the pale blue walls—cozy and safe feeling.

The house was quiet except for the invading chorus of crickets and frog songs coming from the yard below. Without a television in the room, Addy pulled out her cell phone and let it search for a Wi-Fi network. While it connected, she got into her pajamas, brushed her teeth, and washed her face for bed.

Propped up with her feet tucked beneath the cool bed linens, Addy checked emails and then read an industry article about the furlough. Her friends were right, trying to wait it out was a foolish idea. The downturn was in sharp decline. If hired by Fray Enterprises, the temporary job would buy her a few months to find another permanent airline position. As much as she hated to admit it, she needed this job right now. She needed to trust Janet.

The next morning, Addy awoke, already nervous. She hadn't had a job interview in years. She showered and tried to stay calm. Though it was forecast to be another hot day, she dressed professionally in a white long-sleeved, collared blouse with tailored V-neck and black slacks.

When she opened the door of her rented room, the smell of brewed coffee lured her down the stairs. Instinctively, she turned left at the bottom, already knowing the way to the kitchen.

Six-year-old Juli sat on one of the three stools at the breakfast island, the gentle waves of her side-parted blonde hair pushed behind her ears, watching her father pop frozen waffles into the toaster.

"Good morning," Addy greeted them.

"Mornin'," Jack said without looking up. "Glad you found your way to the kitchen."

Addy wanted to say, "I know the location of every room in this house," but she wouldn't because then she'd have to explain how she knew. *She'd lived in this house.* Well, not this house exactly, but one so much like it, she felt home again.

"Miss Addy," Juli said, her smile excited. "Do you like waffles?"

"Sort of, but I think I'll just have coffee this morning if that's okay." She glanced at Jack again. His snug white T-shirt, a lightweight cotton fabric, clung to his muscular arms and abs, and his dark blue denim jeans and boots definitely put him in the "hot cowboy" category. The man belonged on the cover of a high-gloss magazine. She looked away, then asked, "Do you mind if I pour myself a cup?"

"Yeah, sure, help yourself." Jack set down a butter dish by Juli. "Do you use creamer?"

"Yes, a little."

He went to the refrigerator, pulled out a blue flip-top container, and handed it to Juli, who set it on the breakfast island. "So, no waffles? You want toast instead?" Jack gave a tickle to his daughter as he walked past. When Juli giggled, he said, "Our mornings just aren't right around here without waffles."

"I like oatmeal with lots of brown sugar too," Juli reminded him. "And bacon!"

"That's true, but we ran out, and I haven't bought groceries this week."

Addy lifted her cup. "Coffee is fine. Thank you."

When the front door squeaked open, a feminine voice sailed through the house. "Knock, knock."

"We're in the kitchen, Paige," Jack called back.

Addy turned when a woman entered the room.

"Oh." The solid-color brunette stopped, wide-eyed, at the edge of the kitchen island, her gaze stalled on Addy. "I'm sorry. Jack, I didn't know you had company." She extended her hand. "I'm Paige."

"Addy." The two shook hands.

Jack lifted a cautionary brow to Paige. "Addy's our B and B guest for a few days." He slid two waffles onto Juli's plate, then set it down in front of her with a nearly empty bottle of syrup, then his glance landed on Paige again. "Ready for coffee?"

Paige was exactly the type of girlfriend Addy expected a man like Jack Brown to have. She was a brunette beauty, simple and outdoorsy in her blue jeans and sleeveless red and blue checkered shirt, and cowboy boots that hadn't seen a polishing cloth maybe ever. Her wide smile had surely seen more than its fair share of secret kisses out behind a barn. She was the opposite of Addy in every way.

Feeling out of place, Addy stood. "I think I'll finish my coffee outside at the picnic table." She glanced at Paige. "It was nice to meet you."

Outside, Addy was drawn to a circular bench around the trunk of an age-old pecan tree. She sat, cup in hand, staring up through the limbs at the clusters of green hulls, soon to be edible pecans. Undisturbed by the loud and melodious wrens flitting branch to branch, her childhood memories of tree climbing, laughter, and love overtook her thoughts. This Hill Country home had turned back time. For a moment, her heart felt whole again.

She envisioned her father painting their back porch pillars while her mother knelt in the grass at the edge of a fixed planter, weeding the box with a sweet song on her lips. It was a scene that hadn't played out in her memories for years, but too quickly, the comforting image faded into the tormenting sadness that had followed her for what seemed a lifetime—the heartache that had slammed her childhood to an end. Who could have imagined that her loneliness would last so long?

CHAPTER 4

"Thanks for letting Juli tag along today, Paige," Jack said. "I wasn't expecting her to get a student holiday so soon, or I wouldn't have scheduled these appointments."

"No problem. I'm glad to take her with me. What is staff development day anyway?"

Jack shrugged. "Juli, finish your waffles." He pointed to her half-eaten breakfast. "Miss Paige can't wait all day."

Paige reached out, patting the girl's hand. "Take your time, sweetness. I'm in no hurry."

"It's okay. I'm done." Juli put down her fork and slid off the seat. "Daddy, can I wear my purple shoes today?"

"Those are for school. Why don't you wear your boots?"

"Please, Daddy?" With her hands clasped in prayer, Juli bounced on bare tiptoes.

"Oh, let her wear them, Jack. What good are purple unicorn shoes if you can't show them off at a horse show?" Paige seated herself on the stool Juli had been using.

"All right." Jack gave Paige a sidelong glance before looking back at Juli. "You can wear them as long as you keep them clean. I'm not driving back to San Antonio to find another pair for you, young lady."

"Okay, Daddy!" Juli bolted from the room.

"So, how did you end up with a B and B guest?"

"I guess she had an old brochure," Jack explained. "Her reservation was on voicemail. I didn't even notice the blinking message light until an hour before she got here." The sink was already half full with lemon-scented detergent bubbles when he put the breakfast dishes in and began scrubbing. "You know how it is this week—there's no rooms to rent anywhere. This is the busiest weekend of the year. I couldn't turn her away. Besides, this is a legitimate, licensed bed-and-breakfast."

"Speaking of that..." Paige had her elbows propped up on the center island, holding her coffee cup with both hands. She sipped. "When are you going to give that up?"

Jack kept his back to her but stopped washing dishes. He raised his head, staring into the past through the window above the sink.

When he didn't answer, Paige got up and went to him, putting her hand on his shoulder. "Jack, this was Kaitlin's bed-and-breakfast. She's been gone four years. I was her best friend. If anyone other than you knows what she would want, it's me. And I don't think she'd want you living out *her* dream—I think she would want you to live *yours*."

"I know." He nodded, ending head down. "Even Juli thinks it's silly, and she's only six."

Paige patted his shoulder, then took a folded cloth from the drawer and started to dry the breakfast dishes. "I'm not trying to push you into a decision. I just want you to think about it. That's all."

"I have thought about it," Jack softly said. "But we only have three or four people a year anymore, and they've all been friends of friends." He glanced at Paige. "Like your cousins. When you guys had the family reunion, they stayed here. It was better here than a hotel, wasn't it?"

"Way better," Paige told him. "They loved staying here with you and Juli."

"Addy is the first real, legitimate guest that we've taken in for over a year." He washed and rinsed his coffee cup, then hung it on the mug tree without drying it. "And renting a room for Kaitlin now and then brings back lots of good memories."

"For Kaitlin?" Paige asked.

Jack stopped. He hadn't intended to say *for* Kaitlin. He took the dish towel from Paige and dried his hands. "I just meant the act of renting rooms reminds me of Kaitlin. I have lots of good memories, Paige. You know that."

"I'm not trying to play psychologist, Jack, but that slip of the tongue is very real to your subconscious. You need to stop doing things for Kaitlin and start doing them for you and Juli instead."

Juli burst back into the kitchen. "I'm ready, Miss Paige!"

When Jack and Paige turned to the grinning girl, they both laughed.

"A pink tutu, Juli?" Jack said. "Really?"

"I think she's adorable!" Paige laughed.

"See, Daddy?" Juli's hands went to her waist. She

cocked her head so that long waves of blonde hair flipped over one shoulder. "I'm *adorable*!"

"You're sassy too." Jack turned her around, facing her bedroom. "Go put some pants on. A horse show is no place for a ballerina."

When Juli left the room, Jack grew serious and redirected the conversation back to Paige. "Maybe you're right. I should terminate the license. Turn this back into a home for Juli."

"It's already a home for her, Jack," Paige said. "She loves this place as much as her mama did. You're doing a great job raising her in this house. I just worry that it's all too much for you two. The seed business is booming, and Juli's growing up fast. Too fast." She smiled. "I still can't believe she's in first grade."

"I know. Me either." Jack pulled out his wallet and handed Paige a twenty. "Don't let her eat too much junk today, but a little is okay."

"Oh, it'll be Mick's BBQ all the way."

"Paige, I swear, no barbecue sauce spilled on those shoes. This is her second pair!"

She laughed. "Got it, boss. No sauce on the shoes."

CHAPTER 5

White, cotton candy clouds graced the blue midday sky on the 100-degree day. Unlike much of the pancake-flat state, the Texas Hill Country had rolling, evergreen hills evocative of the south of France that Addy so loved last summer while vacationing in Europe.

From Highway 16, she turned her white Miata onto Mystic Way, a rural paved street that soon became a blacktopped country road without a centerline or shoulder. Two cars would be hard-pressed to share its surface. The road ran alongside a sand-colored iron fence, six-feet high, leading to a double gate with an electronic call box. Addy stopped, then reached out and pressed the button marked "Residence."

"Fray residence," a man answered.

"Hi," Addy spoke to the unadorned metal box. "I'm Addy Piper. I have an appointment."

The low, rumbling hum of the electronic gate flushed an earthy-colored rabbit from its hiding place, sending it darting across the road in front of Addy's car.

She followed the bouncy cottontail with her eyes as the man said, "Mr. Fray is expecting you."

Alongside the drive, amid a meadow bright with sunflowers and droopy-petaled Mexican hat flowers, a herd of exotic Axis grazed. A few of the white-spotted deer had antlers, but even those that didn't, froze like statues, staring as Addy drove slowly past them, their wide eyes evaluating the Miata before lowering their heads to forage again.

It was almost a mile before the residence appeared in the distance. The three-story home was dark olive green with two limestone turrets at its entry. The estate was pure Tuscany in its style.

Addy pulled into the half-circle drive and turned off the car's engine. With a flip of the visor, she looked into the narrow mirror. Satisfied, she flicked it up again and grabbed her slim leather satchel before getting out of the car. She stood, closing the car door as her gaze traveled up, past the third story, to the dark, variegated red tile rooftop, only to drop down again when the front door opened.

A man, thirtyish, dressed in gray pants and a long-sleeved white shirt, nodded to her from the open doorway. "Good afternoon, ma'am. Please come in."

It seemed odd for someone Addy's own age to call her "ma'am," but then again, Texans were notorious for using *ma'am* and *sir*. It was a sign of respect—not intended to denote age.

"Thank you," Addy said. She entered the house, stopping in the Saltillo tile entryway to face the greeter. "This is a beautiful home." She pointed back behind her to the meadow. "Your herd of deer was a surprise."

"They don't belong to us—they roam wherever they

want." He smiled and reached out his hand. "I'm Noah, Mr. Fray's assistant."

"It's nice to meet you, Noah," Addy said, shaking his hand.

"Please follow me to the study. Mr. Fray is just finishing up a phone call in another room."

High ceilings, polished cedar bookcases filled with mostly hardback books, and an antler chandelier gave the study a different kind of feel. Not western, really, but certainly not the chic Dallas socialite-style either. Upper-class Hill Country motif, Addy decided.

She sat, professionally poised, in a leather chair near a big window, watching ducks float on a spring-fed pond not far from the house. In the distance, white-tailed deer grazed separately from the herd of Axis. The room held the scent of recently polished wood.

When the door to the study opened, Addy turned in her seat, then stood when a casually dressed man entered the room, pulling on a dark sports coat as he walked.

"I apologize you had to wait." He approached with an outstretched hand. "I'm Thabo Fray. It's nice to have you here."

"Thank you." Addy gave a practiced smile.

Thabo Fray was not the Texas billionaire she envisioned. He was no taller than her own five-foot-eight height, dark-haired and olive-complected, and although he looked fit except for a slight paunch, he was stockier than she expected. Under his jacket, he wore a black T-shirt tucked snugly into indigo jeans.

He went to a library table, took out a notepad and pen from its drawer, then he returned to the leather chair opposite Addy and sat, angled to face her rather than the window.

"So, Janet tells me the airline handed out quite a long furlough list." He adjusted himself in the chair.

"True, unfortunately," Addy said. "I hoped I'd never find myself in this position, but here I am."

"Good for me, but I'm sorry for your circumstances. Have you flown the G550 before?"

"Yes. Well, not on a regular basis. I was certified last April. It's an amazing aircraft. I normally fly the A321."

"That's an Airbus, right?"

"Yes."

"Bigger."

"Lots."

"Then I take it my little Gulfstream won't be a problem for you?"

"I wouldn't call the G550 *little*, but to answer your question, no, it won't be a problem." Addy reached for her business satchel, laid it on the coffee table between them, and opened it. She pulled out a file and handed it over. "I think you'll find everything you need in here — my airline transport pilot license, first-class medical, FCC license," she pointed, intending the last page, "and my résumé too."

Thabo leafed attentively through the papers, then closed the file. He scribbled a few lines on his notepad, then check marked two of those before glancing up again. "And what about being away for several days at a time? I assume it's normal for your profession, but anyone at home to balk about it?" He directed a hard look toward Addy. "I can't lose another pilot at this point. Janet says she's explained the difficulties you might encounter with Ernst, my longtime captain. To be fair, I want to say upfront that we've known each other many years, and I have no intention of replacing him."

Difficulties? Addy's neck stiffened. Reckless and dangerous was more like it. Absurd stance, even for a nonpilot. "I'd like to be perfectly honest."

Thabo leaned back in his chair—one leg crossed ankle over knee. "Go on," he said, giving an acknowledging nod.

"I couldn't care less about your captain's playboy personality, although it is offensive and unprofessional in every way. But in all honesty, I only plan to be here for a few months until Janet returns from her maternity leave, so I've resigned myself to dealing with those issues. His drinking, though, is another matter." Addy firmed her focus on Thabo Fray, who remained expressionless and motionless. "A pilot who cannot control his liquor is a constant threat to the safety and welfare of his crew and passengers. I will not tolerate it." She needed this job, but not at the ultimate price.

"Understood." Thabo took the file with her pilot certificates inside and bent forward with it, laying it on the coffee table along with his notepad and pen. "I don't have a death wish any more than you do, and neither does Ernst. We don't leave the ground unless he's stone-cold sober, and I would not expect you to be accepting of anything less." His eyes considered her. "Are there any other matters?" When she shook her head, he said, "Good." He stood. "I like you, Miss Piper. You've got backbone. An admirable asset." He reached for a handshake from across the coffee table. "I'll need you to start immediately. I have a meeting in Tucson the day after tomorrow."

"Saturday?" Addy stood too. "I'll need more time. To think about it..." Not just about Ernst and this man's

attitude about him but also about her life and its insta-
bility at the moment. "I can have an answer for you on
Monday."

He withdrew his hand. Shook his head. "No good. I
need to be in Arizona. Both meetings had to be
rescheduled. I've already delayed them once, and I'm
not keen on doing it again."

"I'm sorry," Addy said. "Monday is the earliest I can
have an answer for you."

His look hardened. "Are you considering a position
elsewhere?"

"No, it's not that." A flush heated her cheeks. She
hated to feel vulnerable. "I need to find a new apartment or put my belongings in storage until I'm called
back to the airlines."

"Would you consider waiting a few weeks to do
that? I'm able to give you a week off in late September
to take care of those matters, but I need a second pilot
this week."

Addy shook her head. "I need to be out by the end
of September."

With a furrowed brow, he asked, "Why?"

The last thing she wanted was to talk about why she
was losing her apartment or confess that she'd failed to
save enough money for a rainy day, but this was a well-
paying position, and it fit nicely into the empty slot in
her life. She was putting this job on the line by squab-
bling, but her personal belongings had to be moved
—soon.

"My lease wasn't renewed when I was furloughed. I
don't mean to be disagreeable, but I have no choice
about this. I need to move, even though I'd rather not,
and I can't do that at the snap of a finger."

"I see." Thabo nodded, then picked up her folder off the coffee table.

Her heart fell. No one liked problems, least of all a new employer. She reached for the file. "I'm sorry it didn't work out."

But Thabo held onto the folder, lightly batting it against his other palm. "What if I wrote a letter confirming your new employment? Would they renew your lease then? If so, you could stay, or move when it's more convenient."

He still wanted her? "They require permanent employment—a temporary job won't do. The only way I can stay is if I pay one year in advance." Her lips tightened into a forced smile. "I don't have that kind of money. Thank you, though."

He kept hold of the file. "Would you be willing to sign a firm nine-month commitment with Fray Enterprises if my company pays your one-year lease upfront?"

Addy stiffened. *Hold it together.* "I don't think you understand. My lease is twenty-four thousand a year."

With a titter, Thabo said, "At least you don't live in San Francisco or New York City."

She readjusted, shifting her stance. "Mr. Fray, are you offering me an advance on my salary?"

"Call it a signing bonus."

Addy's jaw released, leaving her mouth slightly agape.

"Will that take care of the problem?"

Her thoughts whirled. "Not completely. No."

Head cocked, his gaze focused on her sharp, hazel-green eyes. "What else then?"

"Your Saturday trip is still a problem. I'll need to get back to Dallas, pay the one-year lease, and pick up more personal items for myself—clothes and things—especially since I can't be guaranteed time off until the end of the month."

"I see." He walked to an intercom near the door and pressed its button. "Noah, will you come in, please?"

When his assistant arrived, Thabo asked him to reschedule Saturday's meeting in Tucson to Monday and move the Phoenix meeting to Tuesday. Then he gave Noah the details of Addy's employment agreement, including her signing bonus. "If Miss Piper does not fulfill the term of her contract, the signing bonus must be repaid within thirty days." He turned to her. "Acceptable to you?"

"Yeah, sure," Addy said, nodding.

"Should Noah make the check payable to you or your leasing company?"

Still taken aback, Addy said, "Before he does that, I need to make a call to be sure I can still reinstate my lease."

"Yes, of course." Thabo stepped away for her privacy.

Addy took out her cell phone and dialed. When the receptionist answered, she asked for Gary Larsen. After a brief explanation to him, she confirmed, "Two o'clock tomorrow? Yes," she nodded, "I'll have a check for the full year." At the end of the call, she turned to Thabo and Noah. "Please make the check payable to Westgard Management."

CHAPTER 6

On the drive back, Addy called Janet with the news she'd been hired but avoided mentioning the details of her hiring or the fact that she hadn't met Ernst—the designated captain and her new flying partner. Her vision of a drowsy-eyed man, puffy from drink, next to her in the cockpit made her queasy.

At the B and B, she went straight to the front door instead of climbing the outside stairs to her rented room. It didn't feel right to disappear up the steps during the social hours of daylight without saying hello to her host. She knocked, then waited.

"Hey," Jack said at the door. He pushed it open for her. "How'd the interview go?"

"It was good," she said, stepping inside. "I accepted the job."

"Congratulations!" He motioned her toward the kitchen, then followed her in, pulling out a stool at the breakfast counter for her. "We should celebrate. Iced tea, coffee, wine?"

"A glass of wine would be nice, please." Inside the opened refrigerator, Addy spotted a familiar bottle of white on the shelf next to the milk. "Is that Pinot?"

"Yeah." Jack pulled the barely green bottle out of the fridge. "Is that okay? I thought it would go with the salmon I'm grilling tonight. You do like fish, I hope." When Addy nodded, he said, "It's Juli's regular date night with Paige, and they're still at the horse show, probably with a plateful of barbecue." He smiled at her. "Juli hasn't acquired a taste for fish yet, but I love a good grilled salmon, so I usually cook it when she's out with Paige."

Jack handed Addy a stemless wine glass and then poured himself one too.

"You're lucky," she said. "I've heard lots of awful stories about kids hating their dad's girlfriend."

Quiet, he pulled out a stool opposite Addy and sat. Head cocked, his eyes inquiring, Jack said, "Paige isn't my girlfriend. We work together. Did it look that way this morning?"

"I'm sorry. I just assumed."

"No, it's not a big deal." Jack lifted his glass in the air. "Congratulations on the new job." After a clink, they both sipped. "I guess I've never thought about how our friendship must look to people who don't know us, but Paige is engaged to a pretty successful horse breeder." He swirled his wine, sipped again, and then set down the glass. "Paige was my wife's best friend. She stepped in to help me with Juli after..." He stopped, silent for a moment, his gaze steady on Addy. "I always thought I'd know what to do with my own child, you know? How to take care of her, understand what she needed. It came as a big surprise to find out I didn't know anything at all after Kaitlin died. Thank God for Paige."

"How old was Juli when it happened?"

"Two," he said. "She'd just turned two years old."

"Was it a long illness?"

Jack focused on his glass, memories chilling him before he looked up. "I'm sorry. What?"

Addy shook her head, not wanting to send him into a darkness she knew all too well. "I didn't mean to pry. We can talk about something else."

"No, honestly, it's okay. I don't mind. I just get lost in it sometimes." Jack got up and took a plate with two pink salmon filets out of the refrigerator. He transferred the fish to two thin cedar planks that he'd had soaking in a pan on the kitchen counter and started to season the filets. Without looking at Addy, he said, "Kaitlin died in a car accident. There's a place on Highway 16 with a curve that shouldn't be there."

"Did she lose control of the car?"

"She wasn't even driving." He stopped seasoning the salmon and turned to Addy. "It was all my brother's fault. He showed up here while I was gone on a marketing trip to Houston. He'd been drinking, and Kaitlin, being the good protective woman she'd always been, insisted that she drive him home. They stopped for gas at this little station just outside of town, but the "pay at the pump" system wasn't working, so she had to go into the store. When she came back to the car, he'd slid over into the driver's seat. When he wouldn't move for her, she got into the passenger side and tried to take the key out of the ignition, but he took off with her inside. Nobody really knows what happened after that, but witnesses say he was driving erratically and going too fast. When they came to that curve, the car veered into oncoming traffic. A commercial van hit them."

"I'm so sorry."

Jack slowly nodded. "Kaitlin was seven months pregnant with our second daughter. I can't even imagine how scared she must have been."

Heavy and unsettled, grief disquieted the room.

"What about your brother? Was he killed too?"

He shook his head. "The van hit the passenger side. My brother claimed he barely remembered it happening. He had a broken rib, a concussion, and some bruises, but that's it."

"That's incredibly sad. I'm so sorry."

"I haven't spoken to my brother since."

Jack picked up the cedar board with the salmon filets and motioned Addy to follow him out the back door. When he set the plank on the side table, the grill was lightly smoking. He went to the nearby rosemary shrub with hand pruners and cut two long sprigs, sprouting tiny lavender flowers. He laid them directly on the grilling grate and then set the planked salmon in between the stalks before he closed the lid again.

"What about your parents?" Addy asked. "Were they able to help you with Juli too?"

Jack shook his head. "I haven't talked to them in almost four years either. Not since they decided to side with my brother." He looked at Addy. "They *defended* him."

His heart hadn't healed. She felt it. The loss of his wife and unborn child still burned hot inside him, and clearly, the loss of his birth family felt like death too. Addy understood all too well.

"Where are they now?"

He glanced her way, but his gaze settled in the

distance. "They all still live right around here. I used to run into them at church, so we stopped going, and rodeos used to be a big thing for us, but seeing them there stopped me from doing that too. I haven't figured out how to stop shopping at the grocery store or going to the gas station. No matter how hard I try to avoid them, I still run into them, but we don't speak."

"Does Juli know? About your brother, I mean."

"No. I could never tell her." Jack opened the grill lid, squeezed half a lemon over the filets, and then closed it again. "Do you mind bringing out the salad I made for us? It's in the fridge. Plates too?"

Addy went inside to the kitchen and found the salad, sealed with cling wrap, and opened the cupboard she'd watched him take plates out of at breakfast. She grabbed forks and napkins, too, and carried them outside.

"Picnic table?" she asked.

"That'd be great." Jack opened the grill lid, slid the cedar plank into his gloved hand, and followed her to the table.

"I'll bet you have better family stories than I do. Tell me one of yours."

It had been a long time since Addy had talked about the death of her parents. She wasn't sure if the words would come out anymore, but here, in this place that looked like home, they didn't seem so stifling.

"Mine probably isn't what you're expecting either."

"I'd like to hear it if you're willing," he said, sliding a salmon filet onto her plate. "I don't get many chances to talk about things other than Barbie dolls or how many first graders have kittens, puppies, or ponies."

Addy watched Jack, smiling when he did. He was

captivating. He was gorgeous. But there were other things about him too.

"Well, let's see..." She straightened. "I was seventeen when my parents died. How's that for an opener?"

Jack put down his fork, his gaze steady on hers. "You're right. I wasn't expecting that. That's a tough blow for a teen. Don't tell me you had to raise your brothers and sisters on your own?"

"No," Addy said, giving an amused titter to lighten the mood. "I was an only child whose parents were onlies, too. Sort of the last in the line, you know?"

"What about your grandparents? Mine were a big influence on me growing up."

"Nope." Addy shook her head. "Both sets of grandparents died much too early. My mom and dad were in their late thirties before they married. I always had the oldest parents out of all my friends at school."

"So, at seventeen, you were left on your own without any family at all?"

She nodded. "An orphan with just a few months left in the court system. At eighteen, they waved goodbye, so to speak, and dusted their hands of my existence. As far as I could tell anyway."

Jack reached for the bottle of wine and refilled her glass.

Addy asked, "Do you have other siblings?"

"No, it was just us two boys, but I have a cousin I grew up with who has a cattle ranch in Legacy, not too far from here." He held up his wine glass with a slight tip. "I'm sure the three of us were a handful growing up."

"I always wished I'd had a sister or a brother or lots of cousins. It wouldn't have mattered which. Big families were way cool in my book."

Addy ate almost ravenously until she caught Jack eyeing her. She stopped chewing and put two fingers to her lips. "I'm so sorry. I guess I was hungrier than I thought."

"Eat up. We've got plenty more salad." He glanced at the remnants of coho salmon on her plate. "The filets were pretty small. Sorry about that. But if it's any consolation, I picked up half a dozen freestone peaches in Stonewall yesterday. They're a great dessert. Juli likes me to peel and slice them and then spray whipped cream on top, but I love them fresh, picked right off the branches." Through the limbs of the pecan tree, light from the setting sun found Addy's face, bathing her in a soft hue. It drew a smile from him. "Everything tastes sweeter in August." His gaze stayed.

"I'm not gonna lie—a fresh peach sounds great. In Dallas, I would have bought one from the farmer's market, which is almost as good as picking it yourself. Maybe I'll have one later, okay?"

"Anything you say," Jack said, the smoky scent of grilled salmon lingering in the air. "You never said how your parents passed away. Was theirs a car accident too?"

Addy shook her head. "Airplane crash."

"And you became a pilot? What made you want to fly after a tragedy like that?"

"I know. Weird, right? But afterward—after the crash—I was obsessed with needing to know how the safest form of travel could kill everyone I'd ever loved, so I decided to enroll in flight school at eighteen, and here I am."

Her circle of friends worked and lived in the commercial airline world. Tonight, it was nice to talk to someone with a different background and not discuss the furlough, or losing her apartment, or failing to save money for a rainy day. Frankly, it was nice to be here with Jack.

They talked as the sun inched down, slowly dimming the day's light. As dusk fell in hues of pink and blue on the western horizon, she caught sight of a bird perched on a metal seed feeder at the corner of the fenced yard. A quiet gasp escaped.

She pointed to it and, talking softly, she said, "Look at that bird. What kind is that?"

Jack turned to see the colorful bird move to the backside of the feeder. "Oh, man. Juli's going to be sad to hear that she missed this." Keeping his eyes on the feeder, he said, "She can sit out here for hours with her dolls, just waiting for one of those birds."

"But what is it? I've never seen anything like it. It has so many colors!"

"It's a painted bunting. We get a few visits from them, but they're shy. I can never get close enough for a good picture of one." Jack took out his cell phone and held it up, and then he walked slowly and quietly toward the feeder. He took several photos with his shutter silenced before the bird flew away.

"Did you get a good picture for Juli?" Addy asked.

Jack returned to the picnic table, eyeing his phone the whole way. When Addy stood to see the camera's photos, he moved closer, holding the screen so that both could see. He swiped from one picture to the next until, "Aha! I got him." He rotated the phone. "Sort of..."

Addy reached up, angling the phone slightly downward. "Look at that," she said softly. "You got all but his tail in the picture. His colors are incredibly vivid. He gets his name honestly, doesn't he? It really looks like someone took a paintbrush and painted all those colors on him." Without much thought, she swiped to the next one. "Red, yellow, green... Is his head purple?"

"Blue," Jack said, focusing on the cell phone photo. "Birders say it's blue."

Unintentionally, she leaned into him, sparking a magnetism—the mere touch releasing a surge through her body. She wanted to pull away, but no man had ever felt so *right*. She looked up, her gaze locked onto his blue eyes.

"Incredible," she mumbled.

Jack lowered the phone, keeping his focus on Addy. "It is, isn't it?" Then softly, "The bird, I mean."

"Yes." The word came out in a sultry whisper, one even she didn't recognize. When Jack turned, fronting her, a shameless urge to press her body, her lips, to his nearly overcame her.

"Just curious," he managed to say. "Do you really have to leave tomorrow?"

Sheer willpower sent her a step back. She nodded. "Yes. Early. I have an appointment in Dallas at two o'clock, but I'll be back. My first flight is on Monday morning. A lot sooner than I expected."

"Will that give you enough time to find an apartment?"

Addy glanced at the big American Foursquare that looked so much like home, then back to Jack. She felt like she'd known him her whole life. "Not likely. Any chance I might be able to stay here until I find a place of my own? It sounds like I'll have a pretty busy schedule for the next few weeks, so you probably won't have to see much of me. I can look for an apartment whenever I'm here."

"Yeah, sure," Jack said, unable to curb a smile. "Stay as long as you need." He reached for her, but the motion sensor light, directed like a spotlight, clicked on, lighting up the yard when Juli and Paige opened the back door and stepped out.

"Daddy!" Juli stopped. She put her hands on her hips, pushing out her bottom lip in a pout. "I wanted to buy a pony today, but Miss Paige said no!"

Laughing, Paige called out, "It wouldn't fit in my car." The two came down the back steps hand in hand, with Juli giggling.

The six-year-old ran to her father and hugged his legs, then she turned, looking up at Addy. "Did you have fun today, too, Miss Addy?"

"I did," Addy told her. She knelt to talk to Juli. "And guess what?"

Juli's eyes stretched wide. "You got a new airplane?"

"I sort of did. Yes."

With a bounce, she said, "Can I ride in it? I want to fly like you!"

"Whoa." Jack reached down, picking up his daughter and swinging her onto his shoulders. "Hold on there, cowgirl. I thought you liked horses."

"I do." Juli giggled again, spreading her arms out wide like the wings of a jet. "But Miss Addy has her very own airplane!" Then from atop his shoulders, she leaned down, planting a kiss on his cheek. "I like Miss Addy, Daddy. Don't you?"

Jack glanced at Addy with a grin. "Yep, kiddo, I do."

"I hate to break up this party," Paige said, "but I need to get home." She glanced at Addy. "Congratulations on the new airplane. So, I guess you'll be leaving tomorrow?"

When the motion sensor clicked, the porch light

went off, leaving them in darkness except for light cast by the half-moon.

"Oh, I, uh, no..." Rarely flustered, the stammer put Addy ill at ease. Steeling her posture, she started again. "I'll be staying here until I find an apartment."

Even in the shadowy moonlight, Addy saw Paige eye Jack.

"Yay!" Juli clapped.

Jack gently swung Juli to the ground, then took her hand in his. "Thanks for taking Juli today," he said to Paige, then he slipped his arm around her shoulders and walked Paige toward the house.

"Staying, Jack?" Paige whispered. "What are you doing?"

Detecting their movement, the backyard spotlight clicked on again.

"I don't know," he whispered back.

CHAPTER 7

The road to Fray Enterprises was deserted Monday morning. It seemed that folks in the Hill Country took their Labor Day vacation seriously and were celebrating the end-of-summer holiday somewhere other than on Mystic Road.

After entering the gated property, Addy had instructions to drive directly to the hangar, down a curvy blacktop road west of the house. She drove slowly, following the road as it wound around a stand of live oaks. Beyond the bend was a section of cleared land, stretching for miles, but a tan metal building was just a short distance away, having six garage doors with an entrance door at the far end, above which hung a sign: *Fray Transport*. No more than another half mile farther out was the hangar and runway.

Parked, Addy slung her brown travel duffel over her shoulder and then headed for the door. Just as she grabbed the handle, a man wearing blue jeans and a tan, short-sleeve collared shirt pushed open the door, holding it wide.

"You Addy?"

"Yes." Addy's gaze fell to his broad square-toe boots and then back up. He wasn't at all what she expected. Thin build. Searing blue eyes. Classic honey brown hair. *Plain.* "Ernst?"

"Naw," he said. "I'm Nick, the airport manager. Come on in."

Addy stepped inside. "I thought the captain was meeting me."

"That's the plan, but he isn't here yet." He let the door shut behind her, then said, "Coffee?"

"Yes, thank you." Addy looked around the one-room office. It had little in the way of décor, and a spray of air freshener would have helped a great deal. In the corner of the room was a coffee bar, minimal in nature, beside a single-door refrigerator. Oversized maps hung on the walls, and two metal desks sat side by side in the middle of the room, each with its own landline telephone.

Addy slipped the bag off her shoulder, but when she looked at the floor, she held tight to its strap. The beige tile hadn't seen a mop in weeks, maybe months. This wasn't at all what she expected after visiting the immaculate Fray residence.

"Hope you don't take creamer." Nick handed her a ceramic cup with a faded moniker filled barely halfway with black coffee.

"Actually, I do." Addy handed the cup back for the addition.

"Sorry." He shrugged. "We don't keep that stuff around here. It's black or nothing, but I can buy some next time I'm in town."

She glanced at the refrigerator. "Do you have milk?"

Nick shook his head.

"So, I suppose the fridge is filled with beer and candy bars?"

Head down, Nick laughed to himself. "Nope," he said, raising his head. "No alcohol allowed. And I don't eat candy." He pointed to the fridge. "But there's bread, ham and cheese, mayo, and mustard inside if you're hungry. Pickles, too, I think, unless Joshy ate 'em all."

Of course, there was no alcohol allowed. *Ernst.* Fidgety, she held onto her cup. "Mr. Fray didn't mention that he had an airport manager."

"I've been here about a year," Nick said. "But he should have given me the title of property manager, slash, airport manager, slash, fleet manager, slash, mechanic. I kind of do it all."

"That's a lot to juggle."

"It's good. Thabo's a great guy to work for, and I pretty much get to do my own thing."

A door in the back of the room, one Addy hadn't even noticed, opened, and in walked a young man. His black plaid shirt had grease stains, just like his hands.

"Hey, Joshy," Nick said. "Come on in and meet Addy. She's the new pilot taking over for Janet for a while."

The boy, barely out of his teens, wiped his hands down the legs of his blue jeans, and then he reached for a handshake. "Pleased to meet you, ma'am."

Addy shook his hand. "Joshy, is it?"

"Josh." He glanced at Nick and then looked back at Addy. "Just Josh."

"Joshy helps me with everything around here. Changes oil, filters, wiper fluid, and keeps the fleet clean and ready to go."

"The fleet?" Addy asked.

"The vehicles. Thabo has four, but the caddy and the Nav are his favorites."

"So, who takes care of the aircraft maintenance?"

"Mostly me. I'm certified A&P. Spent almost seven years in the Navy and two years at Boeing." He went to his desk and sat down. "Worked at Mooney for a while too. Great little planes." With his thumb, he motioned behind him. "Got a nice one in the hangar."

"I'm learning from Nick before I move to Houston for school so that I can get certified too," Josh told Addy as the front door pushed open.

All three looked up. A man, head down, wearing a crisp, clean pilot's uniform, entered.

"Mornin'," Nick said. "Ernst, this is Addy. She was here on time. Where you been, buddy?"

"I'm not your buddy," Ernst said. He stopped when his gaze landed on Addy. Shoulders back, he stepped toward her, hand out. "Well, you're a most pleasant surprise."

"Hello," she said with a handshake.

Ernst gave her a lingering smile, and then he headed for the coffee without a word or glance for anyone else. Pouring, he said, "I wasn't expecting such a beauty as you." He turned back, took a sip, and let his gaze wash over her.

Ernst looked nothing like the man she'd envisioned. His pearly-white hair, classically styled in a vintage Cary Grant cut, had a freshly shampooed glisten and bore the salty scent of ocean air. When he smiled, his ice-blue eyes steeled his charisma—masculine and seductive—and his British accent didn't hurt the package. It was no wonder women tolerated his bad behavior.

"Your credentials are impressive for a woman," he said.

"For a woman?" Addy scoffed at the chauvinistic remark. "My credentials are impressive, gender aside." She motioned around the office. "Where are your qualifications? I wasn't offered the same courtesy of reviewing your file. Fair's fair." She held out her hand, summoning proof of his competence.

Ernst laughed. "My credentials are suitable to our employer—that should be good enough for you."

His white pilot shirt shouldered a pair of four-bar epaulets, and its tapered fit flaunted a hale physique. Although he stood in a stance that invited her appraisal, Addy forced her gaze to hold steady on his blue eyes until he turned to Josh.

"It's already hot out." He started for the back-office door, picking a key off the rack and tossing it to Josh. "Drive us, won't you?"

In the garage, Ernst waited for Josh to unlock the doors of an agate black King Ranch SuperCrew truck. He opened the front passenger door at the *click* and then tossed his flight bag onto the floorboard, pulling himself up onto the leather bucket seat.

Addy slid her travel bag onto the back seat, then got in, buckling her seatbelt while the garage door rolled up, flooding the bay with sunlight.

Josh fired up the engine, backed out, and headed for the hangar, a half mile away.

After opening the biparting doors where the aircraft waited, ready for boarding, Ernst said, "You can go now, Josh. You're no longer needed."

Josh gave Addy a departing nod from the open window and then put the idling King Ranch truck in gear. "See you on the return."

Addy forged past Ernst, up the steps of the Gulf-stream. "Shall we get started?" she said without any other acknowledgment.

Although the aircraft wasn't "off the assembly line" new, its condition appeared pristine. With Ernst follow-ing, Addy walked the main cabin, brushing her hand over the beige wool and leather blend seats on her way forward to the full-service galley. Light oak cabinets housed an array of wine and champagne glasses, two coffeemakers, a microwave and convection oven, and a built-in cooler.

"Does it meet with your approval?" Businesslike, Ernst lent no sincerity to his tone.

"How old is it?" Addy swept past him. It was a beautiful aircraft, but she had no intention of bonding with this man over it. She knew too much about him. Worse, she knew his kind.

He followed. "It was purchased used eight months ago with fifteen hundred flight hours on it."

Midcabin, she stopped and turned to him. "Why a G550? It's equipped for sixteen passengers. It's just him, right? Why not the smaller G280?"

"The choice was mine. He left it up to me, and I'm partial to Rolls Royce engines." Just a step behind, Ernst reached out and lightly brushed a speck off the shoulder of her flight uniform. Then softer, he said, "And aside from a powerful thrust, most women agree bigger is better, don't they?" His gaze went to her hazel-green eyes, but when her serious face held, he coolly directed her onward to the open cockpit door. "Fray Enterprises has over a hundred investors, and Thabo has new interests forming in Thailand and Fiji. He's also partial to Northern Spain. The Bay of Biscay. Basque Country. His grandfather's roots and all. The

G550 is one of the longest-range private jets in the world." He offered a smile, holding it in wait of a return. When none came, he broke, saying, "There's more to our billionaire than just eldercare homes."

"International flights were never discussed with me."

"I'm sure he assumed you knew. Is it a problem for you?"

"No," she said.

The flight deck with Honeywell's PlaneView avionics system had been what had drawn Addy to obtain her G550 certification so many months ago. When she considered going into the private sector as a pilot, she wanted the best cockpit technology available, one focused on pilot performance and safety. Gulfstream hit all the marks.

"What's our departure time?"

Ernst looked at his wristwatch. "You've got two hours."

"Good. I'll pull the weather forecast."

"Nick has already called for the refueling."

"Any crew?"

"Yes, Madelyn, but she'll board at the Jet Center." In answer to Addy's questioning glance, Ernst said, "For the Sky Harbor leg." He held up a folded paper. "Thabo has ten new investors flying with him from Tucson to Phoenix."

"Is Madelyn regular crew?"

"Do you mean competition?" Ernst smiled. "Don't worry, love. Madelyn is a true hot-blooded, red-haired beauty, but you're top billing this trip."

CHAPTER 8

The town's strip mall was a concrete and steel monstrosity, cold, bland, and isolated with barely a living thing to beautify it, which is why Paige hated shopping there, but she needed office supplies, and there was only one store for that in town.

Parked alongside a landscaped island, one sorely lacking a gardener's touch, she opened the door of her blue Subaru Outback to a collective buzz of honeybees, quivering the air over tiny lavender flowers on a neglected rosemary bush. Hurriedly, she shut the door, leaped over the dirt-dry median, and headed for the entrance.

"Paige, wait up!"

She turned. Rebecca Brown was zigzagging between parked cars, hurrying toward her, followed by her husband, Doug.

"It's so good to see you." Rebecca pulled Paige into an embrace, holding on for longer than needed.

Paige pulled back with a thoughtful smile. "Hi," she

said. When Doug caught up to them, she returned his hug too. "You both look well. How are you?"

"Oh, you know us," Rebecca said. "We're always fine. Just fine. How's Jack? And how is Juli? She's already started school this year, hasn't she?"

Paige had known the Browns all her life—Jack's parents. Her best friend's in-laws. But when Kaitlin died, so had their relationship. Still, a decades-old emotional bond tugged at her heart whenever she saw them.

"Yeah, it's hard to believe she's in first grade," Paige said. "She's so beautiful and smart. I wish you could see her."

Rebecca blinked, pushing tears from her eyes. "I do too."

"How's the seed growin' business?" Doug asked, a Texas twist to his words.

"It's booming." Paige laughed, trying to ease the tension. "Almost more than the two of us can handle."

"You know I'd be glad to help," he said. "Tell him, will you?"

"I will." Paige nodded. Then, "Is Nick still sober?"

"He hasn't had a drink in four years," Rebecca said. "He's got a real good job now, and he goes to AA meetings every week like clockwork." She reached out and took her hand, holding it tight. "Those three years he spent in jail changed him, Paige. It did. He's not the same man that he was four years ago. We keep waiting and hoping. Do you think Jack will ever forgive him? Or us? It was a tragic accident. But it was an *accident*. Has he said anything?"

The pain, carved deep into her face, was hard to deny. Paige looked down. "It's not an easy thing to forgive."

"Will you talk to him again for us?" When Paige didn't answer, she said, "Please?"

Paige nodded. "Sure, I will." She gave a squeeze to Rebecca's hand before letting go. Glancing at Doug, she said, "It was good to see you both again."

THE JUDDERING SEED CLEANER IN THE TXUS SEEDS building buried the sound of Paige's car engine and her arrival inside.

"Jack," she said, tapping his shoulder. When he turned, she motioned to the on/off toggle.

After a click of the switch, he doffed his dust mask. "Hey, did you find the supplies you needed?"

"Yeah, and I ran into your mom and dad while I was there too." Paige eyed him, waiting for a reaction. When his shoulders tensed, she put her hand gently on his forearm. "They said Nick's still sober. Four years now, Jack. Your mom said he never misses a weekly AA meeting, and he's holding down a good job. She swears he's a changed man."

Laser-focused, he said, "That still doesn't change what he did, Paige. You know that."

She dropped her hand from his arm and nodded. "I know. But they miss you and Juli so much. Your dad wants to come out and help us get caught up, and —"

"You told him we were behind on orders?"

"No." Paige shook her head. "I just said we had so much business we could barely keep up. That's all."

Jack pulled up his dust mask, fitting it over his nose and mouth. "You shouldn't have said *anything*. You had no right to talk to them." He reached for the on/off switch, but Paige grabbed his arm.

"You can't tell me not to talk to them, Jack. I've known Doug and Rebecca my whole life. I've known them longer than I've known *you!*" She released his arm, then stepped back, taking a deep breath. "I'm sorry, I didn't mean to yell, but you know I've never agreed with shutting out your parents. Nick—okay. I get it. But not your parents."

Their conversation paused when Jack turned his back to her, checking the screens on the seed cleaner. Without looking up, he said, "They're just making obligatory parental inquiries. It's a parent's job."

Paige went to the clean seed container and sifted a handful through her fingers. "I'm not sure that's it, Jack." She felt him studying her, trying to read what she wasn't telling him. What started as a conversation about parents needed to be something more. Steeling herself, she said, "I'd like to take Juli to visit them."

Jack shoved the top screen in with a bang, then turned, jerking his dust mask off. "You'd what?"

"She has a right to know her grandparents."

"She had a right to know her mother too!" He started for the door. "I need some fresh air."

Paige winced when the door slammed. "Well, that was a disaster of a conversation." She looked up, envisioning the shining blue sky of heaven somewhere high above the metal rooftop. "I could sure use some help down here, Kaitlin."

CHAPTER 9

When the Gulfstream touched down in Tucson, it was noon and 107 degrees. The blast of dry heat hit Addy while exiting the plane.

Inside the Jet Center, Thabo dialed his driver, then turned to Ernst and Addy. "I should be back in about three hours." To Ernst, he said, "The investors are arriving here at four o'clock. I'll need you to greet them. When Madelyn arrives, board everyone, give them the tour, and have her get them settled with drinks and hors d'oeuvres." Then to Addy, he said, "You're welcome to come along with me. I thought you might like to see one of our eldercare homes. A few of the residents are retired pilots, and they enjoyed having Janet visit and talk to them about the latest news. They'll be disappointed if I don't bring you."

"I'd love to come," Addy said.

The Navigator was a sleek silver jade with a quiet, well-mannered older driver. Thabo focused his conversation on eldercare as they maneuvered through the

city streets, most dotted with green-trunked Palo
Verde, giant saguaro, and flame-tipped ocotillo.

"Although they didn't raise me, my grandfather and
grandmother were more *parent* to me than my own. I
felt as though I'd failed them when I realized they'd
been put into a nursing home with a despicable reputation. I was living in Spain at the time. I flew home as
soon as I heard, but Grandmother passed before I
could see her again. My father had far more money
than I did at the time to take care of them, but he had
very little in the way of love and compassion."

"I'm sorry to hear about your grandmother. Were
you able to help your grandfather?"

"Yes, fortunately. When I saw the conditions, I
moved him into private care, but then I bought the
facility." He glanced at Addy. "It was my first. With
some money and the right people in place, that dreadful
nursing home is now a premier eldercare establishment.
Today, it has twenty-five permanent residents and
offers a team of nurses around-the-clock, seven days a
week. I've made sure it's affordable."

"What about your grandfather? Did you move him
back there afterward?"

"No, he wanted to live in Florida, so I bought a five-
bedroom house and renovated it into a private assisted-
living home. We're visiting a similar one today.
Although Grandfather is ninety-one now, he does well
taking care of himself. He just needs a little help sometimes, and he doesn't like living alone, so the group
home arrangement works for him." He looked at Addy.
"I'd like you to meet him on our next trip to Destin."

"I'd like to. I never knew my grandparents, and my
own parents passed away several years ago. I miss
having a family in my life."

Thabo gave her a soft glance, then said, "I know. Your misfortune was in the report given to me. I'm truly sorry for your loss."

"You had me investigated?"

"I have an agency that checks the credentials and backgrounds of every employee."

"Personal lives too?"

"Absolutely, yes. Character comes straight from the life you've lived."

The eldercare home was on two acres of lush Sonoran Desert, well outside the city limits. The sand-colored adobe home bordered a mesquite bosque, but its front yard was landscaped with crushed red stone, desert verbena, purple lantana, ocotillo, and sage. A stately three-arm saguaro grew in the center island of its circular drive. It was not what Addy had expected. She assumed the assisted-living home would be a cold, institutional-like facility, but instead, the property was a private sanctuary.

An aproned woman greeted their knock. With her dark hair pulled back, she gave them a genuine smile.

"Mr. Fray." She opened the door wider. "Please come in. You're right on time."

The home's interior was decorated in muted shades of sand and shell, and the furnishings consisted of dark oak tables, a library wall of books, and tan Naugahyde furnishings spaced wide for wheelchairs and walkers. Gleaming, wide-plank oak floors ran throughout.

The scent of roasting chicken permeated the quiet home.

"Please," Lettie beckoned, "come with me. The chicken needs basting, or it will dry out." She hurried through an arched doorway.

The kitchen was cheerfully decorated with wares

from Mexico, and on the wide window sill were small, brightly glazed pots growing all manner of herbs.

Two plump hens, golden but not browned, were side by side in a big roasting pan. Lettie stood basting them.

Looking back over her shoulder, she asked, "Has Janet had the baby already?"

"No," Thabo answered. "This is Addy, my new pilot while Janet is on maternity leave."

The woman stopped basting, slid the big pan back into the oven, and turned. "It's very nice to meet you." She wiped her hands before shaking with Addy.

"Janet still has a few months to go before the baby, but she's far enough along that she isn't permitted to fly for a while. I'm just filling in for her until she can return."

"Well, the boys will be awfully glad to meet you. Janet usually plays cards with them and tells them all about her travels. You will, too, won't you?"

Brows raised, Addy glanced at Thabo.

"By *the boys*, she means the residents. There are seven, and three are retired pilots." To Lettie, he said, "Are they in the game room?"

"Yes." Lettie pointed. "It'll be another forty-five minutes before supper is ready. Plenty of time for conversation."

Thabo led the way through the house. Just as Lettie had said, the men were in the game room. Five were playing cards, and two were shooting pool. When they entered, the pool players stopped and laid their cues across the green felt table to shake hands with Thabo. At the card table, players stood, using walkers to steady themselves, and shook hands, too, but the last man was in a wheelchair, so Thabo walked around the table to him and knelt, talking to him as if they were old friends.

"Boys," Thabo said, extending his hand outward to Addy. "Meet Addy. She's taking over for Janet for a while. I'm counting on you to keep her entertained while I tend to business with the Taylors." He nodded to Addy, then started for the door but stopped, turning back. To the men, he said, "Is everything okay here? Anything you need to talk to me about?"

After a collective "things are good" answer, Thabo left the room.

"You a poker player, Addy?"

"Yes, a little. I'm not very good at it," she admitted, "but I know the rules. I'm better at pool." She gave a laugh. "Well, I can hit the balls anyway. Sometimes I manage to get one in."

The man with a Gatsby cap pulled out a chair at the card table. "Come play a hand while Bernie and Del finish their game." He flicked a sideways nod to the pool table. "Bernie'll scratch on the eight ball before long, and then you can play."

Everyone laughed and then introduced themselves by raising a hand and calling out their name as if it were a daily ritual: Bernie, Del, Carl, Jim, Jimmy, Lamar, and Frank.

"Where are you from?" Lamar, a Black man with graying hair, asked her.

"The Dallas area," Addy said. "You?"

"Me?" Lamar smiled and then sat back, holding his cards close to the vest. "New Orleans originally, but the Air Force sent me to Davis-Monthan more than forty years ago, and I just stayed. I never left Tucson. Raised my family here. Buried 'em here, too."

Without missing a beat, Frank said, "Say, it seems

like there's an awful lot of girl pilots nowadays. It didn't used to be that way. Are you Air Force?"

Addy reached out and gave a gentle touch to Lamar's shoulder to show him that she had heard his sorrow, then she answered Frank, "No." She laughed. "I'd probably flunk out of basic."

"Then what made you start flying?" Jim asked, dealing her a hand of cards. "Usually, it's the USAF that makes pilots out of women."

The men—each eightyish and not at all shy—stared at her in wait of a response. She doubted she could get away with a pat answer, so she didn't even try.

"When I was a teenager, my parents died in a plane crash." She scanned the faces of the men, their silence deafening. Methodically, she rearranged the cards in her hand, then said, "I decided to put myself through flight school to find out how those things happen."

With some prying, Addy relented and told the story that she hadn't told anyone in a long, long time.

"I was seventeen. Too old for a babysitter but too young to stay home alone. Or so my parents thought." The men stopped playing to listen. "Prom was a week away, and my boyfriend had just broken up with me. I was a total mess. I didn't even know Mom and Dad had another trip planned. Anyway, they came into my bedroom to say goodbye and found me red-eyed and bawling, sprawled across my bed. Mom promised they'd be home by noon the next day and said we could talk about it. I recall her kissing my forehead, but I yelled at her about leaving me on the worst day of my life, which sort of made my dad mad. He said, 'Get up, stop crying, and get your overnight bag.' You'd have thought they were invisible by the way I treated them after that. I knew Ivy and Beth were outside waiting for me."

"Your sisters?" Jimmy asked.

"Oh, sorry, no. No siblings. Beth was a girl in my math class—the most unpopular girl in my school. Everybody thought Ivy, Beth's mother, was a witch."

"Mean?" Del asked.

"No, like a *real* witch—Ivy Stinson had tarot cards and always had a candle burning. She usually wore black and was super quiet, which made her kind of mysterious." Addy shrugged. "They lived across the street, which made them a convenient stand-in when my parents needed a place to send me."

Then, "I remember rolling my eyes at Dad, which he hated, and I shouted, 'What-ever.' I was seventeen— old enough to stay home for one night by myself. All I wanted to do was cry and write a letter to Marc that would convince him to take me back, but I rolled off my bed, grabbed the bag Mom had prepacked, and took off down the stairs without even saying goodbye to them." Addy glanced at the men again. "I was really mad. I didn't even tell them that I loved them."

The story rolled out—alive in her memories.

In the faint morning light, Ivy had awoken Addy. "You need to get up, honey." She wore a dark bathrobe, and her shoulder-length red hair was poufy with sleeping tangles.

Words were barely a whisper.

Dead? How could her parents be dead? The thought that it might be true was ludicrous—and in a plane crash? The last time Addy had seen them, they were getting into their car at the curb, dressed to impress. Her mother had on her favorite gray dress with pearl earrings and a necklace, and her father was in a suit.

What was it—a wedding? Dinner with her father's boss again? She hadn't even asked.

Ivy made no sense, and wide-eyed Beth had just stared.

"That's a terrible joke to play on someone!" Addy shouted at the two of them and then nudged her way past Beth to the chair where she'd left her clothes. She pulled on her blue jeans and T-shirt and then grabbed her sneakers. "I'm going home."

Still barefoot, she started down the stairs.

"Honey, wait..."

But she kept going. When she realized Beth was on her heels, she turned, shouting, "Stay away from me, Beth, or I swear I'll tell everybody in school that you're a witch too!"

Addy was across the street and on her porch steps before she remembered she had left her house key hanging on the Stinson's key rack. *Why would they lie?* She dropped down onto the weathered porch swing that she hadn't touched since summer and pulled her bare feet up under her. She'd stay there all day and wait if she had to. Noon wasn't that far off. Just like they'd said, her mother and father would drive up, and then she would tell them about the cruel joke. They'd never make her stay at Beth's house again.

But the next time she looked up, Ivy was dressed and crossing the road. She climbed the porch steps and then stood, eyes glistening, not looking at Addy but past her. The two of them stayed there for what seemed like an eternity without saying a word.

When a white car pulled up to the curb, Ivy started down the porch steps toward it. She met the driver at his open door, her eyes shifting from Addy to the man as she talked. When he got out of the car, Addy stood.

He was a middle-aged man, tall and big-bellied, wearing a baby blue dress shirt with cream-colored khakis. She would never forget.

Coming up the walkway, he called out, "Are you Addy?"

Without answering, Addy went to the front door and jiggled the handle, praying it would magically open. The closer he came, the harder she rattled. She squeezed the knob between both hands, pushing against the door with her shoulder until he laid his hand lightly over her clenched but trembling fists. "Addy, my name is John. I'm with Child Protective Services."

Her body went limp. She slid down, her bottom hitting the porch floor.

He squatted beside her. Softly, he said, "I have a place for you, Addy. The house is in your school district too."

"But *this* is my house." Her throat, cold and hollow, closed on the words.

"Since you don't have other family, the Murrays have offered you a room in their home for a while. They're nice people."

She started to cry, first a trickle then more, because the somber offer to live in someone else's house meant there was no denying the truth—her parents weren't coming home. She was completely and utterly alone.

CHAPTER 10

When he heard the air brakes of Juli's school bus, Jack pushed back his office chair and rose from his desk. Deep in thought, he was halfway down the long dirt drive before realizing Paige was already at the designated stop, waiting for the six-year-old.

Paige Davis wasn't just his lifelong friend—or the legal guardian to his daughter should anything happen to him—she also managed the office of TXUS Seeds and helped work the farm. Her graphic design degree, coupled with her congenial nature, had quadrupled his customers in the last four years. He trusted her. But she was a hard reminder that Kaitlin was gone. The two women had rarely been without each other until the accident, even being born on the same day, at the same hospital, just a room apart. They had an uncanny ability to know what the other needed long before the need was known. His wife's death had devastated Paige as much as it had him, but somehow, she had risen above the grief and then pulled him to his feet.

Paige was family. He loved her like a sister. He depended on her, and so did his daughter.

Juli jumped from the bottom step of the bus, taking hold of Paige's hand. The two started back down the dirt farm road toward him.

With hands tucked into the pockets of his denim jeans, Jack waited, watching, taking in every detail about Juli—his beautiful daughter. Her butter-blonde hair, her smile, her love-of-life blue eyes were so similar to Kaitlin's that just the sight of her sometimes took his breath. *Would Jenna have looked like Juli?* An all too familiar ache twisted inside him. *Their baby.* Lost, before found. They'd settled on a name the night before the accident, but without his wife's final consent, Jack had refused to legally name the unborn child. He'd asked that "and Baby Brown" be added beneath Kaitlin's name on the headstone. Though nameless in granite, she was Jenna, his daughter. Jack had never revealed her name to anyone—not to Juli, not to his parents. Not even Paige. Keeping it secret somehow gave him a bond he needed to the child he could never know.

"It's your move, Juli." Jack tapped the wooden tic-tac-toe game box on the coffee table between them as evening light spilled in through the west windows of the living room.

Propped up on her knees, Juli put an *X* on the board. "Why do we have game day on Sunday? Chloe's mom says Saturday is supposed to be game day. Allison said so too."

Jack placed an *O* marker in the top left corner. "I

guess it's because when I was a kid, we always played family games after church on Sunday."

"You mean you and Grandma and Grandpa?"

"Yes."

"And your brother?"

"Yes."

"What's his name again?"

Jack looked at her. "Who?"

"Your brother." Juli rolled an extra *O* marker across the table to him.

He tapped the wooden box again. "Come on, Juli. Concentrate. I don't even have supper started yet."

"But what's his name?"

Jack hesitated at first. "Nick. Now make a move."

"*Nick*," Juli whispered to herself. "*Uncle Nick*." She set an *X* in the center. "Why don't we ever see them? Junie has an Uncle Mike. He coaches her sister's soccer team. And Allison's grandma and grandpa pick her up on Wednesdays from school, and then they go get ice cream. I wish I had a grandma and grandpa that would take me for ice cream. And Allison has *two* aunts and *three* uncles!"

Jack stood. "I'm done playing. You get to put up the game." Without explanation, he left, leaving Juli alone with their unfinished game.

In the kitchen, he took a package of ground beef out of the refrigerator and put the meat into a skillet on the stove. He used a wooden spoon to break it into chunks, then he stirred and poked at it until it turned into crumbles, but his mind wasn't on the spaghetti sauce his wife had taught him to make. It was on their daughter.

Juli was right. She should have a grandma and grandpa, but he hadn't been the one to deprive her of that relationship. His parents had made their choice the day they sided with Nick. If the whole ugly truth were known about her mother's death, she'd understand, but she was still too young—too tender to learn that her uncle had killed her mother in a drunken state of mind behind the wheel of a car—and too fragile to be told that her grandparents had chosen Nick instead of her.

CHAPTER 11

Addy donned her aviator sunglasses and drove straight back to the B and B from Fray Transport, only taking the time to remove her uniform's black necktie.

Parked in the driveway of the big American Foursquare home was a four-door white F-150 pickup truck, its side doors marked with the words TXUS Seeds. She pulled past it and into the open space next to the outside stairs. It had just been a week, but the house felt like home.

"Hi," Addy said when Jack answered her knock. He was the only man she'd ever known who smiled more with his eyes than his lips.

"It's really good to see you," he said. In the kitchen, Jack poured her an iced tea, then added two teaspoons of sugar and stirred before handing her the glass. "Did you have a good flight? How was Arizona?"

"Hot." She laughed, running her hand through the long side-swept bangs of her pixie cut. "But it's beautiful there. Ever been?"

"Years ago. I was about six and wanted to be a cowboy when I grew up, so my folks took us to Old Tucson for a summer vacation. The whole place nearly burned down a month later, and even though it was rebuilt, we never went back." He glanced at her. "Bet it's changed a lot."

"I'll bet it has," she joked. "So, I take it you weren't a Muppets kind of kid?"

"No." Jack shook his head. "I was hooked on old Westerns. I used to watch them with my grandpa. He'd let my brother and me play with cap guns and have shootouts, which my parents would be shocked to know. They expected me to grow up riding and breaking broncs, which I was pretty good at for a while." He laughed. "What about you?"

"*Xena: Warrior Princess*. What else?" Addy sipped her tea. She was looking too long at him. She knew it, but the line of his abs, creasing the thin white T-shirt, gave her an ache that sent her imagination reeling. And when he looked at her with those amazing blue eyes bearing one spot of gold, it was hard to look away.

Jack rinsed his empty morning coffee cup and set it in the sink. "So, what does a pilot do when they're not flying airplanes? Do you have the rest of the day off?"

"Today, *this* pilot needs to go apartment hunting." She took a swallow of tea and then set down her glass. "Can't stay here forever, right?" Though she dared not admit that the thought had crossed her mind.

"Right," he said with a nod. "But, you know, over half the day is already gone. Maybe you should take the afternoon off and come take a look at the flower fields with me instead."

Addy smiled. It was an unexpected burst of feelings. "I'd like that."

About a mile from the B and B was a tan metal building with a *TXUS Seeds* sign. Jack stopped his company pickup under an overhang, shading the truck from the scorching afternoon sun. He shut off the engine. "So, that's my daily drive to work." He flashed a broad smile. "You fly thousands of miles, and I drive five thousand feet. No wonder Juli thinks your job is more exciting."

Gravel crunched beneath his cowboy boots on their way to the front office door.

Inside the building was a small, windowed office, a seed cleaner, and a wall of shelving where dozens of folded tarps and plastic containers with lids were stacked. Most of the polished concrete floor was bare except for a few flat mats that were neatly covered with tiny seeds. Jack walked her to them.

"These wildflower seeds have been through our cleaner twice, but they need another day to dry, and then they'll go to the mill where they'll come out baggable clean."

Addy stood looking down at the orderly mats. "So, you just scoop up these seeds and put them in paper packets and sell them?"

Jack laughed. "There's a little more to it. After the mill finishes its process, the seeds are sent for testing, purity, germination and such, which takes about forty-five days. As soon as the seeds are certified viable, then they can be packaged for sale." His hand went lightly to her back. "Come on. I'll show you the fields."

As they walked to the rear door, Jack's hand slid lower, resting on her waist, his fingers curling impulsively, but quickly he eased, withdrawing his hand completely. He drew a breath and kept walking.

Outside, separated by a pattern of dirt roads, were

eight defined squares of land, each half an acre. Four were bursting with color. Jack walked Addy to the nearest field of yellow. "These beauties are Maximilian sunflowers." He pointed to the other sections one by one. "Over there are purple coneflowers, the next field has golden tickseed, and then the bluish-lavender ones are called Gregg's mistflower."

"Look at all the butterflies!"

"Yeah, they love the mistflower." Jack pointed to the other squares of land, all dormant. "In the spring, we'll have Texas bluebonnets, red corn poppies, black-eyed Susan, paintbrush, and pink primrose, then this summer, we'll have larkspur, Indian blanket, and more sunflowers." He glanced at her. "Keeps us busy most of the year."

Addy hadn't seen anyone in the building, and she saw no one outside working. "Where are your employees?"

He raised an eyebrow and then gave a side nod to the tan building. "There's just two of us this time of year. Paige and me."

"You two collect seeds from all of these flowers by yourselves?"

"No." Jack laughed. "Not by a longshot." He pointed south. "My neighbor runs a crew that does the harvesting for us. It's a time and labor-intensive job. If we ever expand the fields, we'll have to modernize our methods, but we do okay running it by ourselves most of the year."

"Wow." She sent her gaze across the wide, colorful swath of flowers gently swaying in the barely felt breeze. "Seems like a lot of work for two people, isn't it?"

"It is."

Addy resisted the urge to focus on Jack's physique, but a lingering glance settled on him anyway. His white, tissue-thin T-shirt did a poor job concealing his rippled abs and well-defined biceps. Even the scent of him kindled her fire. A man like Jack wasn't gym built. It was natural, she knew, likely acquired by working these beautiful fields and raising an energetic daughter. He was an outdoorsy man—a farmer of sorts —typically not the type of man who could stop her in her tracks. But he had. She glanced down. His boots were worn out and dusty. *Loyal to the end*, they said. Temptation sparked—she felt hot all the way to her toes.

Addy barely noticed the monarch flitting between them until it landed on the sleeve of her white uniform shirt. Its wings opened and closed, and opened and closed again.

After a moment, the deep orange and black butterfly gracefully lifted off. When it did, Jack reached for Addy's hand. He took her with him as he followed the monarch to the field of lavender mistflowers. As it moved from one fuzzy bloom to another, tasting the nectar of each, Jack silently pulled a silver tool from his belt sheath. When it lifted off again, he took the long stem of a visited flower and snipped, handing the flower to Addy as a keepsake. "Folklore says when a monarch lands on you, it's your guardian angel sending you a message."

If she truly had a guardian angel, she hoped Jack Brown was the message sent. Her gaze settled on him. She was tempted to brush her hand over his short-boxed beard and mustache. She wanted to feel the light-brown stubble against her hand, her face. The urge to be with this man, to *have* this man, was too much for her in the moment. Gripping the flower, Addy raised up on tiptoes and kissed him fully on the lips.

A lustful growl came from low in his throat, and then he was kissing her back, his hands caressing her face. Jack shifted her so that her back rested gently against a wood fence post with the wildflower fields behind her.

A floodgate opened. Addy dropped the flower and then slid her arms around his neck, the scent of him intoxicating. Her hands rounded downward over the slope of his shoulders to his biceps, caressing the line of him. His muscles flexed and tightened.

Barely able to breathe through the brunt of desire, a moan escaped Addy. She was ready to take a step she never expected, but like a bird caught midflight, Jack went still.

He took her hands and pulled them to his lips, kissing one, then the other. He held tight to them, a quiver in his grip. Leaning his forehead against hers, he said, "I hear Juli's bus."

No. Addy gave a whimper. She was trembling. *God, this can't be happening!*

Jack stepped back.

What had she done? She'd nearly seduced Jack — unbridled and out in the open, no less. She had virtually attacked him in the wildflower fields! She didn't know whether she should apologize or pack her bags and leave. She wanted to tell him that she'd never done anything like this before, but if she did, there was a chance he'd think she regretted it. And she didn't.

By the time the school bus arrived at its designated stop, Jack was jogging down the dirt farm road toward it.

Addy walked back to the office. From beneath the

overhang where Jack had parked the truck, she waited, watching as Juli got off the bus, then ran, backpack bobbing, to her father's arms. He picked her up and swung her around before kissing her cheek, and then he carried the grinning girl back to the metal building with him.

"Miss Addy, you're back!" Juli squirmed out of Jack's arms and ran to Addy, grabbing hold of her leg and hugging. She looked up, sweeping strands of blonde hair out of her eyes. "Are you staying again tonight?"

What could she possibly say? This was entirely her fault. The man was simply showing her his wildflower fields and she'd lost control. Not like her at all. She'd always prided herself on her restraint and discipline. Control at all times. She had never let a man distract her. *But this man was different.*

Jack tensed at Addy's glance, but then his gaze settled on her. "Of course, she's staying."

AT THE B AND B, ADDY EXCUSED HERSELF AND MADE her way upstairs. At almost thirty years old, she felt like a teenager confined to her room for being naughty. How could she ever face Jack again?

She sat on the Victorian lounge in her rented bedroom and started to scroll through the local motel listings on her cell phone. It wasn't like she was planning to duck out, never to be seen again. She was simply taking back her moral independence. And decency, if she had any. If Jack wanted to see her, he could. *But would he want to?* A place of her own—somewhere she could think—is what she needed.

"Miss Addy?" Juli knocked. "Are you okay? Daddy wants to know if you're coming down for supper. You are, aren't you?"

Addy cleared her throat. Took a breath. "Hey, Juli. I'll be down in a few minutes, okay?"

"Okay," she said.

She listened to the girl's footsteps down the hall and then down the stairs, relieving a bit of anxiety. *Pull it together, Addy.* At the closet, she took out her duffel and rifled through it until she found her favorite jeans and a plain gray T-shirt. Much better than wearing a disheveled pilot's uniform to dinner.

The evening was warm when Addy stepped out into the backyard, a light breeze rustling the pecan leaves as the late-day sun shimmered off its silvery lichen-spotted branches. At the click of the closing door, Jack turned, his blue eyes finding her, tender, although she sensed something more in them. Regret? Guilt?

"Hey," Addy said, approaching him as he stood at the grill. "Smells good." She waited, hoping he would set the tone of their conversation.

Jack glanced out across the yard, locating Juli under the pecan tree with her dolls. "Addy, listen..." Quieter, he said, "I'm sorry about this afternoon."

"You? Oh, no, Jack, it's me who's sorry. I shouldn't have —"

But Jack reached down and took hold of her hand. With a gentle squeeze, he whispered, "It's just been a long time for me."

Her heart thudded. *Oh. My. God.* He hadn't been attracted to her. He was a sex-starved widower! A hot flush pulled her hands to her face. "I'm so embarrassed," she mumbled.

Jack took a breath, then focused on the grilling chicken. "You must hate me."

Addy stiffened, running her fingers through her short blonde hair. "I'll find a place to rent tomorrow."

Head down, Jack nodded. "Okay," he said.

HE HAD BEEN COMPLETELY OUT OF LINE, AND HE knew it. He'd ruined everything. Why hadn't he just kissed her back? Left it at that? But, no, he had encouraged her and then dumped her at the sound of a school bus.

The woman was beautiful. Natural. Her spirit gave him life again. And the mere sight of her sent his testosterone skyrocketing. He was a man with needs—stronger than he'd realized—but more than that, it was *this* woman who had set him on fire. She'd reminded him that he was a man, not just a father.

And he didn't want her to leave.

CHAPTER 12

On a highway headed south, past the town's newest subdivision, was Green Ridge Place. The property, on partially wooded, rolling hills had walking and bike trails, river access, a duck pond, and an open range to the west for a perfect view of the Texas sunsets. What the only available furnished unit didn't have were enough windows to see the beauty of it all.

"So, what do you think?" Candace, the leasing agent, cocked her head, purposely flicking her red curly locks over one shoulder, smiling at Addy.

"The balcony is nice," Addy said. "But the whole apartment only has two windows."

"I know." Candace turned to the dining area like a game show hostess turning letters—her arm sweeping its tiny expanse. "Cozy candlelight meals, even in daylight. Seductive, right?"

Addy had already been to five other complexes and marked them off her list. With a sigh, she glanced around the 620-square-foot apartment again. Antique-white walls, gray wood-veneer floors, blue fabric couch and chair, coffee table, dinette set, and a queen bed and two nightstands in the single bedroom.

"The tenant who's moving out was the first renter to ever live in this unit, and he was only here for six months, so you're getting a practically new apartment."

"Do any of the kitchen items stay? Like dishes, or pots and pans?" Addy asked.

Candace shook her head. "You'll need your own things. Just the furniture comes with the place, but Marty's Discount Store on the square downtown is still having a back-to-school sale, and they have just about everything you'll need. All the college kids go there to buy things for their dorm rooms or apartments. Great prices, too, but get there before the weekend, or they'll sell out of the good stuff."

Addy nodded. "Okay." The knot in her stomach twisted. "How soon can I move in?"

"It'll be ready on the fifteenth." Candace smiled again. She reached to shake hands with Addy. "You're just going to love it here! We've never had a pilot before."

Back at the rental office, Addy signed the month-to-month rental agreement and paid her security deposit. Her move-in date was still a week away, but it was the soonest available unit. Before leaving, she asked Candace, "Can you recommend a hotel—a decent one —where I can stay until the fifteenth?"

"Sure. Just off I-10 as you're coming into town, you'll see a big red-roofed hotel. It has Saltillo tile floors and a great bar."

The hotel was on the other side of town, and after the day she'd had visiting a half dozen apartment complexes, she was exhausted. It was four o'clock, and she was hungry after skipping breakfast and lunch, plus her bags and toiletries were still at the bed-and-breakfast.

On her way back, Addy went through a fast-food drive-thru and bought a burger and fries, and almost as an afterthought, she ordered a fruit cup for Juli. Just the thought of the girl made her smile.

The long main street of the small Texas town was crowded and slow, mainly with pickup trucks and drivers wearing cowboy hats, so Addy took the on-ramp to the adjacent highway, her thoughts focused on Jack. How had she lost herself in this man? She was an urban woman, not a rural country female, yet this farmer—this man who didn't fit her picture of a cosmopolitan man at all—was a tinderbox to her desires. She needed to force a more distant relationship from him or risk another embarrassing misstep.

With the top down on her Miata, she pulled into the B and B driveway and then parked in her usual spot. She planned to leave the fruit cup in the fridge for Juli and then head straight up to her room without any interaction, but as she got out of her car with her purse and the food bag, she heard a loud clatter in the backyard.

Jack's voice sounded strained. "Juli, can you get the gate for me, please?" Then louder, "Juli, honey?"

Addy set the bags on her car seat and trotted toward the backyard.

Inside the yard at the back gate was Jack, red-faced, with a yellow-and-black tool bag weighing down his shoulder. He was struggling to unlatch the gate while balancing a folded aluminum ladder.

"Hey," she said. "Need help?"

Jack's eyes jerked upward, landing on Addy in

surprise. "Hey," he said, then the ladder nosedived over the fence. "Look out!"

It landed with a bang and a clank, narrowly missing Addy.

Jack shrugged the tool bag off his shoulder and then jerked open the gate. "Are you okay?"

"Yeah," she said to him. "I'm fine. Looks like you were a little overloaded."

"I was supposed to have help." He looked behind him. "Juli, where are you?" When she didn't answer, he started back through the yard, followed by Addy.

On the far side of the picnic table, Juli crouched, staring silently up at the bird feeder.

Halfway to the table, Jack stopped, his arm jutting out to halt Addy. With a glance, he whispered, "Painted bunting."

When the bird flew, Jack sighed. "Did we scare it away?"

The girl stood. "No," then, "I don't know. It didn't stay very long." The disappointment in her voice drew a frown from Jack. He went to her and knelt.

"Sorry, my girl," he said. "Maybe it'll come back."

"But you said they're gonna leave in a few weeks, and I haven't even been able to talk to one yet."

Unable to stay away, Addy quietly slid onto the picnic table bench near the two, listening.

"Talk to it?" Jack was curious. "You're trying to talk to the bird? Why?"

Juli lowered her head. "Because." Then quieter, she shyly said, "I just want to."

Jack gave a fleeting glance and shrug to Addy. "Okay, sweetie," he said to Juli. "You know, you can tell me what you want to say, in case I see one before you. I promise to tell it whatever you want."

Juli shook her head. "No. I have to do it." Then she looked at her father, raised her hand, and let her fingers brush across his short-cropped beard. "I just need to ask it a secret question."

Jack bundled her in his arms. "Got it." He planted a kiss on her forehead. "Do you still want to help me with the sign?"

"Yes. Sorry, Daddy," she said. "Did you drop the ladder?"

"Yes," he said and grinned at her. "Sorry it scared your bird."

At the gate, Jack picked up his tool bag and slung it over his shoulder, then reached down for the ladder as Juli held the gate open.

"I can carry the bag for you," Addy said. "Where do you want it?" She slid it off his shoulder, wanting to linger at the mere feel of him.

"Thanks," he said. "Out front." He started down the gravel driveway alongside the big house.

Addy followed with Juli, and then set the tool bag down on the front porch steps while Jack balanced the ladder directly under *The Bluebonnet House* sign.

He took a drill out of the bag and climbed the ladder with it.

"Are you taking down the sign?" Addy asked.

"Yep," he said.

What had she done? Had he given up on keeping his wife's dream alive because she'd kissed him? "Jack, are you sure you want to do that?"

He readjusted himself on the ladder and then looked down at Addy and Juli. "On second thought, if it's okay with you guys, I'd kind of like to do this alone."

"But..."

Juli took hold of Addy's hand. "Want to see my new playhouse?"

Addy's gaze was glued to Jack. "Are you sure, Jack?"

"Positive."

Juli tugged Addy's hand. "C'mon, Miss Addy. Come see."

By the time they got to the backyard, Addy's guilt had peaked. In a daze, she let Juli pull her across the lawn to the pink cottage—the outer edges of the far-reaching pecan limbs shading the playhouse from the late afternoon sun.

"Isn't it pretty?" Juli asked, her head peeping through a playhouse window that still had a newly manufactured hard-plastic smell. "Daddy put it together for me today."

"Yeah," Addy mumbled. "It's really great." After a moment, she leaned closer, looking in through the little window as the girl pretended to wash dishes in the play sink. "Hey, Juli, I just want to say that I've really enjoyed being here with you and your dad, but tonight's going to be my last night, okay?"

Juli spun toward her. "You're leaving? Why? Don't you like it here?"

"There's just some things grown-ups have to do, even when they don't want to."

"Like Daddy taking down the sign?"

Head cocked, Addy said, "I guess so, sweet pea." She reached in through the window and brushed stray strands of blonde hair out of the girl's eyes. "If your daddy doesn't want to take down the sign, why is he?"

Juli shrugged. "That's why I need to talk to the bird."

"The painted bunting?"

She nodded. "Daddy and Miss Paige said Mommy is an angel, and I think she must be because when I see her in my dreams, she has a yellow crown."

"That's beautiful. I'll bet your mommy is an angel too."

"But when she flies away, she looks like that bird." Juli lifted her eyes, but not her head, to see Addy. "If I could talk to her, she might tell me how to make Daddy happy again."

Addy's hand went to her heart. "So, you think that bird might be your mommy as an angel?"

Again, Juli nodded. "Don't tell Daddy, okay? He gets real sad when we talk about Mommy."

Addy turned away, her misty eyes filling with tears. "Cross my heart."

ADDY PUT JULI'S FRUIT CUP IN THE KITCHEN refrigerator and then retreated upstairs to her room with her fast-food bag. She looked, but from her windows, she couldn't see Jack, though his hammer, drill, and the racket that came with moving an aluminum ladder from spot to spot told her that taking down the sign was a lengthy, painstaking job.

She stood at the window that lent the best view of the backyard, ate her burger and fries, and watched Juli play in her playhouse.

For a decade, Addy had been a fastidiously dedicated career woman. She loved flying, long hours, no attachments, and unabashed one-night stands. She didn't feel bad about it either—the need for human touch was instinctual. A natural, basic need. But the truth of it was that men were never smitten with her for too long, so a commitment stopped being a requirement long ago. Relationships only led to break-ups, hard-to-bear separations, and broken hearts, mostly her own. Her life had no room for love, especially unrequited.

So why did she feel like crumpling into a sobbing heap at the mere thought of distancing herself from Jack?

Addy dropped what was left of her burger into the bag and tossed it into the trashcan in her bathroom. She had to get her mind off Jack. At the blue Victorian lounge near her room's window, she kicked off her shoes and sat, scrolling through the day's news on her phone.

The airline industry had been hit harder than expected by the economic downturn and had given in to a second round of furloughs. Her decision to take the job with Fray Enterprises had been right.

She was so engrossed in reading the industry news that the absence of dismantling sounds in the front yard went unnoticed until the scent of smoke from the back-yard grill caught her nose and her attention.

A knock at the door brought her straight to her feet. "Yes?"

"Hey, it's me," Jack said.

Her heart pounded its way to the door. "Hey," she said casually at the sight of him.

"Is it all right if I come in?"

"Sure, yes, of course." She stepped back, giving him room to enter.

"I take it you're the one who left the fruit cup for Juli in the fridge?"

"I hope that's okay," she said with a grimace. "I should have asked you first, shouldn't I?"

"No," he said. "She loved it. I wanted to say thank you."

"Oh, well then, you're welcome. She's a great kid."

"She told me you're leaving tomorrow. Are you?" When Addy nodded, Jack asked, "So you rented an apartment?"

"I did, but it won't be ready 'til the fifteenth. I'll just stay in a hotel until then."

"Stay, Addy." His soft-spoken words drew her eyes to his. "Here, with us. I don't want to be the reason you leave. Juli has gotten attached to you. She's heartbroken you're leaving. It's just for a few more days, and I think it's good for her to have another independent woman as a role model. Someone other than Paige."

Juli was heartbroken. Not Jack. The reminder sent an awful ache straight to her heart. "I don't know, Jack. Don't you think it would be better if—"

"No." He shook his head. "Just stay until the fifteenth. It's silly to stay in a hotel." Jack held his hands up in surrender. "I promise, I'll keep my distance." He crossed his heart. "I'll stay three feet away at all times."

She felt the faintest tug of a smile. "Maybe I should be the one making that promise, not you." Surely, she could handle a week in the same house with this man, couldn't she? She eyed him briefly, but it was still long enough to force a deep breath from her. He had a magnetism that was hard to resist. Did he even know? Maybe a vow to stay three feet away was warranted, after all.

"Okay," she said. "For Juli."

Jack nodded. "For Juli."

CHAPTER 13

The office of Fray Transport was empty when Addy arrived Saturday, but country music, played by a deep, satin-voiced DJ blasted from the multivehicle storage garage on the backside of the building. She peeked through the window of the adjoining door to find a steely-eyed blue heeler, staring back. *Dare she open it?*

After a moment of watching the dog watch her, she pushed the door ajar a pencil-thin crack. "Hey, boy," she said, eyeing him through the narrow opening. "Are you friendly?"

His docked tail wagged, but with the radio so loud, Addy couldn't be sure whether or not she'd detected a growl.

She closed the door and turned, her eyes scanning the office interior. Atop a file cabinet was a box of dog treats. Addy took a hard, bone-shaped biscuit from the box and then she reopened the door to perked ears. She tossed a biscuit to the dog. When the heeler ran for it, Addy headed for the blaring radio.

Beneath the hood of the black Escalade, she found Nick bent over the front grill, an oil rag hanging from his back pocket.

"Nick?" She tapped his shoulder.

He raised up, smiling when his eyes met hers. "Oh, hey..." he jogged to the radio on the work counter and turned it off. "Sorry. I didn't hear you come in."

"No wonder," she gave a side nod to the radio.

"Yeah," he chuckled. "We play it kinda loud out here."

Addy looked behind her, then back at Nick. "Is your dog friendly?"

Nick glanced around the concrete-floored building until he caught sight of the heeler, crouched, crunching the treat. He smiled. "I can't believe that bum let a dangerous character like you in here without so much as a bark."

"I threw him a dog biscuit."

"Ah, well, you obviously have a way with animals."

Addy glanced at the dog again. "Not at all, actually. Is he friendly?"

"He's a guard dog," Nick said. "Maybe the worst one in history." He gave a low whistle, then called, "Pax? Come here, boy."

The heeler trotted straight to Nick, who reached down, palm up, and waited until the dog put his paw in Nick's hand. "Good boy!" He rubbed the dog's head. Then to Addy, he said, "It's a little early for his treat. You'll probably be his favorite person now."

"Hi, Pax," she said to the dog. "Can I pet you?" The heeler moved closer then sat, looking up at her with a lolling tongue. Addy scratched behind an ear and then gave a pat to his head.

"Ever had a dog?"

"No," she said. "We didn't have pets when I was growing up. No cat, hamster, not even a goldfish. I'm completely inexperienced with animals."

"Oh, man. I love animals. Dogs mostly."

There was a comfort to Nick. A familiarity. She was at ease around him. "Did you grow up in a big family?"

"Naw," he said. "We had more pets than humans. Dogs, cats, horses, sheep. Mama even had a big cage of budgies."

"What are budgies?"

"Parakeets," he clarified. "She couldn't stand to see them in pet store cages. Dad used to tell her that bringing them home and caging 'em wasn't any different than leaving them caged in the store, but she used to tell him the difference was love." He shook his head. "She's a good lady with a soft and forgiving heart."

Their conversation was light and easy, precisely what Addy needed to get a feel for her new work environment and the people in it. She missed her friends since leaving Dallas and the airlines, but not one of them had called to see how she was faring in the furlough. Of course, she knew they were busy with their own lives in the aftermath of the layoffs, but being lonely and alone was wearing on her. When she lived in the city, she could at least pretend she wasn't all alone. Every place she went had people. Lots of them.

"I know there's no flight scheduled today, but I overheard you tell Ernst that you'd be adding a lockable storage box in the aft lavatory. I thought I might be able to come along and keep you company, and maybe you could explain a few things, like the flight scheduling around here. It seems pretty sporadic."

Nick smiled. "Nature of the beast—the *beast* being the private transport business. You go when they call."

"Right," Addy said with a chuckle. "But some insight would be appreciated."

"Sure, except that I actually put that installation on the schedule for tomorrow. Joshy took today off to spend it with an old school buddy who showed up in town unexpectedly, so it was up to me to get the Escalade ready for Thabo's trip to Houston."

"Houston? He's driving?"

"He always drives to Houston. He has friends along the way that he likes to stop and visit."

"I guess I should have checked with you first before driving out here."

"It's not a problem. I'm glad you caught me before I left for the day." Nick pulled the mechanic's rag out of his back pocket and wiped his hands, then he closed the hood and leaned against the Escalade. "Hey, any chance you'd like to go to a rodeo tonight? Joshy was gonna go, but he bailed on me."

Although she was born and raised in Texas, she had never been to a rodeo. Feeling a bit like a misfit, Addy gestured to her clothing. "Sounds fun, but I'm not dressed for it."

He smiled, his eyes doing a scan of her. "I think you look great."

"You sure? Jeggings and a pink pintuck popover don't really scream *rodeo!*"

Nick looked down, his smile roused, then back up at Addy. "That's sure what it's sayin' to me."

∽

THE ARENA WAS A FLURRY OF ACTIVITY, SENDING dust from the barrel racers into the air. Nick and Addy edged past a small crowd at the concession booth and then started through a passageway that shot through the middle of the metal, rust-colored grandstands. Spectators, most donning cowboy hats or baseball caps, seated themselves throughout the stands while a smattering of others stood at the steel-tube rail fence surrounding the arena.

Nick turned and looked up at the highest seats, his own straw cowboy hat a sunshade over his eyes.

"You want to go to the top?" Addy asked.

"Not really," he said, staring into the grandstands. "I'm lookin' for my folks. They're here somewhere."

Nick hadn't mentioned anything to her about meeting his parents, but as more people arrived and the stands started to fill up, she searched too. Spotting a couple about the right age, she asked, "Does your mom have long red hair?"

"Brown. Short. Dad will have on a straw Stetson." The two stood staring into the stands.

"Who you lookin' for?" a man asked from behind them.

Nick turned. "There you are. We must have stood here ten minutes looking for you." He hugged the woman in blue jeans and boots and then gave a handshake to the man. With a hand on Addy's back, he said, "Addy, these are my folks, Doug and Rebecca."

Addy reached for a handshake. "It's nice to meet you both."

"Nice to meet you too," Rebecca said, giving a glance to her son. She smiled. "Nick said he was bringing Joshy."

Doug snickered. "You're a damn sight prettier than Josh."

Heat flushed Addy's face. "I'm just a last-minute fill-in. Hope you don't mind me tagging along."

"Not at all," Rebecca said, smiling at Addy. "We're glad to see Nick making some new friends."

"Addy is part of the crew now," Nick explained, his face flushed.

"Oh, how nice!" Rebecca reached out and touched Addy's hand. "I'll never understand how you girls manage to serve drinks without spilling a drop."

It was a common mistake. Passengers often mistook her for a flight attendant simply because she was a female. "Actually, I'm a pilot."

But the distinction passed unnoticed when Doug pointed up into the stands and said, "There's some seats about four rows up," which sent them all up the steps.

Addy sat between Nick and his mother. Not by choice, but once the line started down the narrow aisle, that's where she ended up.

After sitting, Nick leaned forward, and to Doug on the far side of Rebecca, he said, "Any of the broncs yours today, Dad?"

"Boy howdy," Doug answered in a drawn-out Texas drawl. "Good ones too. We got Turquoise Toy and Stutter Step."

Addy glanced at Nick, then whispered, "What does that mean?"

Nick pulled back until even with Addy. "Dad used to be a pretty big stock contractor for the Cowboys Professional Rodeo Association, but he had to sell a few years ago." Nick briefly lowered his head but then continued. "Well, most of it anyway. He still owns a percentage of the business, but I think it's just because he can't quite let go of something he loved so much."

That brought Jack to the forefront of her mind.

The rodeo crowd seemed as enamored with each other as they were with the event riders. Their chatter sounded more like a huge family reunion with shout-outs to each other, backslaps, and hugs. Everywhere Addy looked, she saw young cowboys and cowgirls wearing jeans, boots, and straw hats. When a group called the "Kindergarten Kowgirls" took to the arena in their pink skirts and white cowgirl hats during a break, Addy laughed, thinking of Juli in her pink tutu and unicorn shoes ready for the horse show.

"Cute, aren't they?" Nick said. "There's a preschool group called 'The Little Buckaroos' that will come out riding stick horses after this." He grinned at her.

"I know a little girl who loves the color pink. She loves horses too," Addy said to Nick and Rebecca, then she tapped her temple. "Hey, she would be great as a 'Kindergarten Kowgirl.' Well, except that she's in first grade."

"Do you have children, Addy?" Rebecca asked her.

"No, no kids for me. Never married either."

"But you like kids, don't you?"

"Sure." Addy nodded. Feeling Rebecca needed more, she said, "Kids are great."

Nick leaned, whispering in Addy's ear, "Mom keeps hoping I'll give her grandkids."

Addy whispered back, "But we're not dating, so why does it matter whether or not I like kids?"

Laughing, he leaned forward, looking at Rebecca. "Mom, me and Addy aren't dating. We work together. We're just friends."

Rebecca leaned forward, too, with her eyes focused on her son. "A mother can still hope, can't she?"

At the rodeo announcer's mention of Stutter Step, Doug stood. "Here we go!"

Nick and Rebecca popped up, necks straining to see the chute, so Addy stood too. All eyes were on the juddering metal gate beneath the announcer's stand. When the gate to the chute flew open, a chocolate brown horse with a numbered rider bounded out, bucking.

Addy knew enough to ask, "How long does he have to stay on?"

"Eight seconds," Nick yelled above the crowd's roar.

With every rise into the air, Stutter Step gave a double kick out his left shank and turned, catching the rider unaware.

"Oh!" Addy grabbed hold of Nick's arm. "I thought he was going to get thrown off!"

Nick took hold of her hand and held. "If he's gonna score, he's got to make this a fluid ride and stay on." Then he yelled to the bronc, "Come on, Stutter Step!"

The rider went flying before the buzzer sounded.

"No score!" shouted the announcer. The cowboy limped away with a mouthful of arena grit, shaking his head.

"Yee-haw!" Doug yelled with a wave of his Stetson. "Helluva try!" Then he looked at Nick. "It's lookin' better and better."

Addy was confused. "Didn't we want the cowboy to win?" she asked Nick.

"Depends." He leaned into her to be heard above the crowd's chatter. "This is a PRCA sanctioned event, so we either want the cowboy to score big, or get handed a no score. Stutter Step needs to be known as the bronc to beat or a high-scoring bronc that every rider wants to draw. Dad's hinging on him going all the way to the Houston Livestock Show and Rodeo, but we try never to miss a small-town rodeo if we can help it. The big cities can afford elaborate festivals and head-liner concerts at their rodeos, but the heart of Texas beats strongest in a small town."

Addy was standing ready when the next chute opened. It wasn't her beloved city life, but the Texas Hill Country held a special *something*. And rodeos were more fun than she expected. She'd had lots of Texas friends who had lived a country cowboy-type of life, but she never had, and tonight she was beginning to understand the lure of it all.

After the rodeo, back at Fray Transport where she'd left her Miata earlier in the day, Nick walked Addy to her car. It was dark, except for the outside security lights on the building. "I had a great time today, Nick. I'm really glad I went," she told him. "Thanks for inviting me."

"Me too," Nick said. "You're a whole lot more fun than Joshy." They both laughed.

Addy opened her car door but stopped at the feel of Nick's hand on her shoulder. When she turned, his arm slid down over her shoulder, finding its place under her opposite arm. Tenderly, he drew her to him. His lips, soft and gentle, met hers.

Briefly, her eyes closed, and a low moan slipped through as her lips warmed to his, but then Addy gently pushed away. "I'm sorry, Nick. I can't—"

He stepped back. "Is there somebody else? I should have asked."

Yes! A man she couldn't get out of her mind. A man already taken by the memory of a woman he loved.

"It's not that. It's just that I'm very focused on my career." She forced a smile. "But thank you for today. It was a much-needed break."

Head down, Nick nodded.

She felt his disappointment. "Are we okay?" she asked.

"Yeah. Sure," he said, forcing a half smile. He nodded.

"Okay." Addy got into her snowflake-white Miata and closed the door, but then she rolled down her window, eyes on Nick. "Hey, my first rodeo was pretty great."

◇

NICK WATCHED UNTIL THE TAILLIGHTS OF ADDY'S CAR passed through the electronic gate, turning left onto Mystic Road headed toward town.

For four years, he'd managed to distance himself from relationships he knew he didn't deserve. He'd gambled with the life of his brother's wife and lost it. It was his fault she had died. If his brother couldn't have the love of his life, then he shouldn't either. He'd done well this past year, pushing away any woman who'd shown interest in him. But today, tonight, was different. He'd felt an unusual kinship with Addy. She had a natural spirit about her that settled inside of him. She was self-assured. Smart. And sexy as hell. She made him feel like he was a real person again.

Driving home, Nick forced his mind to return to the dark place it earned, repressing any essence of normalcy he felt today. Any feeling of happiness was not justified.

After the accident, he'd almost welcomed the nightmares. *The crash. Kaitlin's scream. Those last pleading words to save her daughter.* It had taken a long time before the pain stopped tearing his thoughts apart, but it finally had. To a point anyway. He had learned to live with the tormenting grief and the realization of what he'd done.

CHAPTER 14

The summer-hot workday Jack spent in the flower fields had exhausted him. With Juli asleep in the next room, and his own bedroom windows wide open, the cool nighttime breeze lulled him into a deep sleep.

He was dreaming, he knew because he was flying. With arms spread wide, he'd risen into the sky, soaring over massive wildflower fields. Flying beside him was a blonde woman. He knew her. They'd flown together many times. When she smiled, the sun shone brighter, and he became lighter, rising higher and higher as if helium-filled. At the clouds, where the warmth felt good, she reached for him, taking hold of his hand, not letting him ascend into the heavens where he knew he belonged. Willingly, he came to her, and he knew the reason why. Softly, hand in hand, they descended into an immense field of Texas bluebonnets. He reached down, picked a single, long flowering stem, and handed it to her. She took it, whispering, "I love you."

Jack awoke drenched in sweat. Trembling, he sat up, his fingers pressed to his temples. The dream had changed. The angel in flight was no longer his long-dead wife, Kaitlin. This time the whispering woman had been Addy.

※

THERE WAS NO GETTING AROUND IT, JACK HAD BEEN a wreck after Kaitlin's death. Without Paige and a few other close friends, he might not have made it through the soul-fracturing cycles of grief and fury and every emotion in between. He'd shut himself off from almost everyone, even his family. There could never be another Kaitlin. Never *would* be another. Staying single and unattached was the best thing he could do for Juli and for himself. He had no right to allow another woman to take Kaitlin's place as mother or wife. Paige gladly provided Juli with female guidance. He would provide his daughter with all the rest.

And he'd been doing fine so far. He was not one to be easily derailed. Not by women, not by work, not by anything, and he wasn't about to start now. Addy Piper was not a life raft. And he didn't need rescuing. He needed to let her go.

After breakfast, Jack walked Juli to the bus stop and waited with her until she boarded, and then he walked back down the dirt road to his TXUS Seeds office. He couldn't get his mind off Addy or his dream from last night. She was the first woman since Kaitlin to affect him in any meaningful way. And as much as he wanted to deny it, he was drawn to her. Why had he urged her to stay until her new apartment was ready on the fifteenth? He shouldn't have talked her into it.

"Mornin', Jack," Paige said as she walked past with

a stack of invoices ready for mailing. "I've got a few things I need to talk to you about." She waved a paper in the air.

"Mornin'." Even though it was Paige, the intrusion into his private thoughts niggled him. He needed space. "Not today, okay? I want to drive over to Legacy and see if we can increase their seed inventory."

Paige stopped. "Didn't you call on them last month?"

Jack nodded. "Never hurts to be seen. You're the one who taught me that little sales angle, remember?" When she didn't answer, he said, "Do you have a problem with me leaving?"

"No, Jack, I don't have a problem with it."

It would take him an hour to get to Legacy, and if he ran into his cousin, Jace, he would probably stay longer, then it would take another hour to drive home. He would be back in plenty of time to meet Juli's afternoon school bus, but still, it was a busy day. The seed packets had to be ordered, or they'd miss the special sale pricing, and the henhouse chickens needed tending. It was irrigation day in the fields too. He wasn't himself, but he couldn't help it. He was a plan-everything kind of guy, not an impulsive person. And he never just walked out on the day, but that's exactly what he intended to do.

"Good." He grabbed a file and his truck keys. "Daily chores are yours today."

Paige set the stack of invoices on her desk. "I guess you'll have to wait 'til tomorrow." She stood at the window while he drove away.

≈

ADDY WOKE LATE, SHOWERED, DRESSED, AND THEN meandered down the stairs through the big, quiet house. Alone, she made herself a single cup of coffee and then decided to take a morning walk while drinking it. The place looked deserted, but she felt Jack's energy in every fiber of the property. Still, that awful loneliness settled inside her without him. She couldn't explain why. It wasn't just pent-up tension, though heaven knew, that played a part. Something deeper pulled at her.

She needed to walk off her thoughts of him. Urges she had for him. She needed to shake the attraction. Maybe she shouldn't have brushed off Nick so quickly. He was good-looking. A sweet guy. Sexy in a country kind of way. A few of his qualities even reminded her of Jack—but he *wasn't* Jack.

After wandering down a rural dirt road behind the house, Addy found herself in front of a wood-and-wire chicken coop with a dozen cackling hens, second-guessing her decision to leave Dallas. There was no denying it, she missed her friends and coworkers and the farmer's market, where she was recognized as a regular. She missed her Dallas high-rise apartment with windows all around. She also missed *things* like the chic cafés, coffee shops, cocktails on rooftops, music at Fair Park, and Saturday morning yoga in Klyde Warren Park. There were harder to define elements, too, like the energy of the place—pure *purpose* infused the air.

Absorbed in being homesick, Addy hadn't noticed that she was no longer alone.

"I'm surprised to see you way out here." Paige held a white wicker basket, its handle over her forearm, with a plastic feed bucket in her other hand.

Addy glanced back at the big American Foursquare in the distance. "I didn't realize I'd walked so far." Through an embarrassed grin, she said, "Guess I was daydreaming."

"Easy to do around here." Paige hung the wicker basket on the fence's corner post, then reached into the pail for a fistful of feed. As the hens gathered, she tossed handfuls of scratch onto the ground. "Were you out here looking for Jack?"

"No," Addy said. *She wasn't, was she?* "Everyone was gone when I woke up, so I decided to take my coffee and go for a walk. I just got lost in thought."

Paige steadied her eyes on Addy instead of watching the clucking hens peck the ground for the mixed grain. "Jack seems a little unsettled since you arrived."

"Is he? I hadn't noticed, but then I guess I don't know what he was like before."

After tossing another handful of scratch, Paige opened the gate and went inside the pen to refill the galvanized feeder. "He's been drifting off a lot, can't stay focused, and his patience wears thin pretty quickly. That's not like him. You wouldn't know why, would you?"

Addy shook her head, dismissing the mistrusting tone.

Empty pail in hand, Paige walked back to the fence where Addy stood. "So how long do you think you'll be staying at the B and B? I thought you'd be gone by now."

Clearly, Paige had doubts, but at least she was straightforward enough to address them, and Addy couldn't deny her the right to do so. "My new apartment will be ready on the fifteenth. Jack suggested I stay here until then." With courteous intent, she said, "I'm not pursuing Jack if that's what you're worried about."

"I am, a little." Paige nodded, her eyes unyielding. "Jack's been through a lot. Juli too. They don't need any complications in their lives."

"I'm not a *complication*." Then, harsher than intended, Addy said, "Look, Paige, I'm not some scheming woman out to steal Jack away. If you knew me better, you would know that, but you don't, so I forgive the accusation. He's a single dad with a daughter, and he's carrying a lot of baggage. I'm a pilot with a professional career. The two don't mix."

"All right," Paige said, slowly nodding. "Okay then." She pushed open the gate to the chicken pen, holding it, the tension between them lessening. "Ever gathered eggs? It goes faster with two."

Though her heart raced in defense of her intentions, Addy followed Paige into the pen, taking her lead on gathering eggs, putting each one—some brown and some white—into the wicker basket. When they'd collected them all, Paige handed the basket holding the eggs to Addy.

"You don't mind taking these back to the house with you, do you? I need to rake and clean the chicken coop before I start irrigating the fields."

"No, I don't mind."

The midmorning September sun felt good on Addy's bare shoulders as she walked the dirt road back to the house carrying the basket. Not too far away were the flower fields, swarmed by monarch and swallowtail butterflies, some drifting close in search of easy nectar, drawn to Addy by her colorful tank top.

When a monarch landed on the front of her shirt, its wings aflutter, she stopped. Her thoughts flashed to Jack and their afternoon together in the flower fields.

She'd never meant to complicate things for him. On the contrary, her relationships were notoriously cool and *uncomplicated*. Either she had feared falling in love and ended it, or the men she dated grew tired of her arm's length commitment, and they ended it. It was standard procedure. She just wasn't good at romance or relationships. No one stayed for long, and losing people had become too hard. The problem was Addy liked caring about someone. Thankfully, she had never felt the magic deep down in her core that told her she'd met her soulmate.

But the truth of it was that one-night stands, or short-term boyfriends more curious about her profession than they were of her, wasn't what she wanted either. Her relationship rules were clear, though—no getting serious—which left her cold and lonely too many days.

Alone in the kitchen, she took a wet rag and wiped the eggs clean, and then put them into a glass bowl. She set it inside the refrigerator, then pulled her phone out of her back pocket.

Addy had grown accustomed to a regular monthly flight schedule—three days flying, three days off, or some semblance of it, so only flying when the boss beckoned was unsettling. Still, the pay was good, and the job would tide her over until the airlines called her back.

She dialed Thabo Fray.

"Hi, Noah, this is Addy Piper. I was wondering if there's any kind of flight schedule for the month?"

"Miss Piper, yes. I've just revised the flight itinerary

for the next two weeks. Would you like me to email it to you?"

"Yeah, that'd be great. Thank you." Through the kitchen window, Addy spotted Paige crossing the front yard, heading in the direction of the TXUS Seeds office. "Noah, real quick, can you tell me when my next flight is scheduled?"

"Tuesday. To Destin."

"Great. Thanks, Noah. I'll watch for the email."

Three days to kill before her next flight.

Addy hurried through the front and jogged to catch up to Paige. "Hey," she said when she reached her. "I was wondering if you could tell me if there's a bookstore in town?"

"A small one," Paige said. "For one of those big stores, you'd have to go to San Antonio. The city library is pretty good, though."

Addy raised her hands, palms angled. "Not a resident. Can't get a card."

"Oh, that's right," Paige said. "Well, the bookstore is on the square downtown, near the county courthouse, but you're welcome to borrow my card if you'd rather go to the library. The bookstore isn't stocked very well unless you're looking for Texas history. They seem to love that kind of thing."

"No fiction?" Addy scrunched her nose.

"Not much, unless you're into the owner's favorite Westerns or murder mysteries, Texas-style."

"The library's looking better and better. I've got a few days off and just wanted to grab a good book."

"Here," Paige said as she pulled out a slim bifold wallet from her pocket. "Use my library card." She handed it to Addy, then said, "You're not a book thief, are you?"

Addy laughed, flashing the card. "Too late. Should have asked before you lent it to me."

At the library, Addy walked the quiet aisles, stopping at a row of new romance novels. Not her favorite genre, but grabbing her attention nonetheless. In the end, she walked away from the love stories, leaving with two books after being unable to decide which best fit her mood—a psychological suspense novel written by her favorite author or a comfy beach read she'd left unread on her nightstand back in Dallas.

As she walked back to her car parked in the library parking lot, she caught a glimpse of a Thai restaurant almost hidden by its lush surroundings. It was almost noon, and her stomach had started to growl.

Seated out on the high-rise patio overlooking the Guadalupe River, Addy ordered pad Thai and tea and spent the next two hours reading the suspense novel. It wasn't until the waiter approached with news that the restaurant closed daily between two and five o'clock to prepare for dinner that Addy realized she had overstayed. "I'm so sorry," she said, gathering her things.

"It's okay," the waiter said with a smile. "Please come again."

Being a pilot, Addy was an expert at adapting to new places where she knew no one and was constantly in unfamiliar surroundings, but once in a while, she craved the feel of a home. For her, the B and B was the place that felt most like it.

When she pulled her Miata into the driveway and parked, it was a quarter to three in the afternoon. She climbed the outside steps to her second-floor rented room, breathing a relaxed breath at the coolness and light offered by the comfortable room. She kicked off her shoes and curled up on the bed with her novel.

It was four o'clock before Addy heard Jack and Juli downstairs. She sat up. *Was it rude to stay in her room?* Yes, it was. Being a loner was comfortable, but being alone in a house full of people wasn't. She slid her canvas slip-ons onto her feet and headed downstairs, only to meet the father and daughter at the top landing.

"Oh, hey," Jack said at the sight of Addy. "Didn't mean to disturb you."

"Miss Addy!" Juli ran to her. "Daddy told me not to bother you, but you're already here so I can talk to you, can't I?"

"Sure, you can talk to me."

Jack stood with hands on his hips, looking disgruntled at his daughter.

"Guess what?" Juli asked, doing a tiptoe bounce.

"What?" Addy grinned at the girl.

"I get to go camping with Allison and her *whole* family!"

"Apparently," Jack told Addy, "having a big family is way better than just about anything else." He opened the playroom door. "Go on, Juli, and find your Giselle doll."

Addy leaned against the doorway of the perfectly pink room, watching as Juli rummaged through her toy box. "So, what's Allison's big family going to do together on this camping trip?"

Juli turned to answer, her voice straining in excitement. "They're having a family reunion party! Allison's grandma and grandpa, and aunts and uncles, and cousins..." A giggle popped out. "They're *all* coming, and we're going to sleep outside in tents, and roast marshmallows over a real fire, and have a picnic on an enchanted rock!"

"Juli, the park is *named* Enchanted Rock. It has nothing to do with Princess Giselle from the movie *Enchanted*, okay?"

Julie's hands went to her hips. "Daddy, they wouldn't call it *enchanted* if it wasn't."

Jack stuttered a laugh. "Okay, fine. Now, find your doll so we can pick out your clothes and pack them in your backpack for the trip."

When she started searching through her toy box again, Jack shifted his attention to Addy. "She's never stayed overnight anywhere other than with Paige. I think this is harder on me than it is on her."

"Doesn't she have school?"

"We decided to let the girls take a few days off for the reunion." Jack's brows scrunched, second-guessing himself. "You think it's okay that she's missing school?"

"Sure, it sounds fun," Addy said in a reassuring tone. "It'll be a great experience for her, and she'll get to play with some new friends too. I always wanted cousins."

"No, actually, that's why they invited Juli. Allison's younger than everyone else. All her cousins are teenagers. She wouldn't have anyone to play with unless a friend went along, and Juli is her best friend."

Addy's hand went to her heart. "That's so sweet."

"Found it!" Juli shouted, holding up the Barbie-like doll with long red hair, wearing a formal pink gown.

"Good job," Jack told her. "Now, let's go get packed." When Juli bolted down the stairs, he looked at Addy. "Hey, would you like to go out to dinner with me tonight?" He gave a side nod toward the downstairs. "You know, to help me get my mind off Juli going somewhere without me?"

How could she deny time to a lonely father? Especially one so sexy that her heart skipped a beat just looking at him. She could do this without falling in love, she told herself. Besides, it seemed impossible to say no when he looked at her with those beautiful blue eyes.

"I'd love to have dinner with you."

CHAPTER 15

Although the Michelin-star chef at Lookout Peak deserved a black tie and tails clientele, this was Texas. Diners in blue jeans and boots, or slummed-down versions of a Texas tuxedo, filled the hilltop restaurant.

Jack nodded his acknowledgment to several people as the waiter led both him and Addy through the dining area to a table for two near a long wall of floor-to-ceiling windows.

For a moment, the sunset, with its horizontal ribbons of deep blue, orange, and amber, stopped her. She stood at the windows, deaf to the chatter from dining patrons or the clinking of drink glasses. She loved the sky—the one sure thing she had in her life. Tonight, it was the crown on a vista of rolling green hills dotted with oak trees and acres of trellised grapevines, reflecting a countryside so similar to Tuscany that the only thing missing was the iconic Tuscan cypress—tall, thin, evergreen spires that epitomized Italy's image.

"Wine for you?" the waiter asked.

She turned. "Yes, Pinot Grigio, please?"

"Certainly," the waiter said before asking Jack, "and for you, sir?"

"Dark beer. No glass."

Jack pulled out a chair for Addy, then seated himself across the table from her so that she had a full, unhindered view of the Texas Hill Country.

When the waiter returned with their drinks, Addy held up her wine glass, clinking Jack's brown bottle. "This is very nice," she whispered over the table to him.

"It used to be our..." He stopped, hesitated, and then started again, slower. "It used to be my favorite restaurant. The cook is a 'starred chef.' He trained in France and England, but he came back here to Texas when his dad got cancer." Jack took a sip of his beer, then sent a glance over the dining room. "I haven't been here in a long time."

"Right," she teased, thinking back on the several diners and wait staff who had greeted him with a recognized nod or word. "How long has it been? Like a month?" Addy looked about the twenty-six-table dining room, elegantly set with white tablecloths and black napkins. There wasn't an empty table in the place.

Her scan of the room stopped at the adjacent table where two ladies, both middle-aged, were leaned head-to-head in a whisper, their eyes locked on Jack, who was oblivious to them.

"Longer," Jack said, "but I don't want to go into it. I'm tired of sounding so depressing." He took another sip of his beer, then set it down. "I'd rather talk about you."

Addy's gaze went to the window view again. "I wish you could see my Dallas apartment. It has two walls of windows—big like this, but my view is totally different. Mine is a cityscape, but it's just as beautiful. I can't even describe how much I love it."

"So, you really like living in the city?"

She turned to him. "Oh, yeah," she said, her voice almost lyrical. "I love Dallas. I mean, it's great to be here, but I miss city life."

Jack leaned back and shook his head. "I could never live in the city. I need fresh air and open spaces. I need dirt to dig around in." He laughed, but then his tone hardened. "I'd be scared to death to raise Juli in the city where all the crazies live."

A practiced smile surfaced. "I'm not crazy, and I live in the city."

"I didn't mean *you*."

The two women at the next table signed their dinner checks and then rose, heading for Jack.

"Jack Brown?" The tallest woman, wearing a royal purple dress, rested her diamond-decorated fingers on the shoulder of his button-down shirt. When he twisted to look up, she smiled. "I thought that was you."

He scooted his chair back and stood. "Tracy, it's been a long time." He glanced at the other woman. "Millie," Jack said in greeting, then leaned in, giving each a passive hug.

"It's good to see you finally out enjoying yourself again." Tracy gave a discerning glance to Addy, her eyes doing an awkward scan of her blonde pixie with brown undertones. "And with such a pretty young lady too."

Addy smiled and stood but stayed silent when Jack failed to introduce her.

"How is that little girl of yours?" Millie asked him.

"Good." Jack nodded. "She's good." He shot a look

to Addy, then back to the ladies. "Well, it was nice to see you, but we should probably be getting back to our dinner."

Tracy motioned to the menus on the table. "The waiter hasn't even taken your meal order yet. We watched you come in just a few minutes ago."

In a whisper, Millie said to him, "Jack, we're hoping to talk to you about coming back to church. Do you have a few minutes?"

"No, actually, I don't. Maybe some other time?"

"When?" Millie asked. "We could stop by your house. Bring Reverend Michaels. Maybe we could visit with your little daughter too?"

The line of Jack's jaw tightened.

"And surely you must know," Tracy cut in, "that your mother is still brokenhearted over losing you and that sweet little girl. You do intend to mend the relationship, don't you?"

The napkin Jack held became a tight wad of black linen in his fisted hand.

When his face flushed red, Addy interjected, "Ladies, I hate to ruin this reunion or whatever it is, but my meeting with Jack is very important. Maybe you can arrange another time to chat that won't intrude on mine?"

Tracy stiffened into a crowing rooster stance. "Oh." Her hand rose to her heart. "I'm so sorry." She looked at Millie, then back to Jack, and then to Addy again. "We've been friends with Jack's family for ages. I didn't realize we would be intruding."

Addy gave a tight-lipped nod to the women. "I understand," she said.

When Jack stayed silent, the two retreated,

mumbling their goodbyes. They gave just one look back as they left the dining area.

"Thanks for that," Jack told Addy, uncrumpling his napkin before reseating himself.

"Not a problem." She sat. "I know how it feels to have people think they can run your life just because they knew your parents, as if their acquaintance somehow gives them authority over you."

"That's right," he said, an air of admiration in his voice for her understanding.

"Been there."

Jack smiled. He opened his mouth to speak but stopped. Stalling, he took a long sip of his beer. After a deep breath, he set the bottle down and leaned forward. "Addy, I know it's been awkward between us since that day in the flower fields."

She hadn't expected this conversation, but now that he'd brought it up, she had to face it. "I know, and I'm really sorry about that happening."

He reached across the table, touching her long slender fingers. "I'm not. That's what I'm trying to tell you." When she withdrew her hand, he pulled back his own. "I handled the whole thing like a jackass."

The waiter, unseen before his arrival tableside, said, "Are you ready to order?"

"Oh my gosh..." Addy grabbed the forgotten menu and opened it.

"Should I come back?"

"No," she said without looking up. "I just need a second. Go ahead and order, Jack. By then, I'll be ready."

Jack looked at the waiter. "I'll have a ribeye, medium rare, with green-peppercorn sauce, smashed potatoes, and roasted vegetables."

"Very good, sir," the waiter said. "Would you care for soup or salad?"

"No, not for me. Thank you." Jack handed him the unopened menu, then to Addy, he said, "I have a few suggestions if you need any?"

"Nope, I've got it." She shut the menu and handed it to the waiter. "I'd like the Gulf Coast red snapper with lemon and spinach risotto, please? Nothing else."

"Excellent choice." The waiter gave a nod and then left their table.

Jack leaned slightly forward again. Softly, he said, "What I'm trying to say is that I've given this a lot of thought, and I'd like to pick up where we left off. If you're interested, I mean."

He took a deep breath, exhaling the doubt.

The words hit Addy like a tsunami. She slid back in her chair, her mind tumbling with the meaning. For too long, she stared into his beautiful, seductive blue eyes, waiting for the *but* that was sure to come. His steady silence sent her jutting forward across the table. "You do?"

His nod was slow, barely noticeable.

"I wasn't expecting this," she told him.

"I wasn't either. I wasn't expecting *you*."

Jack Brown had an effect on her like no man ever had. Not her first high school crush. Not even her last *maybe forever* man. Her heart was a magnet, so drawn to his that it scared the hell out of her—but not enough to send her running.

She wanted him, but she didn't want to be the *complication* in his life.

Softly, she said, "That's a big step forward. And every step forward puts a little distance between you and the past. Are you sure you're ready to do that?"

She reached across the table and touched his hand. "I know about this stuff, remember?"

Jack took hold of her hand. "I haven't taken a step forward for so long that I can't even remember how it feels anymore." He studied her face. "But I know I don't want to lose you. And I can't get you off my mind. I think about you all the time."

Before they left the restaurant, Jack ordered a single slice of chocolate mousse cake to go. At home, he put it in the fridge, closing the stainless-steel door just as his cell phone vibrated. He looked at the screen.

"Sorry," he said to Addy. "It's Allison's mom. I need to take this." He turned away and answered. "Hello? Hey, is everything okay?"

Private calls had a way of sending Addy off into the distance. It felt awkward to stay when the call was clearly personal, no matter how close she felt.

Outside, the backyard sang with cricket and frog songs, and the faint scent of rosemary tinged the air.

Addy stood in the crisp evening with her arms criss-crossed around her waist, gazing up at the heavens—its stars glittering like diamonds against the velvety black sky. She didn't hear Jack until he stepped up behind her and lightly rested his hands on her shoulders.

"I couldn't find you," he said, his voice softly concerned. "Is everything okay?"

She turned. "Yeah, sure it is. Is Juli all right?"

"They hiked to the lake where they're camping tonight, and they have a fire almost ready for roasting marshmallows. She sounded tired." He gave a soft laugh. "She asked if I was lonely without her."

"Are you lonely without her?"

His eyes caught Addy straight on. "No, not now."

Jack's kiss was surprisingly tender, unlike anything

she'd expected. It seemed the most natural thing in the world to stand on the tips of her toes and brush her moist lips over his, her heart hammering in her chest, her fingers brushing the rough stubble she found so sexy.

When he released her, it was with an unwillingness that made her heart soar, as though he couldn't bear to separate from her. He took her hand, lacing her fingers with his, and led her into the house. Neither spoke.

In the light that spilled from the kitchen, their gaze caught. Addy didn't know what her eyes told Jack, but his own grayed with uncertainty.

"What's wrong?" she asked him.

His eyes veered toward the bedroom, then wandered back to her. At the lowering of his head, he said, "I don't think I can..."

Addy glanced at the room, its door ajar. *He'd never had any other woman in that room but his wife.* She took his hand tightly in hers. "It's okay, Jack."

He pulled her into his arms again and kissed her softly.

She swayed; her muffled moan lost somewhere behind his lips.

"Jack." She breathed his name as if it weren't a name at all, then she led him into the living room where the moonlight found them.

On the blue poppy fabric couch, Addy settled into the comfort of him, listening to the soft sound of his breath, the faint whir of the ceiling fan, and the beat of her own melting heart.

CHAPTER 16

At sunrise, Addy woke to the sound of Jack opening her room door and stepping out into the hallway, then clicking the door shut behind him. She got out of bed and followed him to the door, opening it after him, to find him in the hallway, shirtless and shoeless with panic on his face, staring down at his iPhone.

"Hey, is everything okay?" she asked.

"Yeah." He looked up at her, breathing a sigh of relief. "It's only seven ten. I thought it was past eight o'clock already."

"What happens at eight o'clock?"

"Paige stops by for coffee."

"Oh." Addy hadn't told Jack about her talk with Paige at the chicken coop yesterday, and now didn't feel like the right time. In fact, she would rather not think about their conversation at all. "Well, I'm going to take a quick shower."

"Hold on a minute." Jack went to her, drew her into his bare arms, and kissed her, then he pulled back with a smile. "This house has old pipes. It's going to take a while for the water to heat up."

"Thanks for the warning."

Jack swept a strand of blonde hair away from her eyes. "I wanted to ask if you're flying today before Paige got here. Are you?"

She shook her head. "Tomorrow. Two days in Florida. Why?"

"Well then, unless you have something else planned, I thought I might play hooky from work, and we could sneak off for lunch to this great little place in Camp Verde. Juli comes home tomorrow, so it'd just be you and me for the day."

There was a new warmth in her heart. "Sounds great."

"I'll meet you in the kitchen for coffee when you're ready."

Addy listened as his bare feet nearly danced down the dark mahogany wood stairs.

In the bathroom, Addy held her outstretched hand under the spray of water, waiting for it to warm, all the while thinking about Jack. Him without a shirt or shoes this morning was sure to make her smile for a week. After a groan in the pipes, Addy felt heat in the water. She adjusted the temperature and then stepped into the shower.

Afterward, Addy took a towel from a wicker basket, unfolded its length, and then dried everything but her pixie-cut hair, which was so distinctly short, except for her long blonde, side-swept bangs, that she could barely tell it was still damp.

She scooted her travel bag out of the closet and reached in for her cropped yellow T-shirt. She stretched it on over her head, pulled on a pair of blue jeans, and slipped her feet into a pair of lemon-colored canvas shoes. With a dab of molding paste, she styled her blonde pixie, brushed her teeth, and then added concealer to her nose freckles.

As she started down the stairs, the faint sound of voices came from the kitchen. *Paige.*

Addy strolled nonchalantly into the kitchen with a plan to say good morning as if it were the first time she'd seen Jack since yesterday.

"Hey," she said, walking across the kitchen to the coffee. When her greeting met silence, she glanced at the two of them, standing a foot apart near the sink.

Paige had an icy glare aimed at her. Jack didn't look at her at all.

"Did I interrupt something?" Addy asked.

"No, but it looks like I did." Paige leveled a hell and damnation stare.

Coolly, Addy glanced at Jack only to realize he was still shirtless and shoeless, wearing unbuttoned blue jeans. *Don't panic. Paige had no way of knowing they'd been alone together last night. That they'd kissed. That they'd felt each other's heart.* A pilot's best attribute was in concealing clearly evident trouble. This was no different. She just needed to maintain an air of calm and innocence for his sake.

"A little casual this morning, aren't you, Jack?" she said, adding a tease to her tone.

Jack glanced at her. Serious, he said, "Paige met me coming down the stairs."

Addy turned away, silent, and poured herself a cup of coffee, then she reached for the creamer still on the counter.

"Not out to steal him away, huh? Was this just a convenient one-night stand?"

"Paige," Jack said softly to her, "this is our business."

Addy turned in silence, stirring the creamer into her steaming coffee.

Paige slung an arm outward in Jack's direction. "Come on, Addy. I've already told him about our little talk yesterday, so why don't you tell him yourself that you're not interested in him. 'No desire for a single dad with a kid,' remember? 'Too much baggage.' That's what you said, right? Oh, and let's not forget the 'I'm not a scheming woman' speech. Personally, I'd like to hear that part again myself."

"Paige, leave her alone," Jack said quietly. "She made no promises. This is my fault, not hers."

Paige poured her coffee out into the sink and then slammed her mug on the counter. "For your information, Jack, that's what all scheming women want you to think." She started for the door but turned to him before storming out. "When did you get so stupid?"

Jack stood, head down, as the door slammed shut.

It was impossible to tell whether the air was thick with anger or sorrow—the two bore the same strength in their moment.

Addy went to him. "Jack, I'm sorry."

"No." He held up a hand. "It's okay. Not a big deal." He turned, looking as if he'd lost something more than his heart before turning back to Addy. "Hey, do you mind if we don't do the lunch thing today? I forgot all about promising Paige that we would do a pest inspection on the fields together."

"Sure. Of course." Her words were weak, but she couldn't pull forth more strength.

Jack nodded, ending head down, walking in the direction of his bedroom.

Left alone in the kitchen, the implication of not defending herself set in.

Addy pressed two fingertips midchest, trying to suppress the ache that came when tears threatened. *He needs time*, she told herself. *Don't run begging after him. Needy women were rarely missed.*

Tears blurred her vision. God, how had this happened?

JACK DRESSED, THINKING THE WHOLE TIME ABOUT Addy—not about the things Paige had said and Addy hadn't denied, but *Addy*, the woman he'd felt love for last night. She'd stirred something in him that he hadn't felt for many years. His spirit had been soothed. He'd lost complete control of himself and his emotions. How had that happened? He should have been stronger. Smarter.

Addy didn't need a lonely man's attention. She already had everything—beauty, brains, a fantastic career, an apartment she loved in Dallas, friends, and men better than him. His life *was* complicated. She was right about that. His story was depressing. And he had a child. Why should he think she wanted anything more than friendship from him?

More importantly, why had *he* wanted anything more than friendship from her?

CHAPTER 17

Addy had stood and let Paige use her own words against her, but she couldn't deny she'd said them. She'd never intended to hurt Jack. Had she known yesterday that he was having second thoughts about her, that he had an interest in her, she would have said different things.

But this morning, after seeing Jack's disappointment in her, she felt like the lowest form of female. Why hadn't she defended herself?

She'd gone from being a woman on top of the world to feeling like a low-down charlatan. He had to know that he *meant* something to her, but an emotional upheaval wasn't going to help. She had selfishly disrupted his carefully controlled world—a place where he could have his pick of women, anywhere, anytime. He didn't need a temporary woman messing it all up for him. And facts were facts, Addy *was* temporary, whether she liked it or not.

As soon as Janet had the baby, she would return to

Fray Enterprises and reclaim her job, and Addy would be out. That was the plan. That was the agreement. Then she'd be free to go home to her beautiful high-rise apartment with windows all around and let the city of Dallas reignite her life. By then, the airlines will have called her back, and her life could return to what it was before she ever met Jack. The Texas Hill Country was just a stopover, and everyone knew it.

The problem was, with Jack, she became the woman she'd always wanted to be.

An imaginary life blossomed in her mind. A world with Jack, here in this house, with his daughter, was too much fantasy to hope for, but at least for now, it felt so right. There was no other place she wanted to be. He was the man she wanted. The one she needed. He was the one who made her feel complete.

Addy set her coffee cup in the sink and then took a deep breath. She couldn't let things stand like this—she had to talk to him.

She started for Jack's room only to stop when the front door opened and closed. From the kitchen window, she saw him get into his truck, heard the engine start, and watched him back out of the long driveway.

It was too late to run out, looking like a desperate woman trying to stop him. And there was no sense in going to the TXUS Seeds office. Surely Paige would be there with Jack, ready to inspect the fields, and her showing up would just make things worse for him.

She would have to bide her time and wait until he came home, then talk to him privately.

Addy went into the living room, pulled her phone out of her pocket, and sat down in an oversized chair with a matching ottoman—its material a soft blue poppy pattern like the couch. She focused on her emails, trying to get her mind off Jack. As she read each one, she answered, losing complete track of time until the sound of a car door closing jolted her.

From the living room window, Addy saw Juli walking down the sidewalk, dragging her backpack alongside a sunburned lady in a one-piece swimsuit and yoga pants.

Addy hurried to the front door and opened it for them. "Hi. I thought Juli wasn't coming home until tomorrow."

"She wasn't," the lady said, her hand on Juli's head, stroking her like she was a puppy.

"I got sick, Miss Addy. I even threw up."

"Oh no..." Addy glanced at the lady who nodded.

"I'm Liz, Allison's mom." She smiled and reached for a handshake. "I'm sorry, but I don't think we've met."

"I'm Addy." She shook hands, then awkwardly, she said, "I'm a bed-and-breakfast guest."

"Oh, I didn't know Jack did that anymore." Liz glanced through the open door into the house. "Is he here?"

"No, he's out in the flower fields this morning," Addy told her.

"I can stay with Miss Addy 'til Daddy gets home."

"Well, I don't know." Liz looked from Juli to Addy. "Are you sure that's okay?"

"Yeah, sure, I can look after her."

Liz smiled but dipped her head. "It's just that I don't know you."

"Right." Feeling justifiably unqualified, Addy said,

"Maybe you could call Jack. I'm sure he'll come right home."

"That's sort of a problem," Liz said. "I can't call him." She held up empty hands. "I lost my phone at Moss Lake, and it had Jack's number in it. Actually, it had everyone's number in it. That's why I didn't call to let him know I was bringing Juli home." She pointed to the phone in Addy's hand. "Maybe you can call Jack for me."

Addy looked at her phone and then back at Liz. "I don't have his number either." She motioned to the check-in desk in the adjacent room. "I've only called the B and B's landline, and it doesn't ring through to his iPhone." When Juli whimpered, Addy knelt. "Sweet pea, do you know your daddy's phone number?"

Juli shook her head, wiping tears with the back of her hand.

Liz sighed. "I asked her that too. That's why I thought it was best just to drive her home first thing this morning."

Addy rubbed her hand gently down Juli's strawberry-red arm. "You got sunburned, huh?" When the girl nodded, she asked, "Do you remember Paige's number?"

"I don't know anybody's number." Juli stared down at her dirty unicorn shoes. "Allison said everybody knows their mom and dad's phone number except me." She started to cry.

"Oh, no, it's okay, sweet pea." Addy lightly brushed Juli's tears, then she stood and said to Liz, "Honestly, I can take care of her. It's okay. Really."

"Well..." Liz said, hesitant. "Juli, are you sure you'll be okay staying here with this nice lady?"

"Uh-huh." Juli nodded, wiping her tears. "Thank you for bringing me home. Sorry I threw up in your tent."

Liz laughed, then gave Juli a soft hug. "I'm sorry you got too much sun, honey. And I'm sorry I let you eat all those marshmallows too. That probably didn't help your tummy ache."

After Liz left, Addy took Juli inside the house. "Are you hungry? I can fix something." Then, "Maybe we should drive over to your daddy's office and see if we can find him." She was totally inexperienced in taking care of a child, especially a sick child.

"I just want to get in my bed under the covers and go to sleep, if that's okay."

Addy felt her forehead like her mother used to do to her when she was little. "Okay."

She followed the six-year-old down the hall behind the staircase, past Jack's bedroom, and into her barely purple room. Juli dropped her backpack in the middle of the floor and then crawled into bed.

"Sweet pea, you might sleep better if you get out of those dirty clothes and put on your jammies. What do you think?" Addy untied the laces on the unicorn shoes and slipped them off her feet.

Juli sat up. "Okay." She slid off her bed and started pulling off her shorts and then her striped tank top. "Ouch!"

Addy lightly touched the girl's shoulder. When she felt the heat, she said, "I'm going to look around and see if your daddy has any sunburn gel, okay?"

"Is it the green stuff?"

"It might be."

"Daddy keeps medicine like that in a basket under

his sink." Juli pointed out into the hall where they'd passed the master bedroom.

"Okay," she said to Juli. "Wait here. I'll see if I can find it."

Addy pushed open Jack's bedroom door, left ajar, but stopped when the scent of him hit her. She closed her eyes and slowly inhaled. Thoughts of him last night rampaged through every feminine zone in her body. When her eyes opened, her gaze landed on a pure white comforter on a dark wood bed. Airy, white cotton curtains draped the windows opposite a wall of photographs. She was drawn to the faces. Wedding pictures mounted in umber wood frames hung beside other photos of Kaitlin pregnant, and pictures of Jack with Juli as a toddler, and Kaitlin cuddling her as a newborn. There was a Christmas photo, a formal family portrait, and the quintessential Texas pose of the three sitting in a field of bluebonnets. Their photographed life portrayed one so much better than anything Addy could ever offer him. She turned away, shunning more comparison.

On the nightstand lay an opened envelope, its letter only half concealed. Addy went to it. The feminine scroll on the outside read *To Jack, My Love*. He was an amazing man. He was fit, attractive, decent, and mannered. She shouldn't be surprised to find a love letter addressed to him. She'd been tempted to write one herself this morning.

Beneath a door, a crack of sunlight caught her eye. The master bathroom, she knew.

It had been renovated—different from the one in her own childhood home, although it still had the same small single window. The tub was modern with a separate shower, and there was a private commode room.

The swirled-gray marble vanity, with its two surface-mounted basins, had a luxe, hotel-like vibe. On the left, the counter was set with lotions, perfumes, and makeup. *Kaitlin's belongings, still here after four years.* The other sink belonged to Jack, she knew, because his shaver and a beard and mustache trimmer were set nearby.

Addy pulled open the cabinet door below his basin and found the woven basket Juli had described. In it was insect spray, sunblock, and aloe vera sunburn gel — green. She grabbed the bottle and slid the basket back into the cabinet, closing the door.

When Addy got back to Juli's room, she found her dressed in a teal-colored nightgown printed with the words *Even the Prettiest Princesses Need Beauty Sleep.*

"Hey, sweet pea," Addy said, her own mother's pet name for her as a little girl was as natural as the affection she felt for Juli. "I found the gel." She flipped open the lid and squeezed a big dab onto the palm of her hand. She dipped two fingers into the green goo, and then gently, she spread it on Juli's shoulders, front and back, and then down the outside of her arms. Remote memory kicked in, and Addy leaned closer, softly blowing on Juli's skin.

"That feels good, Miss Addy," Juli murmured, so tired her eyelids drooped, then popped open before falling again.

"Juli, did you get any sleep at all last night?"

"My sunburn hurt, so I couldn't sleep much. Then when the sun came up, Allison's mom said we were leaving so we could get home before Daddy went to work. I slept some in the car on the way back."

"Oh, my gosh. You're exhausted." Addy rearranged

the girl, then pulled down the covers on her bed and tucked her in.

She waited until Juli was fast asleep, then tiptoed out into the hallway on her way to the kitchen.

Whenever she was sick as a child, her mother had made chicken soup and Jell-O without fail, believing the combination was a cure-all. So, Addy started looking through the pantry for canned soup and gelatin. She spotted the Jell-O boxes right off and picked out strawberry banana, but she couldn't find canned soup other than two cans of beef broth and chicken broth. She'd have to make the soup herself.

Besides flying, cooking was one of the things Addy loved most. The kitchen was a healing place. She'd soothed many a cold, and many a heartache, in her own kitchen. But *this* place, so much like her mother's own, gave her special comfort.

She found a can of premium chunk chicken breast and then grabbed one chicken broth off the shelf. In the fridge were celery and carrots, but noodles for the soup were nowhere to be found. A few strands of spaghetti pasta, chopped, she decided, would have to do. Juli would be hungry when she woke up, and if her tummy was still upset, this should help.

Addy prepared the Jell-O and put it in the fridge, then made the chicken noodle soup, put a lid on the pot, and moved it to the stove's warming burner.

She headed for Juli's room to check on her, but when she found the girl still sleeping, she sat down in the bedside rocking chair and opened the industry news on her phone.

Another five hundred ticket agents were furloughed, along with another two hundred pilots and flight attendants. The furloughs were getting worse, not better. Her employment contract with Fray Enterprises was solid until June, but what would happen if she wasn't called back to the airlines by then? Maybe flying tourists over the Alaskan glaciers with her friend, Erin, wouldn't be so bad, after all. But how could she ever leave Texas? Especially knowing she might never see Jack and Juli again.

CHAPTER 18

It was straight-up noon when Jack's white F-150 truck pulled into the driveway. Addy glanced at Juli, still sound asleep, and then hurried to the front door.

"Hey," she said when he opened it before she could. She smiled when his eyes brightened at the sight of her, but her grin faded when his face took on a pallor.

Jack stepped in and closed the door behind him. "I didn't think you'd still be here." He headed for the kitchen.

"Where else should I be?" She followed him.

He stopped at the kitchen door, raising his nose to the air for an inhale, and then let the simmering scent pull him to the stove. He lifted the lid on the pot. "You made chicken noodle soup?"

"And Jell-O."

"You didn't have to do that for me." His tone turned agitated. "I usually make myself a sandwich for lunch. I'm not big on soup."

"Actually, I made the soup and Jell-O for Juli."

Jack put the lid back on the pot and turned to her. "Juli? What do you mean?"

"She's here." Addy pointed in the direction of the girl's bedroom. "Allison's mom brought her home this morning. She's not feeling well."

"She's sick? Why didn't you call me?" He bolted for Juli's room.

"Jack, she's asleep." Addy stayed behind him the whole way. "She's worn out."

But Jack burst into her room anyway. He went straight to his daughter, reaching for her.

"Careful," Addy urged, giving a cautionary touch to his shoulder. "Her arms are really sunburned."

He stopped, took a deep, controlled breath, and then sat gently on the edge of her bed, softly touching her forehead. "Hey, my girl. Are you awake?"

Groggily, Juli opened her eyes. "Daddy, you're home."

"How are you? Addy said you're sick."

Juli scooted herself into a sitting position. Lightly, she hugged him. "I threw up last night, but my tummy feels better now. I got a sunburn too. Look..." she held her arm straight out.

"I'll get the green gel."

When he stood, Juli said, "Miss Addy already put some on me."

Feeling guilty for doing what Jack wanted to do for his daughter, Addy said, "Just a little. She probably needs more by now."

"When did you put it on?"

"About ten o'clock. She's been asleep ever since."

Jack nodded, then looked back at Juli. Quietly, to Addy, he said, "Thanks for taking care of her for me." He turned; his eyes devoid of anger. "I wish you'd called me, though." Then, "I wonder why Liz didn't call to say she was bringing Juli home this morning? What if we'd been gone to Camp Verde for the day?"

"She said she lost her phone, and it had your number stored in it. And I don't have your cell phone number, remember?"

His shoulders slumped. "I'm sorry. I shouldn't have snapped at you." Jack turned back to Juli. Softly, he said, "Are you hungry?"

"Uh-huh. We were supposed to have pancakes this morning, but then I had to come home, so I didn't get any. Can you make me some?"

Jack's face fell. "You know Daddy can't cook pancakes. Besides, Addy made chicken noodle soup for you, and we have a new box of crackers in the cupboard too."

"Okay." Juli slid her legs out from beneath the covers, her bare feet landing on the floor. "Can I have chocolate milk too?"

Jack grinned, taking hold of Juli's hand. "How about we wait and see how the soup settles on your tummy first?"

Hand in hand, he led Juli toward the kitchen.

"If I eat my soup, can I have some chocolate milk?"

Addy suppressed a grin, following the two. "There's Jell-O in the fridge, but it might need a little more time to jell. Do you like strawberry banana?"

Juli turned with wide eyes. "Strawberry banana is my favorite!" Then, "Daddy, can you put whippy cream on top?"

"Whipped cream," he corrected her. "Sure, why not? It sounds like you're feeling better already." He lifted Juli onto a kitchen stool at the breakfast island.

After setting the bowl of soup, with an opened

sleeve of crackers, in front of his six-year-old, Jack leaned against the kitchen counter to watch her eat.

Within whispering range, Addy said, "I need to talk to you. To explain."

His focus stayed on Juli, but quietly, he answered. "Nothing to explain." He shifted a glance to Addy. "It's okay."

"It's not okay, Jack. I want to talk about it."

"Hey, what are you guys whispering about?"

Jack straightened. To Juli, he said, "You know what? I'm going to get your tablet for you so that you can watch *The Princesses* while you eat your soup."

With the pink tablet propped up in front of the six-year-old, Jack started the kid's show, urging Juli to eat while she watched, then he went back to where Addy waited. "You don't owe me an explanation."

"Maybe not, but here goes anyway." Addy faced him. She whispered, "I told Paige those things yesterday because I thought you weren't interested in me—and because I was trying to convince myself that I wasn't interested in you." She took a deep breath, hesitating before saying what she really wanted him to know. "Jack, everybody I've ever cared about, I've lost. You, of all people, should understand how hard it is to believe that anyone will stick around." Her gaze fell to her yellow shoes. "For some reason, it felt different with you. The moment we met, I..." she stopped. She couldn't do it. Openly admitting she wanted more with him felt like jumping out of an airplane without a parachute.

"You what?" He reached for her, but then his gaze unwittingly darted to Juli. He pulled back.

Addy readjusted, steeling her stance and her courage, her eyes meeting his. "I'm not ready to call it a day on this thing between us, are you?" Fearing a too-quick answer, she put a quieting finger to his lips. "I'm not asking for a commitment—I wouldn't. Both of us are still too broken, so I'd never put us in that position, but I can't just walk away from what we've started. These past few days have been amazing, and I'd like to see if there's anything to it, wouldn't you?"

When Jack's head dipped down, his hands pulled upward, landing on his hips. He stayed quiet.

His silence sent a sinking feeling straight to her core. Addy swallowed hard, sending the tremble threatening her steady voice back to the dark recesses of her heart. "Well, okay then. I'll take that as an 'I'm not interested' answer." She turned and started for the fridge to check the Jell-O, but Jack grabbed hold of her arm, gently restraining her.

"Come back, please?"

"What?" she asked.

"I'll admit, I am hesitant. You're right about people not sticking around, and I'm not sure I can go through it again. Losing Kaitlin..." He shook his head. "I had a close-knit family once, so it was hard to understand why I wasn't important enough for any of them to stick by me when she died. That's when I needed them most." He nodded toward his daughter. "When *she* needed them most." His tone softened more when he looked into Addy's green eyes. "Even Kaitlin's dying felt like leaving. I don't blame her for it—I don't. I just don't understand how she could have made such a risky decision that day. She could have let my brother sleep it off right here instead of driving him home. I would've been back in the morning. I could have taken care of everything."

"I'm sure she thought she was doing the right thing."

"I know." Again, he glanced at her. Softly, he said, "I know that."

"I can't help but think of how awful it must have been for you. For your parents too. Both of their sons had their lives destroyed in one day."

His soft blue eyes hardened into a glower. "He killed my wife. His punishment was a few years in jail. Ours is a lifetime. One son lost a lot more than the other."

"Believe me, Jack, I understand how you feel about your wife's death, but even though you probably don't realize it, deep down you're also mourning people who aren't gone, and that has to be eating away at you." She needed him to know that pushing everyone away wasn't the answer. She knew. Her own loneliness was proof. "People like your parents. And me." Addy hesitated, wary about sounding preachy, but his eyes told her he was listening. "Jack, I can't tell you how to fix a broken heart, but I've learned how to live with one. Isolating yourself and Juli only keeps the grief confined where it grows strongest." Her hand went midchest. "Right here. In your heart. You've got to give it an open door—a way out—or it just gets bigger and scarier." Lightly, she touched his forearm. "Didn't you say that your folks still live around here?" Without waiting for him to answer, she said, "I miss mine so much that sometimes I can't pull my world together." She glanced at Juli who was still watching the show, which was now playing music on her pink tablet before she glanced back at Jack. "If mine were somewhere just down the road, I'd never let them out of my sight again. Life changes when your mom and dad are gone. I'd hate to think you're throwing it all away. For you *and* Juli. You still have parents, Jack. You can still be a whole family again."

Jack spoke so softly, Addy had to lean in to hear him.

"We'll never be whole without my daughter's mother."

Her head dipped into a nod. Clearly, Jack wasn't ready for someone new in his life. As much as her heart was hurting, she understood. It was a risk. And most of the time, it wasn't worth the heartbreak.

He gave a nod in Juli's direction. "She's been asking about her grandparents. She was so young; she doesn't even remember them."

"Done!" Juli pushed the soup bowl away. "Can I have Jell-O with whippy cream now?" She clamped a hand over her mouth, then removed it. "I meant whip creamy. Sorry."

The girl's smile was infectious. "I'll see if it's ready." Addy went to the fridge and gave the glass pan a jiggle. She glanced at Juli with a grin. "Looks jelled enough to me." After setting the dish down on the kitchen counter, she spooned the barely jelled Jell-O into a bowl. With it held out, Jack sprayed a swirl of whipped cream on top. "Here you go, sweet pea," Addy said, setting it down in front of her with a spoon.

Jack leaned back against the counter again, arms crossed, an adoring stare directed at his daughter. Quietly, he said, "Paige wants to take her to meet them."

Addy lowered her head, smiling. Paige had pierced his hardened armor without needing any help from her. As much as she wanted to be a savior to this incredible man and his little girl, her presence hadn't been impactful. She gazed into his blue eyes, ones that had stolen her breath at first sight. Mending his heart and strengthening his forgiveness meant more to her than selfish inclusion into his life. "Well then, Jack, maybe it's time."

THE FLIGHT TO THE DESTIN EXECUTIVE AIRPORT WAS uneventful, except for the number of times Ernst slipped his hand across the divide to rest it on Addy's knee. Sixteen, she'd counted. It might have been more had an unexpected cloudbank not moved in off the Gulf, settling over Pensacola and taking his attention.

Moderate turbulence became a factor, so Ernst made a flight adjustment, but Addy had piloted much worse. She thought of all the bad weather she'd encountered over the years, and how many times it had made her think of the crash that had killed her parents. She had always kept quiet on the subject. After all, pilots didn't talk about those things. But it didn't stop her from wondering if their last thoughts had been of her. She had trained with the intent of keeping every passenger safe, but if she failed in a time of crisis, who would have her last thoughts?

When another bump jostled them, Ernst coolly made another adjustment. Janet had been right about one thing; Ernst was a serious pilot when he needed to be.

Safely down and taxiing in, Ernst glanced at her. "Have a drink with me, love, won't you? I'm all yours for the night to do with as you please."

"*Love*? Seriously?" Addy had disliked Ernst at first sight—maybe even before she met him—and she didn't feel bad about taking him down a peg. "How old *are* you? I haven't heard anyone called *love* in years." When his face reddened, she said, "And, no, I'm not interested in having a drink with you. Not today. Not ever. As a matter of fact, you shouldn't be drinking at all. You're on duty, remember?"

Ernst gave her a smile, radiant and real. "Professionally pretentious. The superior attitude wears well on you." After giving a look to the taxiway, his gaze darted back to her. "You must be a real tiger in bed. The in-control type. Am I right?"

When the G550 came to a stop for deplaning, Addy removed her safety belt, stood, and opened the cockpit door into the cabin, leaving Ernst alone at the captain's controls.

Thabo met her at the exit. "You're still coming with me to meet my grandfather, aren't you?"

With a glance back at Ernst, she said, "I'd love to go with you."

The drive was hindered by heavy coastal traffic, aggressive in nature. It took an hour, but after the chauffeur pulled into the manicured circular drive of the large home on Miramar Drive, he pulled to a stop in front of an elegant, arched entryway.

Thabo leaned forward, saying to the driver, "We'll have dinner here. Expect to pick us up about eight o'clock to deliver us to the hotel, but I'll call when we're ready."

"We're staying 'til eight?" Addy asked as she exited the black Lincoln Navigator. She hadn't anticipated a lengthy stay.

"Yes," Thabo said. "I always spend a few hours with Granddad and his friends, and then we all have dinner together. Is that a problem?"

"No, no problem." Addy shook her head. She'd promised Juli that she would call to check on her before five o'clock, expecting to be back and settled in her hotel room by then, but she'd just have to find a way to excuse herself later and make the call from the Destin home. "I'm looking forward to meeting your grandfather."

The Mediterranean-style home had travertine flooring and coffered ceilings, and the view from the library overlooked a screened lanai with a swimming pool and summer kitchen. Just beyond a low-growing red tip photinia hedge was a suburb golf course.

"That's the fourteenth hole," Thabo said, standing beside Addy. "Granddad loves golf."

"It's beautiful here. Does he still play?"

"Can't keep him away, but nine holes is a full game for him these days. At ninety-one years old, he enjoys the camaraderie, especially with his roommates, much more than he enjoys golf." Thabo chuckled. "I think they like riding around in that cart of theirs more than playing the game itself, but they manage to hit a few balls and get some exercise. It's good for them to get out once or twice a week."

"How many are here?"

"Residents?" he asked.

"Yes."

"Four, including Granddad, and then Mary and Mack are upstairs. They're the live-in managers. Mack oversaw a nursing home for about twenty years, and Mary was a nurse. They wanted to retire in Florida, so this worked well for all of us. There's a cook and a housekeeper, too, but they don't live on-site."

"Thabo?" A man called from an adjacent room. "Where are you, boy?"

"Ah," Thabo said, grinning at Addy. "There's Granddad now." He turned and went to the voice. When he returned, he held the arm of a man whose dark hair was losing its battle against the gray. He was thin with a slight hunch. "Granddad, Mary said the doctor ordered a walker for you this week to help with your hip pain. Why aren't you using it?"

"I can't find it."

"How do you lose a walker while you're walking with it?"

"I don't need that dad-blamed thing all the time," he grumbled, focusing on his feet.

"Just when you're walking, right?"

The man's sharp eyes tilted upward, his twinkling gaze landing on Thabo. "You're a smartass, you know that?" He stopped and raised an arm, swinging it around Thabo's neck. "It's good to see you, boy."

After their embrace, Thabo motioned to Addy. "Granddad, this is my new pilot, Addy Piper. I've brought her along to meet you."

"Hello," Addy said and smiled.

The man looked at Addy, then Thabo. "You gonna marry this one?"

"Granddad," Thabo pressed a knuckle to his lips to suppress a grin, "Miss Piper is a professional pilot, not my girlfriend."

The man glanced at Addy with a sly wink. "Why can't she be both? She's a looker, in case you haven't noticed."

Addy moved closer, holding out a helping hand to the elderly man. "Would you like to sit here?" The chocolate brown leather recliner was the closest chair.

Granddad sat, then looked up at Addy again, giving

a sideways nod to Thabo. "No woman has been able to catch that boy."

"I'm happy being single, Granddad."

"You don't know anything about being happy because you've never had a good woman to spoil. I did, so I know."

Thabo smiled. "True, but I make *you* happy, don't I?"

Granddad gave him a dismissive wave. "In Basque country, we say 'Happiness is the only thing we can give without having.'"

One by one, the other male residents came, with Granddad introducing Addy to each one as Thabo's new girlfriend.

After dinner, Addy excused herself and went out onto the lanai with her cell phone. Jack had not offered her his personal number. Was it an oversight, or hadn't he wanted her to have it? She dialed the number to the bed-and-breakfast.

"Hey," she said when Jack answered. "It's Addy. I just wanted to check on Juli. How's she feeling tonight?"

"Addy." Jack's voice was hesitant. "She's good. Better. Do you want to talk to her?"

"Um, sure..." She wanted to talk to Jack longer. She wanted to fix things between them.

"Hi, Miss Addy," Juli said. "Are you in your airplane?"

"No." She laughed. "I'm at a very pretty home overlooking the Emerald Coast in Florida."

"Is your airplane there too?"

"It's about an hour away. We drove down from the airstrip. Traffic was a real mess." Her mind was on

Jack, not Juli. Talk of traffic jams wasn't what she intended to discuss with the six-year-old.

"When am I going to get to see it?" Juli asked.

"The airplane?" Addy laughed. "Soon. I promise. I'll give you a personal tour, okay?" Then focusing on her reason for calling, she said, "Are you feeling better?"

"Lots," Juli said. "But Daddy had to put more green gel on me."

"Does your sunburn still hurt?"

"It's not so bad anymore, but it hurts if I scratch it."

"And what about your tummy? How is it?"

"It's good, but I ate all the Jell-O you made for me. Can you make more when you get home?"

Home. She didn't want to mislead Juli or make promises she couldn't keep. "I won't be back until late tomorrow, sweet pea, and then I'm moving into my new apartment on Saturday. Maybe your Daddy can make more Jell-O for you?"

"Oh." Juli's tone dropped an octave. "I forgot."

A *clunk* came through the phone receiver, followed by Jack's muffled voice. "Juli, what's wrong?" Then his crisp, clear voice sounded through the receiver. "Addy? You still there?"

"Yeah," she said. "I think I might have upset Juli when I reminded her that I'll be moving into my new apartment the day after tomorrow."

"Oh, is that what it was about?" Jack inhaled, releasing it slowly. "She's gotten really attached."

The sooner she moved out, the better it would be for everyone, but she needed to make things right first. "Hey, since tomorrow will be my last night in the old Bluebonnet House Bed-and-Breakfast, would it be okay if I made Juli pancakes for dinner since she missed out on them during her camping trip?"

"Yeah, sure," Jack told her. "She'd like that."

Good, she could leave on a positive note. "Okay, it's breakfast for dinner tomorrow night then."

Making pancakes for Juli might satisfy the six-year-old, but the only way she might salvage a relationship with Jack was in the leaving itself.

CHAPTER 19

The Texas Hill Country felt a million miles away from the hustle and bustle of Destin, or Dallas for that matter. Life was slower in the cedar-covered hills. Quieter. The air was cleaner, and the breezes softer.

With the top down on her Miata, Addy drove straight from Fray Transport to Grayson's, the only full-fledged grocery store in town. According to the search feature on her phone, other shopping options were a specialty store selling ethnic foods only, or a drive across town would take her to a combination department/grocery store that touted the biggest supply of fishing gear in the Hill Country. She doubted that her favorite Farmstead pancake mix would be shelved anywhere other than the town's major grocer.

As she walked through the store's wide-open entrance, a blast of cold air hit her, the gust refreshing on such a warm autumn day. She missed her old neighborhood grocery store in Dallas where she knew where everything was, so she stopped just inside the entrance to acquaint herself with the layout of this new store. Spotting signs, she grabbed a handbasket and headed for the baking aisle, which advertised pancake mixes. The green-and-white Farmstead canister landed first in her basket, and then farther down, she picked up a box of organic brown sugar before heading to the dairy section located on the back wall.

She slowed when she recognized the shopper standing at an open chiller display. The woman, wearing jeans and a floral split-neck blouse, was engrossed in reading label after label on a variety of yogurt drinks before returning each to its shelf.

"Rebecca?" Addy asked on approach.

The woman turned, tucking her short brown hair behind an ear. "Addy, what a surprise!" She glanced behind, searching the wide aisle. "Is Nick here with you?"

"No. I'm just back from a flight and needed to stop and pick up a few things."

Rebecca's eyes darted to the handbasket. She pointed. "Oh, I've heard that's a really good pancake mix."

Addy looked down at the Farmstead label. "My favorite, actually."

"So, tell me, did you have a good time at the rodeo with Nick?"

"Actually, I had a lot of fun. I've lived in Texas my whole life, but that was my first rodeo."

"No, I can't believe that!"

"Yes, it's true," Addy said with a laugh.

"Say, Addy, why don't you come to the house with Nick this weekend? Doug is smoking a brisket, and I'm making potato salad. We can all have a nice evening together."

She liked Nick and had it been another time, another place, things might be different between them. But it was here and now, and she didn't want to give Nick the wrong idea. Jack was the man who consumed her thoughts. If she couldn't have him, she didn't want any man. She hated to admit it, but she had some weird kind of toxic effect on men and her relationships with them. Everyone, including herself, fared better when she stayed career-focused, men-free, and allowed her personal life to lay dormant in the darkness. It had always been that way. That wasn't going to change just because she'd fallen in love with Jack—the man who loved another woman so deeply, even death couldn't part them.

"That's a nice invitation, but I'll be moving into my new apartment this weekend, so I'm afraid I won't have time."

Rebecca's smile took a downturn. She reached out, touching Addy's hand. "You're always welcome. Maybe next time?"

"Yeah, maybe next time." Addy reached for a pint of heavy whipping cream. "Good to see you again." She set it in her basket, then gave a polite goodbye, and headed for the checkout.

This was her last night with Jack and Juli. And although she would never tell them, she craved their companionship and dreaded the emptiness she knew would follow. She felt whole when she was with them at the big American Foursquare. All she could think about was getting *home* to them one last time.

∼

Jack stood at the end of the syrup aisle, stunned by the sight of Addy with his mother. How long had they known each other? Was Addy just a ruse to manipulate him into resurrecting a family relationship? He took a deep breath. Even though he felt ready to explode, he wasn't going to ruin this night for his daughter. Juli was expecting Addy. And pancakes. She'd picked flowers and put them in a vase on the table, and when he'd left the house, she had Paige tying ribbons in her hair. He needed to hold it together.

Jack drove home with the bottle of syrup on the seat next to him, anxious and unsettled.

When he pulled into the driveway, he noticed the Miata wasn't parked in its usual spot. He'd beaten Addy home. Jack parked beside Paige's Subaru Outback, grabbed the syrup bottle, and headed for the house.

"Jack? Is that you?" Paige called out from Juli's bedroom.

"Yeah," he shouted back on his way to the kitchen.

When Paige appeared with Juli, she said, "That didn't take long."

"Did you bring me something, Daddy?" Juli hopped up onto a stool at the breakfast island and held out her cupped hands. He usually dropped in a surprise, but not today.

"No," he said. "Just syrup." Juli frowned when he turned his attention to Paige. "You staying?"

"Oh, no." Paige grabbed her crossbody bag off the counter and tossed its strap over her shoulder. "I'm sure I have something else to do." She turned and headed for the door with a high wave just as Addy pulled in and parked. Paige was in her car, backing out before Addy shut off the Miata's engine.

"Miss Addy, you're here!" Juli called out, pushing open the front screen door for her.

"Hey, sweet pea." Addy stopped and reached into her grocery bag, pulling out a packet of pink heart-shaped Post-it Notes. "I thought you might like these." She'd loved sticky notes as a child herself and still kept a variety of designs in her nightstand drawer back in Dallas. When Juli squealed with delight and ran to her room, Addy laughed.

Inside the house, the quietude seemed off. "Jack? Are you here?" She headed for the kitchen to unload the groceries. There, leaning against the counter while scrolling through his phone, was Jack. "Hi," she said.

"Hey." Monotone and disinterested, he didn't look up from his phone.

Addy was an expert when it came to reading verbal and nonverbal cues, and this was clearly a cold shoulder. She set the plastic bag on the counter and started pulling out items, then she noticed the new bottle of maple syrup. "Did you go shopping?" she asked him. "I looked and thought you were out of syrup."

Without lifting his head, Jack's eyes darted to the groceries on the counter and then to Addy. "You expect me to believe the reason you went to the store was to buy syrup when you didn't come home with any? You sure there wasn't another reason?"

The air was tense. Her heart thumped. Something was wrong. "Is everything okay?"

Jack gave a contentious laugh. "I'm not a complete fool, Addy." He set down his phone. His voice was gruff, and his expression matched it. "Look, Juli is really excited about tonight, and I don't plan to ruin it for her. But I know what you were doing at the store."

He held up the maple-colored bottle. "I was there too. And you weren't in the syrup aisle."

Addy slid the pint of heavy whipping cream and box of brown sugar toward him. "I was planning to make my own Dutch honey syrup." Then she reached into the bag for the pancake mix and set it down hard on the counter.

Jack straightened, crossing his arms. "So, how long have you known my mother?"

Confused, Addy shook her head. "What are you talking about?"

"Oh, c'mon, Addy. I saw you two together. Did my folks hire you to come down here and scheme your way into my life? I guess Mom is willing to stoop even lower than I thought. Paige was right all along about you, wasn't she?"

"How would I know your mother? I barely know anyone in this town."

Jack stared at her, his face reddening. "Sorry, I didn't realize the dairy aisle was a formal meet and greet!"

Dairy aisle. She'd only spoken to one person in the store today other than the cashier at checkout. "Rebecca is your mother?"

"Yes, Rebecca is my mother." Jack looked down at the floor and shook his head before his hard glare settled on her again. "The charade is over."

Addy's thoughts whirled, caught in a wind of rationale. If Rebecca was his mother, then Nick was *his brother!* The man responsible for killing Jack's wife. It was all too much. She put a hand on the counter to steady herself. How could she convince him that she honestly didn't know when eventually he'd find out that his brother was her coworker? No wonder Nick reminded her so much of Jack. She needed time to work this out, but the look on Jack's face said time was up.

"I can't believe I fell for this."

In earnest, Addy said, "I didn't know, Jack. I met Rebecca through a coworker. I had no idea she was your mother."

When he gave her a piercing glare, she softly repeated, "I swear, Jack, I didn't know."

Juli bounded into the kitchen with two heart-shaped sticky notes stuck to the tips of her fingers. "Here's one for you," she said as she handed one note to Addy, "and one for you." She gave the other to Jack.

Addy read the words *thank you* and forced a smile. "You're welcome, sweet pea."

Jack stared at his note and then stuck the Post-it to the left side of his shirt over his heart. To Juli, he said, "I love you, too, my girl."

A pleased smile spread across her face. "Can I help make pancakes?" Juli asked Addy.

After a pause to clear the catch in her throat, Addy said, "Sure you can, if it's okay with your daddy."

Jack pulled a high stool up to the kitchen counter for Juli, and then set out a mixing bowl in front of her. "All yours," he said to Addy.

So edgy, Addy's hands shook as she measured out the mix and water, eggs, and vanilla. The kitchen was silent while Addy melted a tablespoon of butter in the microwave.

After adding the ingredients to the bowl, she handed Juli a whisk to stir the batter while Jack heated the griddle.

"That's good, sweet pea." Addy gave an affectionate

pinch to the girl's chin, but her clandestine focus was on Jack.

Addy lightly whisked the simmering pot of whipping cream and brown sugar until it turned into her homemade Dutch honey syrup. The only chatter came from Juli, who hadn't noticed she was the only one talking.

"I never knew you could *make* syrup! I've only ever seen it in bottles. Like that one." She pointed to the unopened bottle Jack had brought home from the store. "And how come waffles are made in the toaster, but pancakes go on a griddle?" Without waiting for an answer, she said, "Wait 'til I tell Allison that I got to have pancakes with homemade syrup off the stove!"

Addy flipped three lightly golden pancakes onto each plate and then used a gravy ladle to spoon warm Dutch honey syrup atop them. Jack carried two plates to the dining table, his and Juli's. Addy followed with her own.

"I picked those flowers for you, Miss Addy. Aren't they pretty?"

A yellow ceramic vase, center table, held six droopy sunflowers, heads down, looking as sad as Addy felt. She reached for the face of one and lifted it. "They're lovely, Juli. Thank you."

After dinner, Addy offered to wash the dishes to which Jack ignored, agreeing by silence. He took Juli to her room. Soon, the sounds of a fairytale filled the house. She washed and rinsed slowly, hoping Jack would return to the kitchen, but he didn't.

With the dishes put away, Addy ventured out into the backyard. She stood staring out at the horizon as dusk settled into a brilliant orange, yellow, red, and bluish-gray horizon. A warm breeze shivered the leaves of the pecan. She closed her eyes and raised her nose, catching the scent of rosemary and mint. It was only a whiff—the healing kind that never stays long enough to heal. With it came the all too familiar sense of loneliness.

The feeling of not belonging anywhere never got easier.

CHAPTER 20

Addy awoke from her sleep fully dressed beneath the white coverlet, which she must have pulled over herself during the night. Her usual morning energy was painfully absent, replaced by a dark lethargy. She rolled, pulling the coverlet over her head.

Today was the last day—her last few hours—in this place that reminded her so much of a home lost long ago. In such a short time, Juli had stolen half her heart, and Jack had tossed away the rest. The emptiness left an aching void. If there was ever a man she'd never be able to forget, it was Jack. She hated to leave. Moreover, she hated to leave *like this*. She'd somehow managed to cut every tie the two of them had together.

No one was home when Addy packed up her meager belongings, so on her way out, she stopped at the check-in desk and wrote her phone number and new address on a notepad, along with a request to send her the final bill. When she set down the pen, she caught sight of a *Bluebonnet House* business card. On it was a handwritten phone number and the name *Jack*. Did he intend it for her? Hope convinced her to slide the card into the back pocket of her blue jeans.

By ten o'clock, Addy had the keys to her new apartment.

In the dimly lit living room, she stood at the window and gazed out at the rolling, oak-dotted hills lined with manicured walking and biking trails. It seemed the sky went on forever, but the feeling of home was gone. Jack and the bed-and-breakfast felt as far away as her beloved high-rise apartment in Dallas. She was a stranger in a new land.

Disturbing most of all was that this life-altering furlough had torn her world apart, piece by piece. Her career as a commercial airline pilot had disappeared before her eyes, her comfy city life had been hijacked, and now the man she feared she'd fallen in love with mistrusted her, perhaps even loathed her.

In the bedroom, she took her clothes out of the travel bag, refolded them, and put them in a dresser drawer. She had no hangers for the closet and no iron or ironing board with which to press her uniform. She'd even neglected to buy sheets, pillows, and blankets for the bed. Had she been so obsessed with Jack that she'd overlooked the simple necessities of life? Everyday things? She shut the drawer harder than intended and went into the kitchen for a sip of water to settle her jittery stomach, only to realize she didn't own a drinking glass. No plates or cookware either. And the sink faucet was dripping. She called for maintenance, and then she grabbed her keys and headed for the car. Her life was out of order. She needed to get it under control.

The parking lot of Marty's Discount Store on the

square downtown was overflowing with cars. She should have listened to the leasing agent when she advised her to get there early before the incoming college students bought everything home-related for their dorm rooms.

Inside, the store appeared ransacked by crowds of day-after-Christmas shoppers, even though it was only mid-September. Bags, boxes, and open cartons of broken items were strewn down the aisles, and all of the cashiers looked frazzled.

Addy grabbed hold of an empty shopping cart as it rolled unattended toward the return counter and then made her way to a lopsided orange sign advertising *Bedding*. This frenzy was not at all what she needed today.

Little remained on the shelves of the plundered aisle, and what was left was blocked from view by the backs of at least a dozen frantic female shoppers. Slyly, Addy reached between two women and grabbed hold of the first pillow she felt and pulled it back through. She tossed it into her cart and moved a foot farther, then she reached through again, grasping a package of sheets beneath a *Queen Bed* placard. Priding herself on her bold ingenuity, she glanced into the cart for a peek at her rewards. Her breath hitched at the sight of a turquoise Mongolian faux fur pillow and a set of pink pelican sheets.

But the fight to try again wasn't worth it—not today—so she moved on to another aisle where she found a boxed set of white porcelain dinnerware, four blue plastic tumblers, some stainless-steel flatware, a two-slice toaster, and most importantly, a coffeemaker and coffee.

She wanted to run for the exit when the loudspeaker inside the store announced a special sale on laundry items, but there was no getting around it. She needed detergent, clothes hangers, an ironing board, and an iron. Every stitch of clothing she had needed laundering and pressing, and although she preferred the dry cleaners for her uniforms, some things she had to wash, dry, and iron for herself.

The cashier scanned the ironing board and the carton of dishes from the cart and then bagged the rest at checkout.

Groceries were needed, too, mainly coffee creamer and a loaf of bread for morning toast, but Addy couldn't bring herself to go shopping at another store, especially the one that had caused the rift between her and Jack. She'd have to settle for pizza delivery tonight and forego coffee tomorrow morning.

The afternoon sun made her regret parking the Miata at the far end of the crowded lot. Hurriedly, she pushed the cart across the blacktop, popped open the trunk, and put the bagged items into the small space, and then she wedged the carton of dishes into the passenger seat before realizing there was no room left in her sports car for an ironing board.

"Hey, Addy!"

She turned, looking for the familiar voice. An aisle away, she spotted Nick, waving from his pickup truck. He pulled up next to her and stopped, then leaned with his arm out the window.

"Does your ironing board need a ride home?" When she gave him an embarrassed smirk, he laughed.

"I guess I didn't think this through very well."

Nick pushed open his door and slid out, then took hold of the ironing board and put it in the back of his truck. "How 'bout I just follow you home with it? Where do you live?"

"Green Ridge Place. Do you know where that is?"

"I do. Nice place."

She wasn't exactly prepared to entertain a guest on the first day in her new apartment, but she was at ease with Nick, and frankly, she enjoyed his company. He was so much like Jack that their friendship felt natural. Dare she tell him about his brother? No, she decided, it wasn't her place to link the two.

They carried the store-bought items up the outside stairs to her new apartment.

Inside, Nick leaned the ironing board against the short divider that separated the kitchen and living room, and then his eyes scanned the apartment. "You don't have a TV?"

"Nope, but I've got my phone and an iPad."

"Do you need help moving in the rest of your things?"

Addy glanced around the minimalist living room. "Sad to say, but this is it, except I still need to grocery shop." Then with an embarrassed smile, she emptied a shopping bag out onto the couch and held up the turquoise faux fur throw pillow grabbed sight unseen at the discount store. "And go back for pillows. Real ones. I mean, seriously, how awful is this thing?"

Nick pointed to the other contents of her bag. "Are those pink pelican sheets?"

Addy glanced at the square see-through package. She wrinkled her nose. "And go back for sheets too."

They both laughed.

"Mom said she ran into you at the grocery store yesterday and invited you out to the house for Dad's weekend brisket. Why don't you come along with me tonight and have supper with us?"

"Oh, I don't know, Nick." She felt the sudden pangs of deception. If Jack found out, he would surely believe his conspiracy theory. And even though he'd made it clear that he wanted nothing more to do with her, she still felt a responsibility to his feelings. "Thank you. That's very nice, but I really should stay here and figure out how to make this," she waved an indiscriminate hand to indicate the apartment, "a home. At least temporarily."

"Okay then, how about I go get us takeout and bring it back here, and then I can help you get settled in?"

"Nick, no." She said it softly, but it sounded harsh.

He stood before her, hesitant. "Look, Addy," he said, his tone straightforward. "I'm not up to anything if that's what you're thinking. It's just nice to have a friend, isn't it? I mean, you don't really know anyone here, and I just don't get out much." He took a deep breath before giving it a slow release, then he set a hard-truth focus on her. "There are some things you don't know about me. Nothing to worry about, but I was *away* for a while. When I came back, I found out that most of my friends hadn't grown up at all. They still wanted to drink beer and hang out at the river like we used to do as kids, or they all had their favorite bar where they'd meet up to party for the weekend." He dipped his head with a snigger. "I don't drink anymore, so here I am, turning thirty next month, and my parents have turned out to be my best friends." He looked at her again. "How sad is that?"

She knew his story. One side of it, anyway. But

now, having a face—a real person—to attach to the situation made it different somehow.

Her relationship with Jack was clearly over. His choice, not hers. And even though she knew it might take years to pry him out of her heart, all Nick wanted was a friend. Neither brother would ever need to know she knew the other. She'd be gone after a few months anyway, and Jack had chosen to scrub her from his life. There was little chance she would ever see him again. He'd banished her to the emotional outlands, just like he'd banished Nick. His parents too. God knows, she wasn't judging Jack, but she wasn't sure she had a right to judge Nick either.

"You know what?" she said. "I've changed my mind. I'd love to come over for your dad's weekend brisket."

Miles outside of town on a rural country road where the rolling hills gave way to level land, cattle pastures, and fertile fields, stood a two-story farmhouse with a big wraparound porch. Although the home was probably more than fifty years old, it didn't look it with its fresh yellow paint and newer roof. It wasn't that the *Field of Dreams* style home was all that unique, but its front yard, with its half-acre of wildflowers instead of grass or gravel, and its stone walkway that meandered through the blooms to the front porch steps, made it a showstopper.

"Addy," Rebecca greeted her when Nick pulled open the front screen door and ushered her inside. "We're so glad you came."

The kitchen seemed to be the gathering place, so Addy joined Nick, Doug, and Rebecca there for glasses of sweet tea while the scent of smoke from the outdoor grill filtered in through the screen doors.

This home had a real family—one with laughter, heart, and understanding. Paige was right. Juli deserved to know these people. It was heartbreaking to know she never would.

"Ever ridden?" Nick asked Addy.

"As in..."

"Horses." Nick laughed.

"Oh. No." Addy glanced at Doug and Rebecca. "Silly, I know." Then to Nick, she said, "But I'd like to learn someday."

"How about now?"

"Here?"

"Yeah." Nick reached around the corner to the hat rack and grabbed his cowboy hat. He started through the house. "C'mon."

"Don't be gone too long," Rebecca called after them. "Supper will be ready soon."

Addy walked with Nick through the house and then out the back door, past a cornfield where browning silk hung from the ears of corn. To the west of the house were the horse barn and round pen.

Nick slid open the heavy stable door. "We only keep three riding horses these days, but Dad has another six that he's boarding for a friend right now. When I was growing up, we'd have twenty or thirty at a time. Nick took her to the first stall and stopped. He reached his hand out to the waiting roan, giving a soft rub to her thick white blaze. "This is Butterscotch. She's a Welsh-Quarter Horse cross. She has a wonderful, calm, sweet personality, and she's a great lead-line horse. Mom bought her five years ago, hoping she'd have grandkids by now that she could teach to ride. Can I saddle her for you?"

Addy stepped back a step, her nerves rattling. "I wasn't expecting to ride today."

"And you don't have to if you don't want to, but Butterscotch is the best horse you'll ever find to learn on." He opened the stall gate. "I'll tell you what, how about I saddle her, and then we can walk her to the round pen, and I'll just let you get to know her a little bit. If you decide you want to ride, we'll just walk her around the pen a time or two with you on her."

"Okay," Addy said. "But I wasn't this nervous when I took my first solo flight."

They both laughed.

Nick led the horse out of the stable to the round pen and then demonstrated to Addy how to mount a horse, then he moved aside, holding the lead.

Following his instructions, Addy took hold of the reins and mane, lifted her left foot into the stirrup, and took hold of the saddle horn, raising herself into a balance before swinging her right leg over.

"Hey, I did it," Addy said.

"You sure did. First time too."

Nick led Butterscotch with Addy on her around the round pen several times, talking horse etiquette until an old-fashioned outdoor dinner bell rang.

He laughed, looking up at Addy. "Mom's way of saying we've been out here too long."

Halfway back, the smoky scent of a hot grill filled the air.

"That's not brisket I smell, is it?" she asked Nick.

"No, I'll bet the brisket has been done and resting for an hour already. That smells like Mom's grilled corn on the cob. She uses fresh rosemary on the grill."

Rosemary. Same as Jack.

During dinner, Addy found her eyes wandering to

the walls of the home. In trying to keep her glances discreet, she'd laugh when they did and say, "Oh, how interesting," to conversations she hadn't been able to follow. Her focus was on the family photographs hung everywhere in the home. Jack and Nick as little boys at Christmas, and the two of them on horseback, side-by-side, in a dusting of winter snow. There were also pictures of Jack and Kaitlin on their wedding day with Nick as best man. And then a double frame with one side displaying a baby dressed in pink and the other holding Juli's birth certificate.

She clearly understood the circumstances of the estrangement. And if she were in Jack's shoes, she might feel exactly the same, but she couldn't help but think this was one of those rare families that should never have been torn apart.

BETRAYED. THAT'S HOW JACK FELT. EVERY TIME HE closed his eyes, he envisioned Addy in his arms. Touching her soul. Her eyes so true. So gentle. How could he have been so wrong about her!

He'd been manipulated into trusting her. *Loving her.* Why hadn't he seen it coming? His mind went back to the day she'd come so unexpectedly into his life. Truth was in the details. She hadn't used his personal number. She'd called his landline phone to reserve a room on a holiday weekend when no other rooms were available in the entire Hill Country. His parents—who had to be behind this charade—didn't know his personal number. The only number they had was the house phone, which she'd used. He'd changed his cell phone number after the accident four years ago when they sided with Nick, and he'd made sure they never had access to it. *Cutting ties*. It made sense that Addy wouldn't have had his personal number either. And then the flower fields. She'd kissed him for no reason. *That first touch.* Other than the pilot's uniform she wore, was he even sure she was a pilot? She'd never mentioned the name of her new boss or his company name, or given him details on any of her flights. And she didn't have to go to work every day. Didn't pilots have other job responsibilities too? He was doubting everything he had believed.

Alone in his room, Jack sat on the edge of his bed. He pulled open his nightstand drawer and took out Kaitlin's letter, written so long ago.

To Jack, My Love -

Tradition says our first anniversary should be celebrated with paper, but paper is so very plain—everything you're not. You deserve so much more. But I'm a traditional girl, so on this, the first anniversary of our wedding, I want to give you the gift of our future and our past, written on this parchment for you to remember always.

So many times, I've heard people say, 'I loved him at first sight.' It sounds so cliché, doesn't it? But you, Jack, I truly loved you from that very first moment. I knew that as long as we both had breath in our bodies, we belonged together. It wasn't because your beauty stole the air from me, or because of any words we said to each other, or even this crazy passion I have for you! It was something my soul just understood. You are that part of me I never knew was missing. I looked into your eyes, and our future flashed like a picture before me, and you were the center of it all. I can barely breathe when I think of how much I loved you then and how much more I love you now.

If we somehow lose each other along the way, please come

find me, Jack. I can't bear the thought of living without you. But if life somehow separates us, my wish is that you'll find another who loves you as much as I do. I know—I can hear your thoughts—but it is possible, and I can't bear the thought of you living life alone, without someone to love you like I do. So take off that shiny armor, my knight, and remember that true love doesn't come to you, it comes from *you.*

Real love stories never end, so just know that my whole heart belongs to you forever.

—Kaitlin

Jack scanned the perfect handwriting on the page. The memory of her face, her touch, was fading. He glanced at the photographs on the wall, and then he refolded the letter into its envelope and slid it back inside his nightstand drawer. Kaitlin had had no idea what he would be up against.

CHAPTER 21

Addy sat in the cockpit of the G550, studying the Appleton airfield layout. She'd piloted many flights to Milwaukee and Green Bay but never to ATW. Gulfstream had recently invested forty million there for the expansion of a private hangar capable of housing twelve jets in addition to offices, back shops, and general support space. Clearly, Nick and Ernst had made a good airport choice for Thabo's two new Appleton and Oshkosh properties.

She checked the time. *Where was Ernst?* Thabo expected to be in Appleton by five for a dinner meeting, and it was almost two o'clock now. She double-checked flight duration — two hours and fifty minutes.

Addy released her safety belt and exited her seat. She opened the flight deck door and stepped out into the forward galley to talk to Marie, a petite, well-manicured flight attendant who had boarded just before Addy. "Are Mr. Fray and his guests all onboard and settled?"

"Yes, everyone has boarded," Marie said. She handed her the manifest.

"Everyone except the pilot flying," Addy mumbled. Then, "Thank you." After reseating herself, she contacted Nick.

"Hey," Nick answered.

"Hey, Nick, do you know what the holdup is?" Addy asked. "Where's Ernst?"

"He's on his way to the plane as we speak."

"Did he say anything about why he's so late?"

"You know better than that. He doesn't talk to Joshy or me unless he wants to boss us around about something."

"Yeah," Addy said. "Okay. Thanks, Nick."

"Safe flight, lady friend." Nick clicked off.

Within minutes, Ernst came through the door. His appearance was neat and tailored—his profile the epitome of a Hollywood star—but still, his personality had a chill to it today. He took his seat, then removed his captain's cap and settled in.

"Everything okay?" Addy asked.

"Quite," he said, not looking at her.

His cool aloofness hinted at a problem. "Hey," she said, her voice stern. "I need to know you're okay. Can you look at me?"

Ernst twisted in his seat, facing her. "Happy now?" He turned back to his preflight checklist without any explanation for his black eye.

"Jealous husband?" Addy asked.

Calmly, he answered, "Yes, apparently so."

"Did you get yourself checked out?"

"It's a black eye, for pity's sake. Not a stroke."

"Look, I'm not going to criticize you for dating a married woman, but—"

Ernst slapped the checklist against his leg. "I wasn't *dating* her. I was *screwing* her. And this isn't any of your business."

He began, again, his preflight checklist, completing it in silence.

It was a clear afternoon—no forecasts of bad weather expected the whole trip. Takeoff was smooth and uneventful, and Ernst stayed quiet in a solemn sort of way. Cruising at 41,000 feet, he turned off the seatbelts sign in the cabin, only to have Marie knock seconds later.

"Mr. Fray has requested a pilot's visit for his onboard guests."

Addy glanced at Ernst, who kept a forward focus.

"You go," he told Addy. "Make an excuse if he asks for me."

She wasn't accustomed to making up excuses for other pilots, but she did feel a bit sorry for Ernst. His reputation as a ladies' man seemed as important to him as his reputation as a pilot. This had to be an embarrassing ordeal, and she was sure that before this trip concluded, he would have some explaining to do to Thabo. She saw no reason for it to be now.

Thabo stood when his glance caught Addy's approach. Her professional stature, dressed in her starched white pilot shirt with epaulets, black pants, and sensible black shoes, drew all eyes.

"Good afternoon, gentlemen," she said, triggering the three men, each one fortyish and dressed in tailored suits, to stand with Thabo. She extended her hand. "I'm Addy Piper, First Officer for your flight today. It's nice to have you here."

Thabo smiled at her with a nod of encouragement to engage.

"Are there any questions I can answer for you about today's flight?"

"Yes." A balding, paunch-bellied man held a high-ball glass of bourbon on the rocks.

Shoes had a way of saying a lot about a man, much more than his clothes or choice of drink. When the man took a sip from his glass, Addy glanced down. Contemporary Italian with elaborate detailing—she guessed he enjoyed a lavish lifestyle, hated to be left waiting, and liked to command a room. Her hazel-green eyes met his.

"So, you're not the actual pilot?"

Addy held the sting behind a forgiving smile. "Both the captain and first officer are full pilots, each capable of flying this aircraft, so you're in doubly-good hands today."

After an amused laugh, another asked, "Is this the biggest plane you've ever flown?"

"No, the biggest for me was the A321," Addy said. "Before joining the transport division of Fray Enterprises, I flew an Airbus for one of the major airlines."

"That's a pretty big airplane for a woman to fly, isn't it? How many passengers does one of those carry?"

Sidestepping stereotypical sexist questions without offending the passengers had become second nature to her. "Typically, between one hundred and eighty and two hundred and twenty passengers."

The quietest man retook his seat. He glanced up when everyone took notice. "Sorry. The stale air onboard an airplane tends to make me nauseous."

"Then you're in luck," Addy said to him. "This jet has a one hundred percent fresh air ventilation system. Perhaps it's our cruising altitude instead. Can we get you a ginger ale?"

"Yes," the man said, dabbing a handkerchief to his forehead. "Thank you."

After summoning the flight attendant, Addy continued to answer aircraft questions while the seated passenger remained quiet, sipping his ginger ale when Marie delivered it.

The bourbon drinker stood with a comfortable grip on his glass. "I was on a private flight a few months ago," he sipped then rattled the ice, "when the owner of the aircraft said the fans had stopped working. I thought, 'What's the big deal?' but the pilot returned to the airport. We had a full day's delay because of it." He held his near-empty glass in the air and rattled the ice again to summon Marie, then he turned his focus back to Addy. "I'm curious, what would you do if the fans on this plane stopped working right now?"

She held his focus. "Probably start sweating." She laughed when the men did, but then in a serious yet professionally polite demeanor, she clarified. "FANS is actually an acronym for Future Air Navigation System. Basically, it provides real-time position updates and enhances communication between pilots and controllers."

"Really?" the man said, a bump of turbulence sloshing his fresh glass of bourbon.

"If you'll excuse me, gentlemen." Addy returned to the front of the aircraft.

Thabo followed, stopping her short of the flight deck. "I'm impressed. You presented yourself very well." He glanced back at his guests and then looked at her again. "These investors are especially important to the properties I'll be acquiring in the Great Lakes region. I appreciate your knowledge and profession-alism with them."

This job had its drawbacks, Ernst for one, and the sporadic flight schedule for another, but Thabo Fray seemed to be a good and decent man and a pleasant boss. Until reinstated as a commercial airline pilot, flying for Fray Transport was an easy fit for her.

If she hadn't lost Jack, everything would be grand.

ALONE IN THE COCKPIT, ERNST REACHED BACK, unzipped a pocket on his flight bag, and pulled out a titanium flask. Straight Balmorhea bourbon is what he needed. Just another sip and he'd be fine. He took a swig and then rolled the clear deep mahogany liquid over his tongue, briefly holding it before swallowing. He leaned his head against the headrest and closed his eyes, taking an extra sip before returning the flask to his bag.

A night jailed on assault charges was sure to get back to Thabo. When you had big money like the woman's husband had, everyone wanted to be your informant. Someone would snitch. They always did. How long before they did it was the question. Before the return flight? No, whomever it would be, they'd wait until he was home. There was still time to come up with a convincing story to clear his name.

FROM THE RIGHT-HAND PILOT'S SEAT, ADDY SLANTED a wary glance toward Ernst. He hadn't made a single attempt to flirt or caress a knee this flight. And he'd been quieter than usual. He hadn't even bragged about his latest conquest. Then again, he had come away from it with a black eye.

"You sure you're okay?" she asked.

"Dandy."

She hesitated before saying, "Thabo's bound to see your black eye. Are you planning to tell him the truth when he asks about it?"

His facial features tightened. "We've had a long relationship." Faced forward, he threw a side-eyed glance to her. "I know exactly how to handle Thabo. I've been doing it for a decade."

"You know that sounds disloyal and condescending, right?"

Ernst sent his gaze rolling downward over her, stopping at her lap belt. "Are you wound as tight between the legs?"

"You really are an asshole, you know that? No wonder the pilot before me quit."

With his blond brows raised, Ernst said, "Is that why she quit?" He gave an amused titter. "And here I thought she rather enjoyed our knee trembler."

They flew the last thirty minutes almost silent, only speaking when necessary, but when Addy had a visual on the airfield, she made an arrival announcement to the passengers.

When she finished, Ernst radioed air traffic control. "Appleton Tower, this is Gulfstream six-niner-seven on a northeast approach."

"Gulfstream six-niner-seven," the male controller responded, "maintain one hundred and eighty knots to runway two-one."

"Roger, Appleton. Gulfstream six-niner-seven to one-two."

Addy swiveled a look at Ernst. "Runway two-one, not one-two."

"Negative, pilot lady," Ernst said to Addy. "I heard the tower and repeated."

"Confirm again, please," Addy said. "Last I checked, Appleton one-two was five hundred feet too short for us." She grabbed the ATW airfield information.

Ernst continued his approach as chatter at the busy airport continued from the tower.

Addy's tone was steady but hard. "ATC has his hands full and didn't hear the error—I'm telling you, you're coming in on the wrong runway. Request a go-around and confirm."

Ernst glanced at her, his one good eye squinted into an unapologetic glare. "Appleton tower. This is Gulfstream six-niner-seven. Confirming runway one-two."

There was a break in chatter, then, "Gulfstream six-niner-seven. Approach should be two-one. Repeat, you're cleared to land on two-one."

Perspiration beaded above his brow. "Roger, Appleton tower. Gulfstream six-niner-seven going around."

Addy had her focus on Ernst whose hands had a tremble. He used his shirtsleeve to wipe the sweat off his brow, a thing she had never seen him do. This cool, calm pilot whose collected demeanor was rarely rattled, was rattling like a jar full of marbles.

When the tower approved with turn instructions, Addy reached for her controls. "I'm taking us in."

"No. I just need..." he glanced back to his flight bag.

Something was wrong. Addy hated to think that she knew what it was, but she was responsible for seven lives.

"Ernst," she said. When he looked at her, she said again, "I'm taking us in."

White-faced, Ernst nodded. "Yes, all right. You take us in."

CHAPTER 22

It'd been three days since Addy moved out of her room at the B and B. Three miserable days spent with Jack rethinking every word of their last conversation a hundred times over. He had to stop thinking about her. Stop dreaming about her. She wasn't the woman he thought she was. She'd lied to him about her intentions from day one, and she'd finagled her way into his and Juli's life, obviously through manipulated tactics devised by his family. He'd not only put his own heart at risk, but he'd risked Juli's heart and that was unforgivable.

And just when his life had started to rebound.

Now that he knew about the deception, Addy was probably long gone, returned to some other life he knew nothing about. So why was it so hard to get her out of his head? He closed his eyes, trying to force her from his mind.

"Daddy," Juli asked from the doorway of his master bedroom. "Why aren't you dressed yet?"

Jack jerked open his eyes with a glance at his

daughter. "Sorry, my girl. I guess I was daydreaming." He grabbed his black T-shirt and pulled it on over his head.

"About Miss Addy?"

Was it so obvious? "No," he lied, shaking his head. "Other things. Important things. Are you ready for your big day?"

"Uh-huh, except Miss Paige said she would help me pick out my riding clothes. She said shorts are out." Juli's lips turned into a pout.

"Do you have your homework done?" Jack asked her. "There won't be enough time for it by the time we get back from the stables tonight."

"All done. I had to write my ABCs in lowercase. Do you want to see?"

Jack gave her a grin. "I'd love to see."

Juli turned and ran to her room but returned with a single sheet of paper upon which she'd neatly penciled her letters. She handed it to Jack.

"Teacher said everybody who gets perfect marks on their homework will get extra time to draw tomorrow. I want to draw a horse. Did I do mine all right?"

Jack studied the paper. Juli was an amazing kid. Smart. Beautiful. She was good at so many things. He regretted only having Paige to share her with as she grew up.

"It's very good," he told her.

"Hello, hello!" Paige called as the front door opened and closed. "Any horseback riders in here?"

Juli met her halfway to the bedrooms and then leaped into her arms. "Me! I'm a horse rider!" She giggled as Paige twirled with her.

"Hey there," Jack said to Paige. "Juli was waiting for you to pick out her riding clothes."

Paige set Juli down. She looked at Jack. "My god, you're depressing. Have you looked in a mirror today?"

No, he hadn't. "All I said was that Juli was waiting for you. How is that depressing?"

"It's your tone, Jack. And your *oh, so sad* face. Where's the happy man I knew a month ago?"

Jack shook his head. He didn't want to talk about it in front of his daughter. "Juli, why don't you wait for Miss Paige in your room, okay?"

"Why do I have to go to my room? Are you mad at me?" Juli asked him. Her eyes jutted from Jack to Paige.

"Oh, no, Juli." He knelt. "I'm not mad." Playfully, he pinched her chin. "Daddy just wants to talk to Miss Paige about grown-up things before we leave for the stables, okay?"

"Okay," Juli said, then turning to Paige, she asked, "but you're still coming to help me pick out my clothes, aren't you?"

"Absolutely," Paige told her. "Find your comfiest blue jeans and your pink boots, okay? I'll be in to help in just a minute."

When the girl bolted to her room, Paige asked Jack, "What's going on?"

"You were right," he said. "Addy wasn't the person I thought she was."

"What happened?"

"I found her with my mom a few days ago. I think this whole thing with her showing up here out of the blue was a setup to get me to forgive them."

"Oh, Jack. I don't know. Are you sure? I can't see Doug and Rebecca doing something like that."

"Took me by surprise too." He looked down. "Not just about my folks, but Addy too."

"Hey," Paige said, gently laying her hand on his forearm. "I'm not keen about the woman, but I have a hard time believing it about her too. She's pretty straightforward. She doesn't seem like the type to be in on that kind of betrayal."

Jack looked at Paige with a raised brow. "I thought you hated her."

"I don't *hate* anybody, Jack. I just think you can do better. You deserve the best, and so does Juli."

"Yeah, well, Juli, for sure." He ran his hand through his hair. "I don't know what I was thinking."

"I do," Paige said. "You were thinking about living again, finally. And you *should* have a girlfriend. It's been four years since Kaitlin died, and you haven't so much as looked at a woman in that time." She sighed with a roll of her eyes. "Well, until pilot lady Addy showed up. What's so special about her anyway?"

Although unintended, Jack smiled. "Everything, Paige. Did you know that she put herself through flight school after her parents died in an airplane crash? She lost them when she was seventeen. She worked her way up to flying one of those big planes for the airlines, and she's not even thirty yet. She's amazing." His thoughts flew to the flower fields, but he pulled them back just as quickly. His smile collapsed. "*Was* amazing, I mean. I just can't seem to get her off my mind."

"Well, for what it's worth, I don't think your parents would set you up like that. I mean, think about it, Jack. Why would they want you to have your heart broken again, especially by a phony girlfriend? It doesn't make sense."

He raised a brow and then nodded. "I guess that's true unless they just expected her to talk them up. Make me miss them, you know?"

"To do that, she would have to tell you that she knew them. Not much of a deception." Paige gave a pat to his shoulder. "I'm no detective, but I think you need to give this some more thought. I'm gonna go help Juli get dressed. Be ready in five, or we'll miss our reserved time."

Juli was only six, but she'd talked about horses — owning horses, brushing horses, naming horses, riding horses — for as long as Jack could remember. She loved horses, even though Jack had never allowed her to ride. Today, he was changing that. Carter Temple owned Hill Country Stables, and he was Paige's fiancé. She worked there as a riding instructor on the weekends, and Jack trusted Paige more than he trusted anyone else in his life. He'd been an overprotective dad for too long, and it was time to ease up.

On their drive to the stables, Jack tried to focus calmly on his daughter's first horse ride, but Paige had Juli so preoccupied reciting horse names that his mind wandered. The only name on his mind was *Addy*. He had to know if the situation with her was a setup, but to find out for sure, he'd need to ask his mother directly, and he didn't intend to open the door to that long-lost relationship.

At the turnoff, with the white-arched entrance to the stables straight ahead, Juli unclicked her seatbelt and popped up onto her knees. She pointed. "Are those the horses I get to ride? Which one is Kit-Kat?"

"Hey, hey!" Jack glared into his rearview mirror at Juli. "Sit back down and buckle that seatbelt until I park and the engine is off, young lady."

Juli flopped down, buckling her belt. "I just wanted to know," she said.

"She's just keyed up, Jack," Paige said. "I was a

little girl once, too, and horses were my dream animals. I could hardly wait until I could take my first ride. We're on private property, and you're only driving ten miles an hour. It's fine."

Jack glanced at Paige. "Not wearing a seatbelt is never *fine*. Do you let her do that when she's alone with you?"

"No," Paige said, head down. "Of course not. She's just excited today."

Jack pulled in and parked near the office. He turned off the engine as Carter came out the door.

Paige had her arms wrapped around the neck of her sandy-haired fiancé by the time Jack lifted Juli out of the truck.

"Really appreciate this, Carter," Jack said. The two men shook hands.

"Glad to do it. Paige has been wanting to get Juli out here for months now."

"I guess I've been a little overprotective," Jack admitted.

"Yeah, that's what Paige said, but I get it, especially after your wife's tragedy. The wreck happened a long time ago, though, didn't it?"

Jack shot Paige a look. It wasn't just a tragedy to banter about on dull conversation days. It was a permanent life-altering reality. *His reality*. And even though he liked Carter, he resented him talking about Kaitlin as if time should have diminished the impact of her death. He wouldn't dignify the remark with an answer. "So, what's the plan today?"

Carter handed Paige a child-sized pink riding helmet. "Safety first, then Paige is going to take this little lady for a ride with her."

"Are you going on the trail ride too?" Jack asked him.

"No, I need to ride out and check fences along the west property line, but I won't be gone long. Aren't you going?" he asked.

Jack shook his head. "I'm told that I need to loosen the reins, you know?" He glanced at Paige, a quiver snaking up his throat. "She'll be fine without me tagging along."

Paige knelt to fit the pink helmet on Juli's head, first tucking stray strands of the girl's blonde hair behind her ears, but then paused for a kiss from Carter before he headed off to the stables.

"You're riding Kit-Kat with me today," she told Juli. After fastening, then adjusting her headgear, Paige stood and pointed to a dapple-gray, unsaddled in a nearby pasture. "But see that mare over there? That's Bitsy. We'll meet her after our ride today. She's a retired schoolmaster, and she's one of the best grade horses I've ever ridden. She's dependable, gentle, and obedient, and she loves kids. Next time you come for a lesson, you'll ride her by yourself."

"All by myself!" Juli nearly squealed the words.

"All by herself?" Jack gave Paige a wary glance. "So soon?"

Paige grinned at him. She leaned in, whispering, "Give me some credit, Jack. I'll have the lead, and I'll just walk her around the rail for a few minutes."

Following Paige, they went inside the thirty-stall horse barn scented with hay and leather, horses, and liniment. The tack hung in an orderly fashion on the solid wood walls. Some of the stabled horses stretched their necks over stall doors, expecting a pat, but Paige kept walking until she came to the second to the last stall. There, she reached in and stroked the soft muzzle of the Quarter Horse, speaking softly.

"This is Kit-Kat," she told Juli.

After a minute, Paige secured the lead and then opened the stall door, winking at Juli who stood back holding Jack's hand. In the grooming area, Paige described every act of the saddling to Juli. "Learning about riding starts long before the saddle goes on," she told the six-year-old.

Kit-Kat was of average size—a rich red sorrel, deeper than Sedona clay after a rain. Paige led the horse out into the big pen with her saddled and ready for the ride, then mounted her. She held out her arms, beckoning Jack to lift Juli to her.

"I thought riding double was off limits out here?"

"It is," Paige said, wriggling her fingers in want of the girl. "But I know the owner."

Jack boosted Juli up with Paige settling the girl on the swell between herself and the saddle horn.

"Look at me, Daddy!" Juli grinned.

"I see you, my girl. Sit still while I take pictures." Jack took out his iPhone and snapped photos of his grinning daughter on horseback, then said, "Do exactly as you're told, okay?"

Juli nodded, her lips held tight in a smile bursting to beam.

Above, the sky was a vivid blue spotted with snow-white cotton ball clouds, drifting lazily on a gentle breeze. The late afternoon temperature was barely eighty degrees.

Talking to Jack, Paige said, "We'll ride up the high trail so I can show Juli the Angora goats on Farley Ranch. They have a nanny up there with twins, maybe a month old. They're so playful right now."

"Don't stay gone so long that I get worried," he said, and then Jack gave Paige and Juli a wave as they rode the horse at a walk through the open gate onto a smooth dirt trail. He watched until Kit-Kat carried them out of sight on the well-traveled path that led into the oak and juniper woodlands of the limestone terrain, so typical of the Edwards Plateau.

Jack sat in his truck, door open, reading the day's news on his iPhone while they rode. Every few minutes, he caught himself glancing up toward the trail in wait of the two.

In the San Antonio regional news, he spotted his father's photo in a headline article:

Douglas Brown, former owner of Heritage Ranch and co-owner of Stutter Step, the Lone Star Circuit Saddle Bronc of the Year, will be inducted into the Texas Rodeo Cowboy Hall of Fame for his 30-year career as a PRCA Stock Contractor.

Cowboy hats and boots. His father couldn't remember birthdays or anniversaries, but he could remember the date on which he'd bought his first pair. He wore both in the photo. In the blurry background stood Jack's mother with a prideful beam. He wanted so much to feel pride, but his heart was shut so tight he no longer knew how.

Jack studied the man. His face was older, worn, but still, the man had so much life inside of him it poured out onto the page. He could saddle a horse, wrestle a steer, rope a calf, and still cradle a newborn. He'd held Juli within minutes of her birth, promising to teach her all the things he knew. Yet all those opportunities were lost the day Kaitlin died. He'd never expected regret and anger to rule his family.

Almost forty minutes had gone by before he caught sight of the sorrel meandering down the return trail, Paige and Juli in the saddle.

He exited his truck and went to the big pen's metal and wood gate, holding it open until they rode through.

Juli wore a big grin. "Daddy, I saw baby goats! Miss Paige says they're called kids, and they're so cute and bouncy!" She giggled. "You should come see them, Daddy."

"Maybe next time," he said. "What did you think of the horse ride?"

"It was *so* much fun!"

Paige pulled back on the reins, halting Kit-Kat, then she lifted Juli up and off the horse, lowering her into Jack's outstretched arms.

When Jack set her down, Juli said, "Do I get to keep my helmet?"

"Paige?" He glanced up.

"It's yours, but let's keep it here at the stables. That way, it won't get lost, and we'll know right where to find it next time you come out." Paige dismounted. "Carter installed lockers for personal belongings." She gave a playful pinch to Juli's nose. "I'll put your name on one."

Jack took Juli aside and knelt to remove her riding helmet. "Say thank you to Miss Paige for buying your helmet and for the ride today."

"Thank you, Miss Paige! I can't wait to come back and ride Bitsy all by myself!"

As Carter approached on his chestnut mare, Paige led her sorrel to the rail and opened the gate wider, pulling it all the way back for his entry into the big pen.

Once he was through the gate, Carter pulled up on

the reins, focusing on Jack. "How'd she do?" He gave a nod, indicating Juli.

"I guess she did fine for her first time," Jack said, his hand atop his daughter's golden-blonde hair.

Juli bounced on tiptoes. "Oh, Miss Paige! Can I show Daddy the pictures of the baby goats?" Abruptly, she charged in front of Carter's horse, sending his mare shuffling backward with a shrill neigh until it rear-ended the gate that Paige was closing, slamming it and popping a two-by-four out of its loose bracket. The board flew off, hitting Paige on the back of the head, and knocking her to the ground.

She lay in the dirt, not moving.

"Get away from the horses!" Carter quickly dismounted, shouting at Juli. "Don't ever jump in front of a horse!"

At the fracas, with both horses skittish, Jack grabbed Juli and ran her to safety. He put her down outside the corral near the main office and his truck, and then he sprinted back to Paige.

Carter knelt by her side.

"She's knocked out," he told Jack. "Thank God she wasn't trampled, but I think we should call 911. I don't want to move her."

Jack pulled his phone out of his pocket and, with shaky hands, he tapped the three digits. On its first ring, his gaze caught sight of Juli, still outside the fence where he'd left her. Her face was red from crying. Between them, the unattended horses trotted around the big pen, ears back and edgy, both coming to a stop near the horse barn gate. He raised his hand and pointed at her. "Juli, stay right there until I come and get you."

"Nine-one-one, what's your emergency?"

"We need an ambulance," he said. When asked, he recounted the events to the dispatcher.

"They're on their way," Jack told Carter.

Opposite Carter, Jack knelt by Paige, and then he put his fingers on her neck, feeling for a pulse. "Paige?" he spoke softly, hoping she would open her eyes or make a sound, but she didn't stir. With his fingers, he tucked her shoulder-length brown hair behind her ears, making her look less disheveled as she lay there motionless on the bare ground.

When the paramedics arrived, Paige was slowly stirring. They checked her vitals, then loaded her into the ambulance.

"Jack, I've got to put up the horses," Carter said. "I'll meet you at the hospital as soon as I can."

With Juli strapped into the backseat of his truck, Jack drove through the arched gateway, following the ambulance onto the main road headed toward town.

"Daddy, is it my fault that Miss Paige got hurt?" Juli wiped her eyes. "Mr. Carter yelled at me."

"No, it was just an accident."

"Like Mommy's accident?"

Instinctively, Jack took a breath. "Mommy's was different." He kept his eyes focused on every turn the ambulance made, never staying more than a length or two behind it.

"Different how?"

Different because Mommy died.

"Listen to me, my girl. This wasn't your fault. Accidents happen sometimes. That's why they're called *accidents*. And she's a tough lady." He glanced in his rearview mirror. "Miss Paige is going to be okay."

He didn't know if that was true, but he couldn't let Juli live with the guilt if it wasn't.

CHAPTER 23

The sky had always spoken to Addy, but as of late, it had gone quiet. Even before the furlough, her kinship with it had stalled above the clouds, leaving her with an awkward loneliness as if life was done biding its time, or maybe she was just being punished for ignoring it all these years.

High above the Mississippi River, flying south toward Texas, her soul found the sky again, or maybe it found her. It was the only place she could be perfectly honest with herself.

Addy glanced out the side window, her gaze bending downward onto the tops of clouds.

She was in love with Jack. Deeply. So much so her heart ached at the mere memory of his face, his voice, his touch. Love wasn't something she'd fallen into unwillingly; she'd freely stepped onto its front porch and knocked. And in truth, love hadn't blindsided her. It'd faced her head-on, honestly, with the most beautiful blue eyes. She couldn't just walk away from Jack and let him believe she'd betrayed him. He meant more. He wasn't some idealized version of a man she kept tucked away in her dreams—he was the one her heart had searched for forever.

Addy checked her flight instruments. Estimated time of arrival was six o'clock.

She intended to find Jack. She couldn't bear the thought of losing him. Facing rejection would be easier knowing she had risked everything, including her heart.

"Why don't you check in with Thabo and his guests?" Ernst said. "Make an appearance, you know?"

Ernst had found a professional attitude since Appleton. He'd been quiet and reserved these past few days. When she'd seen him, at least. He'd spent a lot of time in his hotel room, which had made their stay quiet and uneventful. Exactly the way Addy liked it.

She glanced at him. "He hasn't asked for a pilot's visit."

"Why wait? Impress the boss, you know? Your time to shine and all."

Ernst's black eye had faded from a deep, angry purple to a storm-cloud gray, but it hadn't paled enough to go unnoticed by the passengers.

"All right," Addy agreed, unstrapping her safety belt. "I'll go dazzle the guests."

Marie was in the forward galley with a tray of scotch on the rocks, two red wines, and one sparkling water on her way to serving the passengers.

"Behind you," Addy alerted. "I just want to check in with Thabo."

Marie glanced back. "They're all occupied with their laptops, quiet as mice."

Addy thought about returning to the cockpit without disturbing them, but she'd promised to make a pilot appearance. Ernst had given the suggestion sincerely, and the idea wasn't totally without merit. She made her way through the cabin.

Each passenger wore earphones, staring at their open laptops, riveted to the same white-haired older man on their screens. They simply nodded an acknowledgment to Addy after taking a beverage from Marie's tray.

Without interruption, Addy continued back to the conference area where Thabo sat with his laptop closed, reviewing real estate purchase contracts laid out on the table in front of him.

Thabo looked up. "Addy. Is everything all right?" He glanced forward to the cockpit door and then back to her again.

"Yes, everything's fine. Ernst suggested that I come back for a pilot's visit, but it looks like everyone is on a conference call. Would you like me to come back later to visit with the passengers for a few minutes?"

"No." He stood, glancing again at the closed cockpit door. "If I'd wanted you, I would have asked for you." He reached for the bottle of sparkling water on Marie's tray. "I can take care of everything back here." His eyes motioned her away. "Just stay in the cockpit with Ernst for the duration."

Summarily dismissed, Addy started back toward the flight deck, carrying with her an uneasy feeling. It was a side of Thabo she hadn't seen.

When she reentered the cockpit, Ernst was adjusting himself in his seat. "That was quick," he said to her. "Too quick, dare I say?"

Addy reseated herself and strapped her harness. "He didn't need me." Then she thought better of it. "Actually, he didn't want me to leave the flight deck."

Ernst jerked a look to her. "He didn't want you to

leave the flight deck?"

"No." She shook her head, her gaze analyzing him.

Ernst turned his focus back to the PlaneView avionics system. "Well then. I suggest you stay in your seat. We're just forty minutes out anyway."

Addy had learned long ago that when beads of sweat dotted a pilot's brow, her attention needed to be on the mark. Her internal warning system had bells ringing again.

She glanced at the pilot. "Is everything all right?"

"Dear God," Ernst answered with a backward dip of his head. "Do you know how to ask any other question?" He looked at her. "How long is it before Janet returns? Hasn't she had that baby yet?"

It was no secret to Addy that men found her difficult, pilot or not. And like Ernst, they usually made their feelings known early in the relationship. She could deal with them fine as long as they weren't flying a twenty-four-ton aircraft with her aboard.

Addy lifted her nose. An ever-so-faint hint of alcohol scented the cockpit air. She might have dismissed it as aftershave had Ernst not seemed nervous.

"Have you been drinking?" she asked point-blank. "Is that why you sent me back into the cabin for a pilot's visit? So you could steal a drink?" When he laughed, she bucked up in her seat. "I'm sure I don't need to tell you that liquor impairs a pilot's ability to perform the required tasks during the operation of an aircraft. It's an invitation for disaster."

His lips tightened under the grit of his teeth.

Addy settled back and checked the flight instruments. "I'm taking over."

"The hell you are! You're forgetting that I am the

captain." He donned his cap. "This aircraft is under my command."

"Not as long as you're under the influence of alcohol, it isn't." Addy shot Ernst a look as hard as the glare he gave back.

Pilot disagreements were rare, but not unheard of, it had just never happened to Addy. Or to any pilot she'd ever known for that matter. She needed to calm the situation so that she could assume control.

"Ernst, you're a talented pilot. I'm not saying you aren't. What I'm saying is that even the best pilots can have a bad day. A bad flight. This hasn't been a good trip for you." She had a way of staying levelheaded, even in turbulent times, but today the flush on her face was heating up into a warning. "Either you allow me to take over, or you can explain to our boss why you won't. It's your choice."

Addy piloted the Gulfstream over Texas, touching down on Fray Transport's only runway at five fifty-nine in the evening, one minute earlier than anticipated.

With all that had happened, Addy still had her mind on Jack. Finding him. Admitting she was in love with him. But right now, her primary responsibility forced her to focus on Ernst and Thabo Fray. She unlatched her safety harness and pushed herself up out of her seat, only to be bumped back down into it by Ernst, exiting his seat at the same time.

He stood, grabbed his flight bag from behind the seat, and aimed an icy glare at Addy. "You'll keep your pretty little mouth shut if you want to keep this job."

"Keep my mouth shut?" The nagging thought of flying tour planes over Alaskan glaciers hit her, but she wouldn't tolerate threats. "This isn't working out," she told him. Addy exited her seat, standing face-to-face with Ernst. "This was the last flight for one of us. I won't fly with a drunkard. If I'm wrong about today and you can pass a Breathalyzer test, I'll pack my bags. If I'm right, you need to pack yours."

Ernst pointed his finger at her. "I'm more important to Thabo than you know. Shall we see who's packing?" He motioned to the flight deck door.

Addy exited the cockpit and stood in a professional stance to offer farewells to the three passengers as they deplaned, waiting until they boarded the black Lincoln Navigator awaiting them. Last to the jet's exit door was Thabo.

Ernst shouldered past Addy to him. "We need to talk," he told Thabo.

"Can it wait? I'm tired, and I have a lot on my mind right now."

"No," Ernst said, "it cannot wait. You have a serious pilot problem that needs to be resolved right now."

Thabo lowered his head, double-checking the zipper on his laptop bag. "That's what's on my mind."

Ernst straightened. "Well then, good." He glanced back at Addy, who stood by silently. "I cannot work with this woman any longer. She's insubordinate. Pompous. Insanely rude. And her Pecksniffian attitude is intolerable!"

"You won't have to work with her any longer," Thabo said. He glanced at Addy, but then he turned a straightforward glare to Ernst. "I'm letting you go. This was your last flight."

"Me?"

"Yes, *you*. We've been together a long time, Ernst, and you've helped me through many personal difficulties. I appreciate that, but you knew I'd given my last ultimatum. Stop drinking. Stay out of trouble. That's what we agreed." He removed the leather shoulder strap and set the laptop bag at his feet. "I got a message this morning that explains your black eye. Your night in jail. The drunk and disorderly charge. And the assault charges. Do you realize that man—that woman's husband—is still in the hospital?" He leaned in with a sniff. "Bourbon today, am I right?"

When no answer came, Thabo gave a knowing nod and turned to Addy. "I apologize for putting you and our passengers in danger by not dismissing Ernst the minute he instructed you to leave the cockpit today. I shouldn't have trusted him to pilot this plane the rest of the way. It won't happen again."

"Understood," Addy said. There was no reason to add anything further.

"You can't be serious!" Ernst shouted at Thabo.

Without a flinch, Thabo set his attention squarely on Addy. "We're grounded until I can hire another pilot, but I'm hoping you'll accept the captain's position. For as long as you want it."

It wasn't what she expected. It wasn't even really what she wanted, but it would give her time to try and mend her relationship with Jack. If he would give her the chance.

"Gladly," Addy said. "I have an excellent first officer in mind if you're interested."

Thabo nodded. "Set it up, please?"

"To hell with the both of you!" Ernst yelled. He turned to start down the airstairs, but his first footfall caught on Thabo's laptop bag. He tumbled with a guttural scream.

As an assist in the deplaning, Nick waited below. When Ernst fell, he leaped up the steps, stopping the tumble midway down the eight-step stairway.

Addy bounded down and grabbed hold of Ernst to help Nick stabilize the fallen man.

Ernst cried out again. "My leg! I've broken a leg!"

Nick glanced at the man's limb, contorted into an over-exaggerated angle, and then gave a directing nod to Addy. "I'd say so, wouldn't you?"

Her eyes widened at the sight of the oddly twisted leg. In a quick swivel, she connected with Thabo. "You should call 911."

After Ernst was loaded into the ambulance, Thabo said to Addy and Nick, "I'll ride along with him, but I'll need transportation home after a while."

"I can meet you at the hospital, but I'll need to secure the aircraft first," Nick said. "It won't take long."

"I'll stay too." Addy glanced from him to Thabo. "We'll get things locked up, and then we'll come and pick you up."

Thabo nodded before he disappeared into the back of the ambulance.

When the emergency vehicle departed, lights flashing but only one whoop of the siren, Nick asked her, "What the heck happened?"

"He got fired," Addy said matter-of-factly. She wouldn't feel sorry for a man who had just risked his own life and the lives of six innocent people. "He'd been drinking. I mean, he didn't admit it, but I'm sure of it. When Thabo terminated him, he got mad and tripped over the laptop bag, ending up down here with you." She started back up the steps to retrieve her personal belongings from the aircraft.

"Fired? Are you serious?"

"I am." She tossed the words over her shoulder, but at the top, she stopped and turned around. "Oh, and I've been promoted."

CHAPTER 24

Hospitals were foreign ground to Addy. She'd never been admitted to one herself. Never even seen the inside of an emergency room. And since her parents never had a chance to be saved by one, she'd never even visited, so when Nick pulled the King Ranch Ford truck into the parking lot, she took in the unfamiliar sights, sounds, and feelings with interest.

The Hill Country Hospital stood alone on the outskirts of town as if it wasn't a part of the community at all. Its three-story limestone rock exterior had a sanitized, uncaring feel. Had it not been for the giant copper star hanging above its Texas-themed entrance and the bushy hedge of green-tipped shrubs with slender red blooms hugging the line of its outer walls, the place would have seemed cold and unfriendly.

Nick pulled into a parking space near the entrance then shut off the engine. He glanced at Addy. "You're staring at the hospital like you've never been in one before."

"I haven't." She opened the door and slid out.

"Never?" he asked, walking around to the front of the truck where she stood staring at the building.

"Never."

"Wish I could say the same. This place has got some real bad memories for me."

The accident. She stared at the hospital for a moment more. Had Jack's wife died in this place? Her imagination reeled. Not just death happened here, she told herself. Birth was here too. It wasn't all bad.

The double glass doors were automatic and opened wide at their approach. The heels of Nick's cowboy boots on the stone-like floor drew the eyes of several people in the waiting room, but Thabo wasn't among them.

"Excuse me," Nick said to the lady at the check-in counter. "A friend of ours was brought in by ambulance. We're looking for the man who came in with him."

In the distance, Addy heard the faint voice of a man call to her.

"Addy?"

She glanced at Nick, who stared back at her. "Did you just say my name?"

"No." Nick turned, his gaze scanning the lobby.

The same voice said, "Nick?"

Addy turned, following Nick's line of sight. "Jack!" The sight of him roused joy in her. She started for him. "I can't believe you're here. I was going to come looking for you as soon as we finished. I need to talk to you."

Jack took a step back, his hands glued to his hips. "Do you want to tell me what you're doing here with my brother?"

Nick. She stopped and glanced back. *Jack.* Her

glance swiveled between the men. Panic blazed. "Oh, Jack, no." She felt a fire burning down her dreams. Her words spewed out—direct and uncomplicated— the only way she knew to keep truth strong. "This isn't what you think. I'm here on business."

Jack stared at her in a deafening silence.

She was blowing her chance. Addy started toward Jack again, working the words out in her mind. She didn't want to sound awkward or like she was reading from a rehearsed script of flattery and flirtation. "I know what this looks like, Jack, but please listen. Remember when I said a friend introduced me to Rebecca?" She glanced back at Nick before facing Jack again. "Nick is that friend, but I had no idea he was your brother until you told me Rebecca was your mother. And Nick didn't know anything about you."

"I can tell you that much is true," Nick told Jack, his tone supportive. "I didn't know 'til right now that Addy even knew you."

Jack turned on him. He pointed. "*You* can't tell me anything!"

Nick raised his hands in a quiet surrender and stepped back just as Juli surfaced at Jack's side. She took hold of her father's arm and pulled it down from his hip for handholding.

"Daddy, why are you so mad?"

Addy's gaze dropped to Juli. "Hey, sweet pea," she said, forcing a smile of normalcy.

Juli tightened her handhold but raised her other in a modest wave.

A nurse wearing blue hospital garb emerged from doors marked *No Admittance*, bringing with her a sanitized scent. She stopped at Jack and Juli. "Your friend is asking to see you two."

No more than a dozen people filled the emergency waiting room, most seated against a back wall, stoic like mannequins against the tan-colored walls where abstract art drew the eye.

"Who...who?" Addy stammered. They were in a hospital, so someone was likely hurt or very sick. Juli was beside him — safe. *Dear God, don't let him be here with another woman!* Addy felt the alarm in her eyes when her gaze landed on Jack.

"It's Paige."

"She fell down and couldn't get up," Juli finished.

Relieved in that instant, Addy said, "I know someone who fell down and couldn't get up either." Then the very real possibility of something more serious hit her. "Is Paige okay? What happened?"

Jack glanced at Nick and then Addy again. He shook his lowered head without response. With Juli in tow, Jack walked away, silent, following the nurse back through the double doors.

"Well, that was surreal," Nick said to no one in particular.

Addy headed for the blue-and-beige swivel chairs in the waiting room and plopped down in one at the end. She leaned forward with her head in her hands. "I think I'm going to be sick."

Nick followed. "Hey," he said, a comforting hand on her back. "Do you need a bottle of water?"

"No." Then she sat upright. "Yes." She looked up at him. "I don't know."

∿

JACK HELD TIGHT TO JULI'S HAND AS THEY followed the nurse down an aisleway of curtained cubicles. Finally, she stopped and slid open the barely blue cloth, revealing Paige, awake and sitting up in a narrow bed, side rails raised.

"You're looking kinda rough," Jack said to her, coercing a smile. He leaned, kissed her forehead, and then smoothed her shoulder-length brunette hair. "How are you feeling?"

"Okay, I guess, but I've got a heck of a headache from that bump on the back of my head."

"Sorry I scared the horses," Juli said, barely audible.

Paige gave a pained grin to Juli. "Well, I'm sorry I didn't fix that bracket on the gate. I knew it was loose." She looked up at Jack. "Did Carter come with you?"

"He said he'd be along as soon as he put up the horses, but I haven't seen him." Jack wanted to tell her who he *had* seen, but another discussion about Nick or Addy might not be the best idea. Especially in front of Juli. "What did the doc say?"

"They're waiting for the results of my CT scan to come back. I might have to stay the night."

Jack nodded. He hated hospitals. "Okay." He pulled the only chair close to the bed and sat, patting his knee for Juli. "Did they say how long it would be before the scan results come back?"

Juli inched closer, leaning into Jack instead of climbing onto his knee. She yawned.

"Jack, you don't have to wait here with me. Juli has school tomorrow, and it's been a long day for you guys already. I'll bet she hasn't even had supper yet. Why don't you go on home? I'm sure Carter will be here soon."

"I'm not leaving you alone."

Paige reclined against the raised adjustable bed.

"Well, then you'll have to wait out in the waiting room because I have to pee, and they're making me use a bedpan."

"What's a bedpan?" Juli straightened up, interested.

"Okay..." Jack stood. "TMI, Paige." Her laugh made him smile. He squeezed her hand, holding it longer than needed, stalling. He wasn't prepared to see Addy and Nick in the lobby again, but he couldn't hide in here forever. "Maybe you're right. We should go home. Juli needs supper, and then I need to put her to bed for the evening."

Paige squeezed back. "Hey," she said. "Thanks for coming. I'll call you, okay?"

"Yeah, okay." Jack lifted Juli, who gave Paige a kiss on the lips. "You scared the hell out of me, you know?"

Juli put her hand to Jack's lips. "Daddy, don't say that bad word."

Paige laughed, then grimaced. She put a hand to the back of her head. "Yes, stop it, Jack," she teased.

They left the curtained cubicle as Paige was ringing for the nurse.

Maybe if he walked fast enough, head down, they'd go completely unnoticed on their way out.

"IT WAS AN OLD BROCHURE FOR THE BED-AND-breakfast," Addy explained to Nick. "I left a message that I was coming, but I didn't leave a phone number. By the time I got here, everything in town was booked up. Jack felt sorry for me and rented me a room."

"And you didn't put the last names together that we

might be related?" But right away, he shrugged. "I guess the name Brown is pretty common."

Addy scooted up in the chair, swinging her legs up under her. "You introduced yourself as 'Nick.' I never knew your last name, or I might have put it together. Maybe not, but I didn't even get the chance."

Nick looked down, busy rubbing dirt off the toe of his boot with his fingertips. "So, did my brother tell you about his wife dying?" He kept focused on his boots.

"Yeah," the word came out in a whisper. Addy put her hand on his shoulder. "I know about the accident."

He nodded. Blew out a breath. "You must hate me, like everyone else."

"I don't hate you. I can't imagine what you've gone through all these years, or how you've dealt with the guilt." She took hold of his hand, pulling it into hers. "The thing is, Nick, I'm crazy in love with your brother. And even though these things don't usually work out for me, I have to try. I've never felt about anyone like I feel about Jack."

Nick raised his gaze to meet her hazel-green eyes. With his other hand, he brushed her blonde bangs aside, giving a slow tracing touch from her brow to her temple. Then he smiled. "He's a really good man, Addy. He deserves someone as special as you."

When the double doors marked *No Admittance* opened again, Thabo Fray, and Jack with Juli, emerged. Both Addy and Nick jumped to their feet.

Jack was walking fast, head down, pulling Juli along with him toward the exit.

"Jack, wait!" Addy called out, bypassing Thabo entirely. He was outside, headed for the parking lot before she caught up to him. She grabbed his arm strong enough to stop him. When he turned, she saw more than anger and disappointment in his glare—she saw sadness. Regret. In the thud of a heartbeat, she released his arm. "Jack, you're not giving me a chance."

"Now isn't the time," he said, glancing down at Juli. He started toward his truck again, only to have Addy follow.

"If we don't talk now, we may never—" The word *never* wedged in her throat.

Jack opened the back door to his crew cab truck and lifted Juli inside, securely buckling her into the seat. "Stay put," he said to her before closing the door. He turned with a glance back at the hospital.

Addy took his unoffered hand and curled her fingers around his. She had to say it fast before he pulled away. "Jack, I'm crazy in love with you, and I'm so afraid I'll lose you before I have the chance to tell you why."

He stood silent, waiting. When she didn't speak, he said, "Well, go ahead then. If that's what you need to do to…to…to end whatever this is between us, then go on and say it."

The problem with words is that the right ones never seem to come when needed. Addy felt them all jumbled up inside of her, and every time she tried to pull one out, they gridlocked. *She just needed one word!*

"Backward," she said.

"Backward?" His brows pulled together. "What does that mean?"

"I've been walking backward nearly my whole life, looking for that one missing puzzle piece, hoping to find the lost part of me that would heal my heart and my world. When I'm with you, I feel whole again. I *want* to turn around and see the future." She added her other hand to the hold she had on his. "Jack, your house—

that big beautiful American Foursquare—it's almost exactly like my childhood home." When his head shifted to a tilt with a squint of curiosity, she nodded. For a moment, her gaze lingered on his blue eyes, focusing on that one beautiful spot of gold in his right iris. "That's why I kept the outdated brochure all these years. Something told me your house was the secret to my broken heart. I just didn't know it had you there waiting for me."

"Why didn't you tell me?"

Addy shrugged. "Feelings too dark to talk about, I guess. The farther I ran from my past, the stronger I felt, but nobody told me how lonely I'd be. Grief is a quicksand. It's the place love goes when it has nowhere else to go. No matter what I did, I couldn't shed the darkness of my parents' deaths. Not completely anyway. Not until I found you. You brought light to my life. I can see more clearly now than I ever have." She held tighter to his hand. "Come with me, Jack. Out here in the outside world—together—where this grief and anger and sadness can't punish us for the rest of our lives."

Jack cleared emotion from his throat. "If you're asking me to stop grieving Kaitlin, I can't. If I stop, I'll lose her forever."

Softly, Addy said, "Jack, the only way you can lose her is to stop *remembering* her. I will never ask you to do that. I promise."

When he swept a caress over her fingers, she felt a flicker of something. She couldn't say it was love, but it was something.

CHAPTER 25

J ack opened the passenger side door of his truck.
"Get in," he softly said to Addy. "We can at least
get a burger together."

For a moment, her only thought was to jump in
his truck and drive away from any life that didn't
include him, but she owed Nick an explanation. She
couldn't just disappear.

"I need to..." Addy looked back at the hospital
entrance, but then turned to Jack. "I want to go with
you. I *will* go with you, but I need to grab my flight bag.
I left it in the waiting room." Her nerves rattled a
warning.

Jack glanced at the hospital, then he closed the
truck door. "You're going back inside to see Nick,
aren't you?"

"Yes." Her head nodded of its own volition. "Nick
drove me here. My boss is there, too, and he's probably
wondering why I ran out. I have to go back inside, but
it will only take a few minutes. Please, Jack, will you
wait for me?"

The sun was slowly fading from the Texas sky, its daylight-blue hue turning the western horizon an inky purple. Jack tucked his hands into his jean pockets and leaned against the truck door. "Go on," he said, nodding toward the hospital. "I'll wait."

Addy wanted to wrap her arms around him, press her cheek to his close-shaven stubble, and tell him again that she loved him, but her instincts told her to do what needed to be done so that she could return to him quickly.

She ran through the opened entrance straight into Nick. He took hold of her shoulders, his hands atop her pilot epaulets. He stared intently at her. "What happened? Are you okay?"

"Yes, I came back to tell you I'm leaving with Jack." A hopeful smile came. "And to say thank you."

Nick's hands melted off her shoulders. He nodded but then smiled. He glanced back at Thabo who stood head down a few feet away, talking on his phone. Nick reached down for her flight bag and handed it over. "Go get him, lady friend. I'll take care of everything here."

Addy ran across the parking lot to Jack, her eyes on him the whole way. His repressed smile showed when she bounced to a stop in front of him.

"Ready now?" he asked.

She loved the warm tone of his softened heart. "Yes."

Jack reopened the passenger side door and waited while Addy climbed inside, then he closed it and walked around the front to the driver's side.

From the truck, Addy saw Nick through the hospital glass doors, watching. Her hand went up when his did.

At the drive-thru down the street, Jack ordered a boxed kid's meal with a small drink for Juli, then burgers and fries for Addy and himself. With their food bag and drinks on the console between them, they drove back to the big American Foursquare home on the outskirts of town.

The three sat at the picnic table in the backyard, beneath the old pecan tree, eating their fast-food meals. After finishing their food, Jack carried Juli, sleepy from the day, to her bedroom for the night.

It was almost October, and the fine line between a Texas summer and autumn was harder to define now. Evening temperatures had cooled, and the earth was quiet as if winter was closer than expected.

Addy stared up at the three-quarter moon in the western sky, watching the stars push through the darkness.

When the back door opened, Jack stepped out carrying a battery-operated lantern and a knitted throw in ivory and gray. He came to the table and set down the light, and then he draped the throw over her shoulders before taking a seat on the bench opposite her. For a moment, he stared into her eyes, silent, as if trying to decide whether to say the thing that had kept him quiet most of the evening.

Addy pulled the throw around herself and leaned forward, closer to him. She met his gaze with a smile. "Something's on your mind, Jack. Do you want to tell me what it is?"

"Yes," he answered quickly. "I just don't know how to say it."

"It's okay," she said softly. "Whatever it is, just say it." She was here with him. In the moment. That's what mattered.

Jack reached across the table, summoning her hands. When she gave them, he took hold, his fingers still but steady, withholding a caress. He took a breath, exhaling slowly. "Okay. Here goes," he said. His gaze focused on her. "You've turned my world upside down, Addy, and I'm having trouble adjusting."

Nerves quickened her pulse. Afraid to speak. Worried she might send his thoughts in a direction she couldn't bear.

"I never expected to meet you," he said to her. "And I sure didn't expect a whirlwind love affair. A long time ago, I made a silent promise to myself and to Juli that I'd never fall in love again." His gentle hands began to involuntarily stroke her fingers. "Kaitlin was the love of my life."

Jack glanced back at the quiet house, dimly lit. "Juli doesn't remember much about her mom. Most of what she recalls is probably just memories that Paige and I gave to her, trying to keep Kaitlin alive in her heart." He looked at Addy, a shine of apology in his eyes. "She should grow up knowing that her mother was the only woman I ever loved."

His words were a thousand knives, inflicting pain on her breaking heart.

"Why?" Addy pushed up off the bench. She stood. "Jack, do you think there's only one person in this world for each of us?" She knew her tone sounded defensive, but it wasn't a set-up question. She wanted to know. "Because if that's true—if each of us only gets one—then we are two hopelessly lost souls. You'll go on loving only Kaitlin forever, and I'll go on loving only you."

"That's not it," Jack said with a downward shake of his head. "I think you can have lots of *loves* in your life, but the *love of your life* only comes along once. True love is a one-time thing." He stood and walked around the picnic table, closer to her. "Addy, you deserve to be the love of someone's life. Someone's soulmate. Someone's I-can't-live-without-you love."

Addy pulled the knitted throw tighter around her, tears threatening to unhinge her armor-plated emotions.

In defense of any tender feelings, Jack took a step back. "Besides, you'll be leaving in a few months."

"What if I wasn't?" she asked. "Leaving."

His was a troubled glance. "Addy, don't give up a career you love. Not for me. Not for anyone."

She shook her head. "I wouldn't be giving it up, Jack. I was promoted. I'm captain for as long as I want the job. I just have to decide whether or not to stay after my contract expires in June."

His expression slowly changed.

"What if I stayed?"

Conflicted, he said, "What about your apartment in the city? And your friends? Your routine. You love Dallas and its city lifestyle."

"The things I thought I loved were just paper and glue holding me together," she said softly. "I know that now. I think I could give it all up if my new life included you."

Reality drew a hard breath. Jack closed his eyes. After a moment, he opened them, his eyes fixed on her. "The truth is, Addy, I might not be able to give up mine. To change everything from the way it is now. Not permanently anyway. Kaitlin will always be with me. Every time I look at Juli, I am reminded of her and our life together."

In the lantern light, her welling tears were caught by a glisten. Unsteady, she sat, her back rigid and straight. "So, what are you saying, Jack?" It wasn't anger, but a flare of heat flushed her cheeks. "That you'll let me share your bed, but not your heart? Is that it?"

Surprised, Jack slid onto the bench beside her and took hold of her hand. "No," he said. "I'm saying that I'm trying really hard not to fall so madly in love with you that I can't stop myself from loving you. I'm not sure that I have a right to change our lives—mine and Juli's." He held her hand without pressure. "I want you so badly that I can barely think of anything else. And I don't just mean in my bedroom, Addy. I mean *you*. But I don't know if I'll ever be able to give you my whole, unbroken heart. Part of me is always going to belong to Kaitlin, and you deserve a man who'll give everything to you—his heart, a home, a family, and so much more. This isn't fair to you."

A flood of emotion hit her. Addy leaned her head back, saw the stars of fall, and caught the hitch in her throat. Jack was the man she'd dreamed of finding, wished for, wanted. Yet he didn't understand.

She squeezed his hand, and then her gaze settled on his blue eyes. "Jack, I can find a man that I can live with, but what I want is the man I can't live without."

When the hard lines of his brow softened, Addy reached up, touching his face, outlining his lips with her fingertips. "Don't you know, Jack? I'm not asking for the part of you that will always belong to Kaitlin. I love you more because you still love her. It proves what kind of man you are."

He stood and pulled Addy to her feet. "I can't make you any promises."

Addy had meant her hug to be a comfort—to hold him and tell him she understood—but when she wrapped her arms around Jack, her head falling softly against his shoulder just over his heart, his surrender broke free. He held her to him as if they were one.

"Come with me," he whispered. With her hand in his, Jack led Addy into the house.

All the lights were off, except for a nightlight between his room and Juli's room. For a moment, he stood and looked down the hallway toward his bedroom, but then he turned and led Addy up the stairs to the room she had once rented.

CHAPTER 26

Morning rose while Addy slept, stirring only when the rumbling sounds of a school day infringed on her slumber.

She sat up, hearing family sounds downstairs. *She'd overslept.* Addy jumped out of bed and headed for the shower.

When she got downstairs, donning yesterday's flight uniform, the coffee was brewed, but neither father nor daughter was there. She peered out through the kitchen window, spotting Jack with Juli, the two waiting at the stop for her school bus. She watched until Juli climbed the bus steps.

As soon as the school bus turned the corner on its way down the main road, Jack sprinted down the drive to the house. He found Addy in the kitchen, kissed her cheek, then he headed for the coffeemaker and poured himself a cup. He turned with a smile.

"Good morning," he said.

"Good morning." Addy smiled, too, sipping her coffee. "How did you sleep last night?"

"I didn't. Or not much, anyway. I was afraid I'd oversleep, and Juli might miss her bus." He gave a side nod toward his truck parked in the driveway. "I forgot and left my phone on the charger in my truck, and it's the only alarm I have in the house."

Addy set her cup on the kitchen counter and went to Jack. She slid her arms around his neck and kissed him. "You're an amazing father. Juli's so lucky to have you as her dad."

He set down his coffee and wrapped his arms around her.

Softly, she said, "It's nice to be here with you." Then she gave a coy laugh. "Actually, it's *incredible* to be here with you—but my clean clothes and toothbrush are at my new apartment."

"That's right," he said, pulling back a bit to study her face. "I'd almost forgotten." With her hands still clasped around his neck, he smoothed her white shirt, and then he reached for his cup and took a sip. "You've got no way to leave, do you?"

The tease in his voice caused her to laugh. "Totally dependent on you."

Jack leaned, kissing her just below her ear, and then he whispered, "Thank you for last night."

Addy kissed him, then released him.

He emptied his coffee into a travel mug that had been washed and set upside down on a folded drying towel and then grabbed his truck keys while Addy retrieved her flight bag.

"What's your new address?" Jack asked.

Blankly, Addy stared at him. "Oh, my gosh. I don't remember."

"But you know how to get there, right?"

"Not from here, I don't think so." When Jack gave

her a suspicious head tilt, Addy said, "I have the address in my GPS. I just turn it on and go."

"That's good, except your GPS is with your car, and where is that, by the way?"

"Parked at Fray Transport." Then, she said, "Oh, wait! I gave you the address."

"Me? When?" He gave a laugh. "If I'd had your address, I'm not sure I could have resisted coming to see you."

Addy headed for the B and B check-in counter. Still there, exactly where she'd left it. She picked up the note with her phone number and new address written on it. "Here you go." She smiled as she handed it to him.

Jack read the note, then glanced at her. "Send the final bill, huh?" He pushed the paper into his back pocket then pulled her to him, kissing her. "Do I get to collect whenever I want?"

She brushed her fingertips over his lips. "You most certainly do."

INSIDE ADDY'S APARTMENT, JACK WENT ROOM TO room, inspecting it as if he were renting it himself. He turned to her. "It's sort of a plain boxy place, isn't it? And it only has two windows."

"I know. That's exactly what I said to the leasing agent when I rented it, but she referred to it as 'cozy' and made that sound like a good thing." They both laughed.

Jack went to Addy and slid his arms around her. "It's amazing to be with you. It's like I've found part of myself again."

"You have," she said, her gaze settling on his gorgeous blue eyes. Then, she corrected herself. "*We* have. I feel the same way, Jack. I think I've been looking for you my whole life."

His breathing changed, landing a hard focus on Addy. Without warning, he swept her up into his arms and turned toward the bedroom, stopped by a knock on the door. Jack looked at her. "A welcome to the neighborhood visit?"

"I don't know."

"Then we don't care." He started again toward her plain, unadorned bedroom.

"Jack, put me down," she whispered with a laugh. "It might be maintenance. I called about a leaky faucet."

"So?" he said. "They can come back later."

"They have a key!" Her strained whisper was loud.

Jack had never rented an apartment, so he'd never given much thought to the rights of landlords or how maintenance worked. Hurriedly, he set her down.

Addy smoothed her blonde pixie and caught her breath on the way to the door. She turned the deadbolt, then opened it.

"Hey, lady friend." Nick held up the pilot's cap she'd left behind at the hospital. "I thought you might need a ride to work since your Miata is still at the office this morning." He stepped inside with an easy smile. "And how are those pink pelican sheets working out for you?"

Jack stood in the bedroom doorway. A glare lit his eyes. "What the hell are you doing here?" Then his stare turned to Addy. "And how does he know what your sheets look like?"

"Jack," Nick said, switching his focus between the two. "Sorry, man. I didn't know you were here."

"How do you even know where she lives?" Before Nick could answer, Jack challenged again. "And how many times have you been on her sheets?"

"Jack!" Addy turned with a fire in her eyes. "How dare you think I'm sleeping with Nick after the things I told you last night!"

When an unknown man and woman stopped outside her opened door to gawk, Addy slammed it.

"We *work* together. We don't *sleep* together!" Addy walked a tight circle of fury in her living room—a fist-hold on her short blonde hair. She wasn't the type to lose control. And she rarely lost her temper.

Jack turned, looking for his keys.

"Hey, Addy," Nick said quietly. "I'm really sorry. I didn't mean to cause any problems."

Jack snatched his keys off the kitchen counter. He headed for the door.

"Where are you going?" Addy snapped. She sprinted for the door and then leaned with her back against it. "You can't leave." When Jack stopped, she said, "I have something to say."

Jack steadied dismissive eyes on her, never looking at Nick. "Addy, get out of my way."

She felt the cold. "Why? So you can walk out on me too?" She hadn't meant to say it. *God, how she loved him!*

His eyes flickered. Visions of his late wife in that crumpled car with Nick unfurled in his mind like scenes from a movie.

"How about I leave instead?" Nick started for the door, only to be spun back for a fist to the jaw. He fell.

Addy screamed, "Stop it!" but Jack had already pulled Nick up by the shirt collar and was punching him, again and again before dropping him back onto the floor.

"Fight, damn you!" Jack shouted down at him.

"No," Nick said, wiping the blood from his split lip onto his shirt sleeve.

Addy pushed between the two men, yelling, "Stop fighting over me!"

Eyes ablaze, Jack turned. "This isn't about *you*!"

She stepped back—her thoughts spinning out of control. She had to get out. She grabbed Jack's dropped keys off the floor and ran. Out the door, bumping the waiting gawkers, and down the outside stairs. Addy ran through the parking lot to Jack's truck and got in. She only looked back once.

CHAPTER 27

It wasn't that she *wanted* them to fight over her, even though it probably looked that way to Jack when she ran out of the apartment, essentially stealing his truck and then disappearing in it. The heartbreaker was in realizing it wasn't her who mattered to him.

She was an invisible woman, lost in the memory of another. Her heart just a throwaway thing. She had never been enough. Not for anyone. Jack had been honest, so why had she fooled herself into thinking their relationship could be different?

Addy kept her tears at bay, deciding to drive until her thoughts cleared and the vise grip on her heart loosened.

Although Jack's pickup truck was bigger than her sports car, she wasn't intimidated, after all, she'd flown a ninety-three-ton Airbus without a flinch. Even so, there was more traffic on the ground than there was in the wide-open sky, and she had no notion of where she was going on these narrow, unfamiliar streets. Where was her PlaneView avionics when she needed it?

An hour of driving nowhere nudged Addy into the parking lot entrance for the Guadalupe River Trail. She parked, got out, locked the doors, and started walking. Alone with nature, in the sky or on the ground, was sometimes the only place solace could be found.

The trail hugged the river's edge, its wide waters flowing past towering bald cypress trees whose fluted trunks grew from the banks. Hackberry, oaks, pecan, Ashe juniper, and others grew on shared land inside the park where dozens of squirrels played, and many-hued ducks and geese waddled back and forth to the water. The river, with its earthy-scented banks, infused the air with the essence of a woodlands retreat. It was easy to love a place like this, but it was a hard place to lose love, especially when it had all felt so natural.

What was she doing here in this town that felt so foreign? Her home was in Dallas. Her people were in Dallas. Her life was there too.

When the cooling breeze picked up beneath the midday sun, thrown shadows hinted of places Addy had once longed to see. Spending her days where she didn't belong shouldn't be a prison sentence. She needed the job at Fray Transport, but no one ever said that lonely days of downtime were a requirement. She had no one waiting for her at home. There were plenty of places to travel, and no one there expected anything from her. Places far from Jack.

Her faraway dreams had been stuffed into a box rarely opened. Bucket-list adventures. She'd planned to hike the John Muir Trail in California, and bike through the wine country in Napa, even take a trail ride down into the Grand Canyon—just as soon as she learned to ride a horse. Nick had taken her one step closer with Butterscotch, but she'd delayed everything for her commitment to the sky.

As much as she loved the heavens, she wanted to love the earth too. Not just the ground beneath her feet but the things that grew from it. Wildflowers and farms. Life itself. She had never even planted a seed, yet Jack had grown field after field, nurturing each little seed until its life sprouted and took hold. Those things hadn't taken on any urgency for her until now.

Addy looked down at the bare dirt beneath the trees strewn with October's dry leaves. She squatted, sweeping leaves from a spot, and then scraped up a handful of dry dirt, squeezing it so tight that the grains lodged beneath her fingernails, just like Jack's hands had looked the day she first met him.

Jack favored the earth. She preferred the sky. He shunned family. She craved it. He'd had the love of his life. Until now, she'd never been truly in love. They were on opposite ends in the spectrum of life. And between heaven and earth, there was no middle ground.

On the path back to the parking lot, she walked silently through her thoughts. She could do life alone. *She could.*

Near the top of a gently sloping hill near the parking lot, Addy spotted the white F-150 parked right where she left it, sunlight glinting off its rear chrome trim. It was still the only truck in the lot. She pulled the keys from her pocket and walked toward it. She needed to return the pickup to its owner. How to face Jack doing it was a whole other matter.

∾

NICK LAY ON THE FLOOR, JACK TOWERING OVER HIM. Both had their eyes trained on the slamming door.

"Don't let her go, Jack. Go after her," Nick quietly said to his brother.

Instead of responding, Jack reached into his back pocket. He pulled out his iPhone and the note with Addy's address and phone number written on it. He dialed the number only to hear the phone ringing a room away. Holding his own to his ear, he walked toward the sound. On the bed was her phone, chiming from his call.

Jack hung up and then walked back to the living room where Nick had pushed up onto his feet again.

"Now what?" Nick asked.

A glare flashed. "What makes you think we're having a conversation?" Jack walked to the living room window and looked out, scanning the parking lot for his truck. When he didn't see it, he mumbled, "She's already gone."

Nick pulled out a dining chair and sat. "Jack, brother, you know it's been four years since we talked." He dabbed his busted lip with a knuckle. "I never got to tell you in person how sorry I am about Kaitlin."

Jack turned. "You make it sound like she died in some sort of unavoidable accident." Bitter, he said, "You *killed* her, Nick. You killed Kaitlin *and* our baby."

"Yes," Nick said softly.

"Are you expecting me to forgive you? Is that what this is all about? Because that's never going to happen."

"I know, and you have every right to hate me," Nick said. "I don't expect you to forgive me. I can't forgive me. I just wanted to say I'm sorry." He looked straight at Jack. Eyes steady. "I'm sorry. Sorry for it all."

Jack went to the couch and sat, leaning forward

with his head in his hands. For a long while, neither man spoke.

A jangle of keys finally broke the silence. "I've got my truck," Nick said.

"What?" Jack glared at him.

"Keys." Nick jangled again. "We can take my truck and go look for her."

The two drove mostly in silence with Jack looking out the side window, trying to spot his pickup truck in strip mall parking lots and gas stations. On the outskirts of town, Nick turned left, driving out to the rodeo grounds, but the truck wasn't there either.

Jack kept his focus on the passing scenery. Somber, he asked, "Did she say anything?"

"Addy?" Nick asked. "Yeah. She's in love with you. It's so obvious."

Jack glanced at his brother. "I meant Kaitlin."

Nick fell silent, focusing on the road ahead. After a moment, he said, "I barely remember any of it, Jack."

"But you do remember something, don't you? You hesitated, so tell me."

Nick stared straight ahead. He nodded. "We were both trapped in the car. I heard sirens and some guy yelling at me, then I felt Kaitlin's hand. I told her to hang on."

At the next stoplight, Nick glanced at Jack. "She asked me to save Jenna. If it came down to a choice, she wanted the paramedics to save the baby instead of her."

A sob broke free from Jack.

When the light turned green, Nick pulled into the next parking lot and stopped. He sat quietly, giving Jack time. After a few minutes, he started again.

"When the paramedics got there, I told them she was pregnant. I said she wanted the baby saved."

Jack used the bottom hem of his T-shirt to wipe his face dry, then he adjusted himself in the seat. "She told you the baby's name."

"Yeah," Nick said. "I hear it every time I close my eyes."

Jack nodded. They sat silent for a few minutes. "Was there anything else?"

"No," Nick said softly.

After another minute of silence, Nick pulled out onto the road again.

At the park entrance near the river trail, Jack pointed. "There it is," he said.

Nick turned into the lot and parked next to the white truck emblazoned with *TXUS Seeds*. He idled his engine.

Jack sat, staring at the empty truck. Addy wasn't inside.

When Jack didn't open his door, Nick asked, "You got an extra key?"

"Yeah."

Still, Jack sat, his eyes on the pickup truck.

"She's worth it," Nick said. "But you already know that."

Jack opened the door and got out of his brother's truck. He closed it, then walked to the front of his own truck and gazed out at the long river trail. The Upper Guadalupe narrowed through the park, flowing gently. Peacefully.

Nick got out, too, but left his door ajar with the engine running. He walked closer to Jack. "I can wait with you."

"No." Jack shook his head.

Nick hesitated. "If you'd rather take off, I can stay and give her a ride to her car or back to the apartment."

Jack didn't answer. He knew that if neither stayed, Addy would be left high and dry at the park without a vehicle or a phone.

Softly, Nick followed up with, "Are you okay to stay?" Met with silence, he waited, then said, "I'm not trying to aggravate you, but you've always been a hard man to read."

Jack turned to him. "Addy isn't your responsibility."

"I know, but—"

"Did you hear me?"

"All right," Nick said. He returned to his idling truck, reluctant to put it in gear until Jack climbed up onto the hood of his SuperCrew and sat. Only then did Nick back out of the parking space and head for the exit. After a glance into his rearview mirror, he turned onto the traffic-heavy street, leaving the park behind.

Jack checked the time. It was almost two in the afternoon. Juli's bus was due home in about an hour. Either he or Paige had always been home to meet her bus, but Paige was probably still in the hospital. Again, he looked at the time. He didn't want to have to choose between stranding Addy at the park—especially after the way he'd acted—or deserting his daughter.

As Addy got closer to the parking lot, she saw Jack, waiting. He'd found her and come to reclaim his truck. Just as well, she thought. Since she was destined for a life of solitude, she might as well get started on it.

"Hi," she said on approach, holding out his keys. "Looking for these?"

Jack walked to her, an air of calm between them both. He held out his hand and let her drop the keys into it.

"I was looking for *you*," he said.

For a moment, Addy hesitated, wondering if she had gotten it wrong. She gave it a quick, judging thought. It was an expensive truck she'd taken, that's all.

"Any chance you can drive me back to my apartment so I can get my phone and keys? I'll call an Uber for a ride out to my car."

"Yeah, sure," Jack said, gently. "But you don't need an Uber. I can drive you to your car." He checked his iPhone for the time again. "I've got to pick up Juli first though, okay? Her bus is due home in about twenty minutes."

Addy nodded and walked to the passenger door. When she heard it click, she got inside, buckled her seat belt, and turned her face to the side window.

Jack was ready to back out of the parking space, but he kept his foot on the brake. "Addy, I'm sorry about yelling at you back at the apartment and for saying the stupid things I said, but Nick deserved that punch in the jaw. It's been a long time coming, and things just got away from me."

"I understand," she said without looking at him. "I hope Nick's okay."

"Nick's fine. That guy never gets hurt."

Addy turned to look at Jack. "I don't think that's true. I think Nick hurts all the time, and I think everyone is so wrapped up in themselves that they never stop to see his pain."

There was no response as Jack pulled out and onto the main road, his eyes fixed forward.

The breeze shivered the leaves on the roadside trees and sent gentle waves over the native grasses on their way back to the big American Foursquare at the edge of town. It seemed autumn was fighting for its rightful place against the weakening summer season.

Addy kept her gaze focused out the side window. The houses along the way reflected the families within —swing sets in the yards, picnic tables, treehouses, and dogs with wagging tails in wait of a school bus that always arrived. In a pasture scattered with live oak, a group of green-vested 4-H kids worked with a herd of buff-colored Angora goats.

Just let go of it, Addy. These families belonged here, but this place would never be her home. It was just one more place she didn't fit.

Jack pulled up behind a yellow school bus and followed it to its stop at the end of their driveway, and then he put the truck in park. "I'll be right back," he said to Addy. He got out and walked toward the opened door of the bus, then waved to the driver. When Juli jumped from the bottom step with her backpack, Jack smiled and took hold of her hand. He walked with her to the truck, opened the back door, tossing her pink backpack onto the floor, and then he lifted her onto the seat.

"Miss Addy! You're here!" Juli stretched forward for her as Jack was trying to buckle her in.

Addy turned and reached back, taking hold of the girl's outstretched hand. "Hey, sweet pea. How was school?"

"Juli," Jack interrupted, straightening the ruffles on her drop-waist dress from beneath the seatbelt.

"We're going for a ride with Miss Addy. Do you need your afterschool snack now, or do you want to wait until we get back home?"

Juli scooted back on the seat as Jack tightened her seatbelt. "Now, please? Can I have a juice box too?"

"Yep," Jack said to her, then to Addy, he said, "It'll just take me a minute." Jack closed the door and then sprinted down the long driveway to the house, loping up the steps, and then disappearing inside.

"Miss Addy, guess what?"

Turned around, Addy said, "What is it, sweet pea?"

Juli pursed her lips to hold her grin inside, but when it came out anyway, she leaned forward and whispered, "I got to talk to the bird."

"The painted bunting?"

"Uh-huh." She nodded. "And guess what?"

"What?"

"*You're here.*" Juli clamped her hand over her mouth, suppressing a giggle.

Jack pulled open Juli's door. "Here's a juice box and a bag of fruit chews for you." He opened the small bag for her. "You okay now?"

"Yes." She grinned and took the snacks, her legs in a happy bounce, and poked her straw through the juice box for a sip.

"Good." He kissed her forehead and then closed the door.

On the drive to Addy's apartment to get her keys and phone, Jack, keeping his voice low, asked, "Will you have dinner with us tonight? Let me make up for today?"

"I don't think so, Jack." She didn't want to sound sorrow-filled or regretful. Just firm.

"What about tomorrow?"

"No." Her tone was kind but decisive. She glanced at him. "Work is going to be busy for a while. Now that I'm the captain, I need to help hire a first officer to replace me as copilot. No new flights until a second pilot has been hired, and Thabo has several trips planned."

Jack nodded. Faintly, he said, "Okay."

Parked near the exterior stairway to her apartment, Addy got out of the truck.

Before closing the door, Juli called out, "Aren't me and Daddy coming, too?"

"Not this time, my girl," Jack answered his daughter. "We're going to wait here together." With that, Addy closed the door.

Once inside her apartment, Addy glanced around. The earlier fight between brothers hadn't disturbed much of anything, other than leaving behind a residual air of anger. She picked up the pilot's cap that Nick had returned to her and took it to the bedroom, tossing it onto the bed.

For a moment, thoughts of Jack, his hands on her, his lips to hers, brought her breath to a standstill. She closed her eyes. How would she ever stop loving him? *She had to try*. They could never last. The mere sight of Nick had sent any thought of her to the farthest corner of his mind. Next time, she might be left there forever, in the aloneness that somehow always found her.

CHAPTER 28

Addy gave Jack directions to Fray Transport. At the entrance gate, she hopped out of the truck and input the security code for the gate herself. After returning to the truck, she directed him down the blacktopped drive, west of the Mediterranean-style residence.

"The office and hangar are at the end of this road," she told him, keeping all emotion out of their togetherness.

"I've never been out here," he told her. "Didn't even know this place existed."

"Are we going to fly in the airplane?" Juli asked.

Jack gave a chuckle. "It's not a carnival ride, my girl. Someday we'll get to fly in an airplane, but not today, okay?"

"Okay," Juli said with a pout.

Around the final bend was the tan metal building with the *Fray Transport* sign. In the distance was the hangar.

Jack pulled in and parked next to the Miata and Nick's truck.

"Thanks for the ride," Addy said, opening her door, trying hard not to look at Jack. She had ahold of her keys and phone.

"But I thought I was going to get to see your airplane!" Juli cried out from the back seat. "You said I could..."

Addy glanced at Jack, who glanced back at her. "I did promise to show her the plane. She might not get another chance." The reminder that she might never see Jack or his daughter again stabbed like a knife through her heart, but she stayed steady.

"Addy," Jack said, his arm draped across the back of the passenger seat. "*His* truck is here. That means he's here too." He gave a side nod to the backseat. "And I have Juli."

Addy stood for a moment, understanding he didn't want Juli to meet his brother. "But I made a promise to her, Jack." She looked at him with more answer in her heart than she wanted to give. "Promises are serious business."

"She *promised* me, Daddy."

Conflicted, Jack fixed his gaze on Addy, his mind calculating the options.

"Let me go inside and check," she said. When Jack gave a nod, Addy told Juli, "Sit tight, sweet pea. I'll be right back."

"Yay!" Juli clapped. "We're going to see the airplane!"

Inside the office, Addy heard the radio playing in the fleet garage. She grabbed a biscuit for Pax and opened the door. She tossed it to the dog and then headed for the first vehicle with a raised hood.

"Oh, Josh, it's you."

"Hey, Addy," Josh said, smiling. "Congrats on the promotion to captain."

"Thanks. It wasn't exactly how I wanted to earn the spot, but things happen, you know? Hey, is Nick here? I saw his truck out front."

"Yeah." Josh raised up, pointing in the direction of the hangar. "He's working on his routine maintenance list for the G550. He's at the hangar."

"Oh, great," Addy mumbled. Not what she wanted to hear. Then, "Thanks, Josh. See you soon." She turned and headed back outside to Jack and Juli.

"Well?" Jack said.

"Not here. He's at the hangar. With the airplane."

"Who's with the airplane?" Juli asked, overhearing the conversation.

"We should just go," Jack said.

"Jack, it's not a big deal. He's working. I can ask him to stay out of the way." Palms up, she shrugged. "Then everyone will be happy, right?"

He glanced into the back at Juli, who was bouncing her feet.

"All right."

They drove to the hangar and parked just as Nick came down the steps of the jet, holding an empty box. He stood at the bottom, staring at the three of them.

When they got out of the truck, Juli pointed to the Gulfstream. "Is that one yours?" She bolted for the airplane.

"Come back here!" Jack shouted. He started after her with Addy following.

When Nick saw the girl, he knelt at the base of the stairs and waited. "Hey there," he said when she came to a stop in front of him. He put a hand up to his chin, a finger partially covering his fat-lipped smile. "I'll bet you're Juli."

"How did you know?" she asked him.

"I met you a long, long time ago. You're a big girl now."

Jack came to a stop behind her, his hand lightly gripping his daughter's shoulder. Addy stood beside him, silent.

"Did you know my daddy a long time ago too?"

Nick glanced up at Jack, then back down to Juli. "Yes, I knew your daddy when he was your age." Instinctively, he started to reach for her but thought better of it and pulled his hands back. "It's really nice to see you, Juli."

Juli smiled. "Miss Addy is going to show me her airplane."

Nick laughed, tears welling. "Oh, it's her airplane, is it?"

"Uh-huh." Juli nodded. She looked up at Addy. "Isn't it your airplane, Miss Addy?"

"It's only mine to fly, sweet pea. Nick takes care of everything else."

Juli looked back at him. "Your name is Nick? I have an Uncle Nick, don't I, Daddy?" She looked up at Jack.

The three were silent, Nick's eyes glistening. He stood. At Jack's silence, he said, "Hey, how 'bout I get out of your way so you can go inside and see the airplane." Moved aside to give them access to the stairs, Nick nodded to Jack and Addy before ducking under the nose gear, disappearing.

"Come on," Addy said, "let's go on up." She looked

back to see Jack lift the six-year-old, carrying her up the steps with him.

"Whoa!" Juli said when Jack put her down inside the jet. She ran to a luxury seat and hopped into it, staring at the laptop-sized monitor jutting out from the sidewall. "Is this a TV?" Then she bumped her head on the round window, looking out. "Look how high up we are!"

Jack scanned the interior, brushing a hand over the high-gloss polished wood credenza and tables before shifting to Addy. "Wood interior and leather seats? Very nice. I've never been on a private jet."

"Much more comfortable for the passengers than a jumbo jet."

Addy led Jack down the aisle way toward the rear of the plane, talking the whole way. "This aircraft seats sixteen and has both a forward and an aft lavatory. The conference room becomes a private bedroom when needed for overnight flights." With Jack in tow, she turned, ruffling Juli's hair on her way past, prompting the girl to jump down out of the seat and follow them to the forward galley.

Champagne and long-stemmed wine glasses hung secured beneath glossy wood cabinets. "We have a wine cooler, refrigerator, microwave, and convection oven." She presented the galley as if she were leading a formal tour. "And for little girls," Addy said, leaning down and grinning at Juli as she opened the fridge, "we have orange juice, tomato juice, and ginger ale."

Juli's mouth dropped open. She shot a look to her father. "Can I have one, Daddy?"

"You just had a juice box," he whispered to her.

"Maybe she can take a package of peanuts home for later?" Addy suggested.

"Peanuts! Can I have peanuts?"

Jack smiled like he always did when Juli was happy. "Okay." He put a hand atop her head. "Tell Miss Addy thank you."

"Thank you!" Juli bounced on the balls of her feet until she was handed the individual-sized bag of honey-roasted peanuts.

At the flight deck, Addy opened the door and then stepped across into the captain's seat. She lowered herself into it, feeling the promotion. Instructor-like, she pointed to the PlaneView multifunction display and described its capabilities.

Behind her, Jack stood immersed in Addy's explanation of the advanced avionics system, oblivious to his daughter, who had her nose pressed to the copilot's window, secretly grinning and waving to Nick on the ground below.

THE SEASON HAD BEGUN TO USHER IN COOLER mornings, turning the leaves of the flameleaf sumac a golden yellow, burnt orange, and red. Jack stood looking out the kitchen window, sipping coffee and listening to Juli talk while she ate her breakfast cereal.

"Daddy, I told my teacher that Miss Addy flies airplanes, and she wants to know if she can come to Career Day."

He glanced at his daughter. "Career Day?"

"Uh-huh. That's when mommies and daddies come to school and talk about their jobs, but I thought Miss Addy could come since I don't have a mommy. Do you think she can?"

Jack had drawn his daughter into a relationship

he'd already ruined. How do you tell that to a six-year-old? "Maybe I could come for Career Day?"

Juli giggled. "Daddy, you just grow itty-bitty tiny little seeds." She pinched her fingers together to show how small. "But Miss Addy flies great big airplanes!"

The groan of a bus engine graveled closer. Jack grabbed Juli's backpack. "School bus, Juli."

The girl jumped down off the kitchen stool and turned so Jack could slip the straps of her backpack over her shoulders, and then they both hurried outside. When the air brakes *hissed* to a stop and the bus door popped open, Juli looked up at her father. "Promise you'll ask her, Daddy, okay?"

Jack nodded without meaning to, then waved to her when she took a seat on the school bus, grinning and waving to him from the window. He stood watching as the bus roared away.

He didn't like complicated, and he surely didn't want any complications in Juli's life, yet here he was with a woman stuck in his heart, in his thoughts, and in his daughter's life.

Before he headed back to the house, he spotted Carter's truck slowing for a turn into the driveway. He waited as they pulled in and stopped. Paige got out of the passenger side, walking slowly toward him with Carter beside her.

"You look good, Paige," Jack said, hugging her, then shaking hands with Carter. "How do you feel?"

"I'm okay," Paige said with a slight smile meant to comfort him. "I got home last night but went right to bed. Sorry I didn't call." They started up the porch steps together. "It's funny how spending a day or two in bed makes you really tired."

Jack pulled out two bar stools for them in the kitchen and then poured their coffee, adding creamer to Paige's cup before handing it to her, then he poured himself a second cup.

"Is Juli here?" Carter asked, his eyes scanning the house.

"She left for school right before you pulled in. Why?"

"Because Carter wants to apologize to her for yelling at her at the stables." Paige glanced at her fiancé. "Don't you?" She looked at Jack. "I was horrified when he told me what he'd done."

"Yeah, honestly, I'm really sorry about that," Carter said. "I just freaked a little."

"Juli understands, Carter. She's a smart kid. She learned the hard way what happens when you spook a horse." He looked at Paige. "Sorry you got hurt." Then a smile he couldn't hold back came out. "Good thing you've got a hard head."

Paige gave a chuckling snort. "Me? Look who's talking." Then, "Speaking of being hardheaded, what'd you end up doing about the lady pilot?"

Jack gave a sigh louder than he intended. "A lot has happened since the accident, starting with your trip to the hospital, but let's just say I blew it, big time, and leave it at that."

"Have you tried sending flowers?" Carter asked. "Usually works for me when I mess up."

Paige looked at Jack. "Flowers aren't the reason I forgive him for the silly things he does, but they are a nice touch. I forgive him because I love him."

Jack set his coffee cup down.

"Uh-oh," Paige said. She bent forward on the stool,

leaning closer to Jack who stood on the opposite side of the breakfast island. "You fell in love with her, didn't you?"

Jack nodded. "I guess so. It's too bad she hates me now."

CHAPTER 29

Addy slid into a booth inside the Pecos Patio Grill. A storm was moving in and the skies were an ominous gray black purple. She had smelled the rain though it hadn't started to fall yet.

The waitress, young and pretty, set a glass of water on the table and handed Addy a menu. "Hi, my name is Lacy. I'll be your server today." She smiled. "Can I get you something from the bar?"

"No," Addy said. "Thank you. I'm waiting for a friend. Can you bring another menu?"

"Sure." The waitress left, returning with another menu. She laid it on the table. "Do you want to wait until your friend gets here to order?"

"Yes, please."

Alone at the booth, Addy sat near the window wall, scrolling through the emails on her phone, stopping when a text message popped in from Nick.

Hey, lady friend. Did you know Janet is back in town?

Yep. Meeting her for dinner at Pecos.
Waiting for her now.

I think something's up. Let me know.

There hadn't been much of a conversation when Janet called. Addy had simply accepted the dinner invitation without question, glad that her friend was back in town.

She was sending a thumbs-up to Nick when a clap of thunder brought the rain down, splattering the window that overlooked the empty patio, its tables bare and wet. Lights strung pole to pole around the perimeter were the night's only outdoor décor.

Addy took a sip of water, her glance spotting Janet across the restaurant. When the hostess pointed, Janet looked up, her eyes meeting Addy's high wave.

Four more weeks of pregnancy had turned her friend's former gait into a gentle waddle. Addy stood at her friend's approach only to have Janet eye the booth, pick up the menu, and set it down at a nearby table.

"You don't honestly think I'm getting this body into a booth, do you?" Janet asked her, pulling Addy into a hug.

"Sorry," Addy said, grabbing her menu and water and changing tables. "Your belly grew while you were gone."

Janet pulled out a chair, lowering herself into it. "Oh, trust me. I know. And I still have six weeks to go." She settled herself. "You know, I thought I'd be all belly with this pregnancy, but I can't tell you how many times people in California stopped me to say, 'Oh, any day now!' When I'd tell them how far along I am their expressions would shift from joy to pity and fear. I could just imagine them saying, 'How big is that baby going to be?' God, who thought the fat party would go to my face and ass too."

"Oh, stop it." Addy laughed. "You're radiant, and you know it. That little guy is just prepping to be a big burly football player, that's all. Have you picked out a name yet?"

"Probably." Janet waved for the server. "Tom likes the name Burke. I do too. He insists that the baby not have the same name as anyone in either of our families, even distant relatives." She gave Addy a hard look. "Do you know how hard that is? We both come from large families, and when you start down the ancestry road, it's a long and tedious mission to find a name no one has ever used."

"Burke is a good name. I like it."

Janet nodded. "Me too. So unless a long-dead relative pops up with the same name before I go into labor, it looks like this little guy will be Burke Lee Bellini."

When their server arrived tableside, Janet said, "Sorry about the table change, but the booth wasn't working for me." She gave an open-handed display to her pregnancy.

"No problem," Lacy said. "Are you ready to order?"

"Past ready." Janet glanced at Addy. "Do you know what you want?"

"You go ahead," Addy said, grabbing her menu for a look.

Janet handed her menu to the server. "I'll have a grilled ribeye with sweet paprika butter, roasted vegetables, steak fries, and a Diet Coke. Oh, and bread pudding. Can you just bring it out with the food?"

Addy gave a sly smile to the waitress but then handed over her menu too. "I'll have the beef fajitas and sweet tea, please?"

Janet waited until the waitress left their table, then said, "I heard about Ernst. I can't wait to hear what happened."

"How did you hear?"

"Marie called. I'm surprised you didn't call."

"I guess I should have. Sorry," Addy told her. "Things have been a little crazy."

"So, tell me. What happened?"

Addy shook her head. "I told you that I wasn't keen about flying with a pilot who had a drinking problem."

"Don't tell me he broke his twelve-hour rule with Thabo."

They both quieted while the server set their drinks on the table but started again when the waitress walked away.

"He had an altercation with a jealous husband," Addy explained. "Which left him with a black eye, so he wasn't in the right frame of mind when he boarded the flight to Appleton, and he was elusive while we were there, but on our way back, I smelled liquor and confronted him. He got mad, of course. Long story short, Thabo fired him and offered me the captain's position."

"You're the captain now?"

"Oh, gosh..." Addy reached for Janet's hand. "I'm sorry. I didn't mean to just blurt that out." Addy scooted her chair closer to the table and then leaned toward Janet. "Look, if you want the position when you come back, I'll step aside. No hard feelings."

Janet sat back and laughed, holding a hand to her pregnant swell. "Well, look at you," she said. "We're barely more than midway through October and you've already scored a promotion, Captain Piper." She leaned slightly forward. "Good for you."

"I mean it, Janet. The position is rightfully yours."

The sizzle and scent of fajitas turned both sets of eyes to the approaching server. Lacy set a clay-colored tortilla warmer on the table, then announced, "Hot," as she set a cast-iron platter on its wooden rest down in front of Addy. Another server brought Janet her grilled steak, fries, and vegetables. "Can I get you anything else?"

Janet scanned the table. "Yes, I think you've forgotten my bread pudding. And ketchup. I need a bowl of it, please?"

"Oh, I'm so sorry!" Lacy hurried away toward the kitchen.

"How can you eat all of that?" Addy laughed. "You used to order a side salad as your entire dinner, remember?"

"I think those days may be gone forever." Janet smiled when the server set the plated dessert and the small bowl of ketchup down beside her plate. "Thank you," she told her.

"So, here's the thing," Janet confessed, already cutting into her steak. "I'm not coming back."

"What? Why?"

Janet took a bite of steak, chewing as she talked. "Tom's family offered him an equal partnership in their Napa winery, which is growing by leaps and bounds. When Tom left there a few years ago, it was a small operation, and he had no say in its management. It's not so small anymore, and they're impressed with what he's done with our little twenty acres here."

"And what about those twenty acres? Are you planning to sell them?"

"He's keeping them for now. Tom still believes the

boom is coming. He has a trusted friend who has agreed to run it for him."

"What about you and your career? It wasn't easy climbing the ranks and getting to where you are today."

"Oh, Addy, let's face it." Janet set down her fork and picked up a steak fry, dipping it into her ketchup. "I want babies. I've always wanted babies. And I want to be part of the whole big Italian family thing they've got going on. Kids are everywhere on their estate, and Tom's sweet old grandmother still does most of the cooking for all of the big dinners." She gave Addy a nod. "Yeah," she admitted, "I loved it there, and I can't imagine raising this little boy any other way."

Addy sat back. Janet exuded happiness. Families did that to people. They made them whole. Complete. They didn't have the missing pieces she had.

"But what about flying?" Addy asked her. "You loved that too. I don't understand how you can give it all up."

"True," Janet agreed, taking a last bite of steak. "And that's the real beauty of it all. They want to buy a Learjet." She laughed. "I told you they're doing really well. They have big plans to expand. I'll be their number one pilot. No pressure, though. I'll fly when it suits me."

Resigning herself to the fact that she was losing Janet—a friend and the pilot she thought she would be flying with—she asked, "So, what did Thabo say when you told him?"

"Oh, I haven't told him yet. I wanted to talk to you first." Janet set her empty dinner plate aside but then slid the dessert over and started to eat. "So, will you stay now that you're a captain? That's the position you've been wanting, isn't it?"

It wasn't about being captain. It wasn't even about having a steady job until her furlough ended. It was about Jack. It was over between them, and Addy knew it—he was a man that never should have happened to her—but the thought of leaving him entirely was too much to deal with right now.

"I'm considering it," she told Janet. "I like working for Thabo. And I like Nick. I love the Hill Country, but I do miss Dallas. I had a different kind of life there, you know?"

"Yes. Probably as different as my new life in California will be to me. We'll both have to adjust, but Fray Enterprises should be a strong contender to the airlines if you truly want a long-term career as a pilot. They're a stable company, and Thabo is—or was..." She stopped with a glance to Addy. "Unless things have changed, the whole reason Thabo bought the Gulfstream was for international travel. I don't know his whole plan, but before I took my leave, he was planning flights to Spain and Italy. The Spanish islands too." Her brows lifted. "And you have to admit, it would be nice to find yourself in Majorca a few times a year. If I were like you, and had no family or attachments, I'd be piloting that plane all over the world with a smile on my face."

PAIGE SPOTTED ADDY FROM THE HOSTESS STATION, but she followed Carter to their table without a word about it. The pilot was hard to miss with her blonde pixie and long side-swept bangs. She was pretty enough, but she wasn't of local stock, that was for sure. She had a metropolitan style. She missed being country by a mile.

After being seated, both Carter and Paige ordered a margarita.

Paige leaned across the table toward Carter, whispering, "Addy's here."

"Who?" he asked.

"You know. The pilot lady I told you about. The one Jack fell in love with."

"Where?" Carter swiveled in his chair, scanning the dining room. Without turning back to Paige, he asked, "The gorgeous short-haired blonde?"

Paige glared at the back of her fiancé's head.

When Carter glanced over his shoulder, he met her stare. "What?"

She sat back, arms crossed. "How did you know that *gorgeous* blonde was her?"

Carter gave a quiet laugh. "Because it's obvious that she's not from around here. She looks worldly."

"Hmmm…*worldly.* I like that way better than gorgeous."

Carter took a second glance. "Well, she is very pretty. Who's the lady with her?"

"No clue. She looks a little familiar, though, doesn't she?"

"If she was dressed up, she might look a little like the lady we met at that wine tasting event you dragged me to a few months ago."

Paige looked again. "Oh, yeah. Maybe so."

When Addy stood, Paige grabbed her menu and hid her face behind it.

"What are you doing?" Carter asked her.

Paige whispered around the menu's edge, "I don't want her to see me."

"Why?" Carter reached and gently pushed the menu aside until his focus found Paige. "If Jack is really in love with this woman, don't you think you should be more friendly? You're the one who keeps saying he needs to find *normal* again."

Paige lowered the menu, laying it on the table. "You're right, Carter. I'm being such an idiot. Thank you." She stood and followed Addy to the door.

CHAPTER 30

At the restaurant exit, Addy reached for the handle to push open the door but stopped when she felt a halting touch.

"Addy, hi."

She turned to the familiar voice. "Paige." Addy took her hand off the door. "Hi. I didn't see you here." All three women stepped back, away from the doors when a family entered the restaurant, then Addy said, "I heard about your accident. Are you doing okay now?"

Paige put her hand on the back of her head. "Yeah, I'll be fine."

"I'm glad to hear that." Addy gave a finger touch to her friend's shoulder. "This is Janet. We work together."

Paige reached for a handshake. "Are you from around here? You look familiar. I think we might have met at a wine event a while back."

"Probably. My husband is quite the winemaker." Janet gave a pat to her rounded belly. "I can't wait to try his new vintage in a few months. I've heard it is perfection in a bottle." When her cell phone buzzed, she glanced at the screen, then said, "Addy, I've gotta run. I'll call you after I meet with Thabo tomorrow."

A bolt of lightning flashed at Janet's exit.

"If you have a few minutes," Paige said with a side nod toward her table, "I'd like you to come and meet Carter, my fiancé."

"Sure." Addy glanced into the dining room. "Okay."

At their approach, Carter stood, reaching for a handshake. He was a clean-shaven, brown-eyed man with a youthful face and a strong hand.

"It's nice to meet you." He pulled a chair out for Addy. "Would you like to join us?"

"Oh, no, thank you." Addy held up a hand to decline only to have Paige point out the window to the sudden downpour that was battering the windows of the tin-roof restaurant again.

"Really, you should stay and give this storm a few more minutes to let up a bit. Besides, it would give us a chance to talk."

Every glance at Paige gave Addy an image of Jack. The two just went together, like best friends should.

Addy sat—her chair pulled out a thigh-length from the table. She folded her hands in her lap. To Carter, she said, "I heard you're a horse breeder. Or was it a horse trainer?"

"Both," Carter said, straightening with interest. "We raise and train well-rounded working horses that fit the needs of all kinds of events, disciplines, and lifestyles, but my specialty is in therapy horses."

"I'm not sure I know what that is," Addy said, her interest spurred. She'd always wanted to know more about horses and riding, but she knew very little about that world.

Carter adjusted, engaged with the subject. "Halos for Hooves and Heroes," he said. "The ranch belonged to my dad, but he passed away while I was in Afghan, so it's mine now. I served twelve months and lost a good buddy to an IED that injured a few other guys in my unit. Lots of vets came home with life-changing injuries, so I decided to add an equine therapy program as my way to help the permanently disabled and those with PTSD."

"Wow." Addy scooted her chair closer. "So how does that work? I mean, how can a horse help a wounded vet?"

"Plenty of ways. Horses feed off emotions, so in order to control a horse, a rider needs to be calm and self-assured. Soldiers with PTSD can regain some emotional strength just by riding and taking care of these horses. Some vets come out to the ranch several times a week because they've bonded with a horse, and that helps break their cycle of isolation."

The same waitress that waited on Addy and Janet came to take Paige and Carter's dinner order. When she asked Addy if she wanted anything else, Addy said, "No, thank you, I'm fine."

After the server left their table, Carter picked up the conversation again.

"Horse therapy helps soldiers who have more severe physical injuries, too, helping them learn balance, modes of stability, and walking again."

Paige interjected. "Carter also offers trail riding horses for the weekend equestrian. That gives him a chance to really use the property." She gave him an admiring smile. "The ranch is a little over five hundred acres of great Hill Country land. We're trying to increase opportunities for kids to learn how to ride too.

We're working on creating some easy trails for them. The ones we have now are for average and experienced riders. We need some flat, easy trails that still offer some nice scenery for kids and inexperienced riders."

Carter reached, touching Paige's hand. "That's really her forte." A soft smile came when his eyes met hers. "Paige is really good with kids."

"I just rode for the first time a few weeks ago. It's been on my bucket list forever. Let me know when you get that kiddie trail finished. It sounds perfect for me," she joked.

"I'd be glad to teach you how to ride," Paige said. "Come out anytime." She handed her a business card.

Addy read the card with a new admiration for Paige. "How do you do all of this and still work the wildflower farm with Jack too?"

"I put in some long hours," Paige said, glancing at her fiancé. "But it's okay. I love doing both."

"After we're married in the spring," Carter explained, "I want Paige to work full-time at the ranch. I've been putting on the pressure, but it's really up to her." He caressed her hand. "My mom and dad worked the business together and I always expected that me and Paige would do the same thing, but her and Jack are like brother and sister. She'll do what she needs to do, and I'll do my best to respect her decision."

Paige gave a squeeze to Carter's hand then took a sip of her margarita, keeping a focus on Addy. When she set down her glass, she asked, "So, what happened between you and Jack?"

"He didn't tell you?" Addy automatically pulled back.

"No, he just said he was stupid and you hated him now."

"I don't hate him." Addy looked down, fingering the edge of the tablecloth, remembering the way Paige had used her words against her once before. "Jack is an amazing man."

"You're right. He is amazing," Paige said. "The way he raises Juli and runs his business, honestly, he's a pretty great guy. All of his customers trust him, and with good reason. He won't send out any product that doesn't meet the highest standards. Even though the seed business is his, he feels like his grandfather's name is still on the packets. I guess it is in a way. Sometimes I think he still feels like he is working for Grammy and Gramps."

Sincerity pushed Addy into a forward lean again. "Paige, he is such a family man. Don't you hate it that he lost his parents over the accident?"

Paige shook her head. "He didn't lose them. He closed the door on them."

When the server brought their order of hamburgers and fries, Paige ordered two iced teas. Glancing at Addy, she asked, "Are you sure you don't want anything?"

"No, I'm good, but thanks."

Paige took the last swallow of her margarita then slid the empty glass to the side before picking up the conversation where she'd left off. "His folks are always asking to see him and Juli. They're really nice people. I've known them all my life, but I've also known Jack that long too. Kaitlin," Paige glanced at Addy for a hint of name recognition, "she was Jack's wife. The three of us were best friends. We grew up together."

"So, then you've known Nick a long time too."

Paige sat up straighter. "How do you know Nick?"

"I work with him," Addy explained. "He's the

airport manager at Fray Transport. That's who I fly for now. Nick is a great guy. I mean, I know the whole story of him and the accident. Jack told me. But I think he's probably changed a lot because he doesn't seem like the same guy Jack talks about. And Nick doesn't drink anymore. We had a good time at the rodeo a few weeks ago, and it looked like everyone had a can of beer, but Nick never even looked at one."

Paige wrinkled her brows, giving a squint to her eyes. "Have you been dating Nick too?"

Fury, indignation, resentment flared. The friendship she'd started to feel with Paige was gone in a flash. "No." Addy scooted her chair back from the table and stood. Her glare landed on Paige. "I haven't been dating Nick. We work together. That's all." This conversation wasn't going to happen. "It was nice to meet you, Carter." She slid her empty chair up to the table.

"Wait," Paige said and stood. "Hang on. Addy, I didn't mean that the way it came out."

Carter stood too. "Paige is really protective of Jack. Even I've had my head bitten off a few times. Don't take it personally."

"But it is personal." Addy looked back at Paige. "For your information, Jack is the best thing that's happened to me. I didn't say he was amazing because he's a good father, which he is, or because he's a good businessman, which I don't doubt. I said it because he's absolutely the most amazing man I've ever met." A blur of tears welled, threatening to spill. Whether it was from emotion or anger, she wasn't sure. "I love Jack." She stopped—the words more intense than she imagined. She'd admitted she was in love, and there was no taking it back now. Addy firmed her stance. "I'm crazy in love with him, and I guess I'm telling you this because he trusts you more than anyone else in the world and I don't want you to think that I've been trying to change his relationship with you, or with Doug and Rebecca, or Nick, or even Kaitlin. But it's for all those reasons that I won't pursue a relationship with him. I need to walk away, now, while I still can. I can't compete with the part of his heart, broken or whole, that he's given to each one of you. There's just not much left for anyone else, and the part that is left is just not enough."

CHAPTER 31

Addy was strangely out of sorts. She was captain of a grounded plane and in love with a man she couldn't have. Life was in crash mode, and she was failing to pull out of the dive.

Her morning coffee was cold, the ceramic mug still full to the brim when she stepped out of the shower. She dumped it into the vanity sink and then rinsed, setting the cup aside while she brushed her teeth and combed her hair. Her mirrored reflection was devoid of the depth she'd once seen in herself.

She went to the bedroom, picked up her phone from the nightstand charger, and called Janet. "Hey, just curious about what time you're meeting with Thabo today."

"Eleven," Janet said. "I'm taking him a nice bottle of Napa Merlot to soften the blow."

"Be sure to let me know how it goes, okay?"

Addy was good at keeping secrets, but she wanted to talk to Nick about this unexpected development. His suspicions had been right, and she hated to withhold the information from him.

Despite the mid-October sun, the gray day offered little warmth. To pass the time while awaiting Janet's call, Addy walked across the parking lot to the bike trails that wound through the park-like setting adjoining the apartment grounds. She pulled her light sweater around her when a breeze pushed across the landscape, sweeping past her with the scent of cedar and earth.

Down a gradual embankment was a natural spring-fed pond as big as the ice-skating rink at the mall back in Dallas. Addy moved closer to the water after spotting four ducks and a goose, paddling or preening. She squatted in the shade of an expansive old red oak, quietly watching the waterfowl until a small dog, dragging his leash behind him, bounded down the embankment and leaped at the nearest duck, causing them all to fly away.

"Free!" An attractive redhead sprinted after the dog, only to slip and fall at the water's edge.

Addy darted down to her, reaching out a helping hand. "Are you okay?"

"Yeah." The woman glanced up. "Thanks." She reached out and grabbed the dog's leash before taking Addy's hand, pulling herself up. She twisted into a rear glance, inspecting the clay-like mud smeared on the backside of her blue jeans. "I've never brought him here before. I had no idea he was a duck chaser." One shoe stuck awkwardly out of the mud, leaving her with a bare foot. "Do you mind?" She held out the leash to Addy, who reluctantly took it. "I just need to get my shoe."

Addy glanced down at the dog, white with black-

and-brown markings, who stood on point, his big round brown eyes studying the water's surface. "He's cute," she said.

The woman gave a snicker as she bent down and swished her muck-covered canvas slip-on in the pond, washing away the excess mud but leaving her with a sopping wet, dirt-stained shoe. "He's a mess, and I don't just mean those muddy feet." She rose, holding the slip-on while taking the leash from Addy, and then she carefully inched up the embankment to the grass and sat down.

Addy followed, sitting down on the ground beside her. "Is your ankle all right?"

"I think so. It just twisted a bit when I slipped." She offered her outstretched hand to Addy for a shake. "I'm Kelsey-Rose."

"Addy Piper." The two shook hands.

"That was really nice of you to come to my rescue." The Jack Russell terrier climbed onto the woman's lap and stood with his two front paws chest high on her blue sweatshirt, tail wagging, intent on licking her face. "Fine. Okay. You're forgiven," she said to the dog as she picked him up and then set him down on the grass beside her, wiping at the muddy paw prints left on her sweatshirt.

Kelsey-Rose reached for her sneaker, but the terrier grabbed it and ran, dragging his leash behind him, the shoe clenched in his jaws. "Free!" she yelled. "Bring that back!" She stood, calling him again, but the dog kept running. With his head held high so that the tip of the shoe barely grazed the ground, he ran until he came to a clump of bamboo growing at the water's edge. He stopped and turned back for a look. "Free, here, boy!" Impaired by the loss of one shoe, she attempted to hobble nonchalantly toward him, coaxing him the whole way. "Come on, Free."

Inexperienced in the art of chasing down a shoe-stealing dog, Addy walked with Kelsey-Rose as she approached the terrier.

"Don't scare him," the woman whispered to Addy.

The tricolor dog stood a few feet beyond, next to the shoe he'd tauntingly dropped, with his ears perked and his tail wagging. His big, round, brown eyes stared unblinking at his master.

Kelsey-Rose got within a step of his loose leash before gently reaching down for it, but before she could grab it, the dog snatched up her shoe in this game he was winning and bounded into the pond with it.

"Okay, now you're in trouble!" Kelsey-Rose stood and sloshed into the water after him, snatching up the dog. Holding him in one arm, she stooped, feeling all around in the dark water. Step by step, she moved and felt.

"Any luck?" Addy finally called to her.

"No." With a grip on the terrier, Kelsey-Rose swished back through the pond water to the embankment, her jeans wet almost to her knees. She glanced at her antique wristwatch. "And I promised Paige I'd be there ten minutes ago to help evaluate the new therapy horses."

"Are you talking about Halos for Hooves and Heroes?"

"Yes," she said, making her way up onto the grass with one foot still bare. "Do you ride there?"

Addy shook her head. "No, but Paige introduced me to Carter, her fiancé, last night. They told me all about the place." She didn't want to mention how the evening ended, especially since she was feeling guilty for reacting badly to Paige's question about Nick.

"You're a friend of Paige's?"

Addy's throat tightened. She looked down before answering. "I don't really know her very well. I met her through Jack—"

"Wait," Kelsey-Rose cut her short. "You know Jack Brown?" Then, friendly, she laughed. "What a weird coincidence. I met Paige through Jack too. We've been friends ever since."

"You know Jack?"

"Yeah, we've been in the same grief counseling group for years." She eyed Addy. "You know he lost his wife in a car accident, right?"

"Yes," Addy said. "Jack told me." Then, "So, you lost someone too?"

Kelsey-Rose nodded. "My fiancé." Her sorrow didn't spill over into the conversation like Jack's grief had.

"I'm sorry," Addy said.

When they were back on the bike path, both headed toward the apartment building, Addy asked, "Do you live here at Green Ridge Place apartments too?"

Kelsey-Rose glanced up at the buildings ahead. "No, I had to pull in when my car conked out. I'm pretty sure it's the fuel pump." She looked back at the pond. "I was just taking Free for a quick pee break while we waited for the tow truck, but you saw how that turned out."

Just a few feet from the parking lot pavement, an Action Towing truck pulled into the lot.

"Oh, there they are!" Kelsey-Rose hurried, half shoeless, across the lot.

Addy arrived car side to hear the woman explain to

the tow truck driver that the engine would die each time she slowed or stopped.

"Yeah," the driver said, "sounds like a bad fuel pump, or maybe a dirty injector." He glanced at Addy, then back to Kelsey-Rose, who held the dog in her arms. "Do you care which repair shop I tow it to?"

Kelsey-Rose sighed. "No, I guess not. My boyfriend is a mechanic, but he lives in Topaz, and that doesn't do me much good here, does it?"

The driver shook his head. "You want me to tow it to Topaz?"

"No," Kelsey-Rose told him. "That's thirty miles."

"Downey's Shop is four miles from here."

"Good, just take it to Downey's."

The driver filled out the paperwork and then handed it to Kelsey-Rose for a signature. She grabbed her purse off the floorboard and then dropped the car key into his hand.

With her sea blue Santa Fe loaded aboard the tow trailer, she reached into the pouch pocket of her sweat-shirt and pulled out her cell phone. "Thanks for staying with me," she told Addy. "I should call Paige and ask her to come pick me up."

Addy checked her own cell phone for the time. "It's only nine, and technically it's my day off. I'm just waiting for a call after eleven to see how the rest of the day plays out." She had nothing to do until Janet met with Thabo, promising to call her afterward, which meant her thoughts had time to drift to Jack and all the mistakes she'd made. She hated the ugly regret that ruled the dark recesses of her mind. Nick was her usual diversion, but she dared not talk to him right now, or she would likely spill the beans on Janet's resignation. "I can give you a lift."

Kelsey-Rose stopped. "Really? You wouldn't mind?" She glanced down at herself again. "I'm pretty dirty."

"I'll just grab a towel for the seat. I need to go up for my wallet anyway. Do you live far from here?"

"Oh, no." Kelsey-Rose reached out, touching Addy's shoulder. "I don't live *here*. I live in Topaz, thirty miles north. That's why I was going to call Paige to come and get me."

"Sorry. I assumed that since you and Jack attended the same meetings..." Addy let the thought drift.

"Jack refused to go to local counseling. He wanted to be in a place where no one knew him, so he used to drive to Topaz once a month." She gave a compassionate smile. "And I drive here to help evaluate and train therapy horses." When Addy nodded, she said, "Maybe you could just take me out to Halos? That's a couple of miles."

"Sure. Yeah, of course."

Not long after the turnoff onto Hidden Hills Road, the white-arched entrance came into view. Addy drove her Miata through the gates, following the directions given to her by Kelsey-Rose.

She parked beside a white pipe fence after Kelsey-Rose spotted Paige in the breezeway with two saddled horses. When they got out of the car, Paige started toward the Miata.

"Hey," Paige called to them as she approached. Then closer, she pointed to the dirty jeans Kelsey-Rose wore. "What happened to you?" Her glance dropped to the one bare foot. "Where's your other shoe?" Then with a hard, creased brow, she stopped at the fence, her eyes darting from Kelsey-Rose to Addy and back again. "I didn't know you two knew each other."

"We don't," Addy and Kelsey-Rose said in unison. Addy finished with, "We just met."

"My car conked out." Kelsey-Rose held up the terrier like he was a prize. "And then this naughty rascal stole my sneaker. I had to chase him into a pond for it, but I couldn't find the shoe in all the mud and muck." With a side nod to Addy, she said, "She came to my rescue."

Paige pointed back behind her to the tack room and wash racks. "Jenny's working today. I'll bet she'd love to give Free a bath for you."

"Great." Kelsey-Rose ducked through the fencing, holding the dog. "I need my riding boots anyway."

As Kelsey-Rose limped across the empty arena, Paige said to Addy, "Sorry about last night. I didn't mean to sound like an overprotective sister."

"I know," Addy told her. "I guess I'm a little sensitive too."

"I stopped by to see Jack this morning before coming out here." Paige steadied her focus on Addy. "I was going to tell him about running into you last night, but honestly, he was so quiet I just didn't want to bring up your name."

"What made you think he was quiet because of me?"

"Because I know Jack." Paige leaned against the white pipe fencing. "It's been a long time since I've seen him like this. I think his heart might be broken again." She reached through the fence for Addy's hand and gave it a squeeze. "I don't want to see him like that ever again, so if you have regrets about calling off the relationship with him, don't. I think he's in love with you."

Maybe it could have been different if the time and place and past hadn't been what it was, but it was clear that Jack loved his wife as much in her afterlife as he loved her before her death.

His heart had no room for Addy, even though she knew Jack was the one and only person she was ever meant to love.

Why was she the only person who seemed to understand the problem?

CHAPTER 32

Addy ironed her blouse twice, waiting for Janet's call to come in. When the phone finally rang, she only saw the flash of a name and answered. "Janet, hi, how did it go?"

"The man is a class act," Janet said. "He wished me the best and had Noah give me my full fourth-quarter bonus while I was there." She took a cleansing breath, then said, "I kind of hate to leave. But anyway, he's going to call you."

She had barely gotten the words out before another call beeped in on Addy's phone. "That's probably him now. I'll call you later, Janet." She clicked over. "Hello?"

"Hi, Addy, it's Thabo. Any chance you're free for a quick meeting today?"

"Yes, of course," she said.

Waiting in the study for Thabo, Addy stood at the window, her gaze searching the land for the herds of deer that had always been there milling around the deer feeder. Today, however, only a breeze visited. There, in the quiet privacy of the peaceful room, an inner voice, devoid of reason or logic, questioned whether she would stay permanently if she were asked to make a choice today.

"Addy," Thabo said in a brisk walk toward her. He reached out for a handshake. "Thank you for coming on your day off." He sat in the leather chair that seemed to be his favorite. "Have you spoken with Janet?"

She hadn't thought to ask Janet whether she'd told Thabo about their conversation, but it wasn't in her nature to lie. "Yes, briefly."

He nodded. "Then you know I need a long-term pilot, and I seem to be running out of those faster than deer corn." Thabo shook his head, not angry, but certainly frustrated. "So, I suppose my first question should be, is there any chance you'll stay long-term?"

"I don't know." The quick answer slipped through her lips.

"There would be a substantial increase in pay, of course, but I have to be honest, Addy. I'd need you to commit to a five-year contract. I'll understand if you can't, but I'll have to fill the captain's position with a pilot who can commit to that. Of course, regardless of your decision, your original contract as first officer will remain in place until June, as agreed."

A permanent position as captain or a short-term seat as first officer. "Can I think it over?" she asked.

"Yes. I need you to be sure about the decision." Thabo stood. "But we'll still need a copilot quickly, and it would be easier if I knew which position I was trying to fill."

He was right, of course. "I have a qualified and

dependable F/O in mind, and she might be willing to accept a permanent position in either capacity. If she agrees, and if she meets with your approval, you'd actually get a few months with her before the final decision needs to be made."

Thabo lifted his chin, interested. "Is this the same pilot you mentioned earlier?"

"Yes, I just haven't had a chance to make the call yet."

"Can you do that today?"

"Yes." Addy nodded.

Addy got into her sports car, but instead of leaving the estate grounds, she turned the Miata toward the hangar office. She pulled in and stopped beside Nick's truck.

"Hey, Nick," Addy said. The radio was playing, and he was head down at the far desk, scanning a dozen scattered papers.

"Addy!" He stood. "I didn't even hear you drive up. What are you doing here today?"

"I just came from a meeting with Thabo. Janet resigned to raise babies in California."

"You're joking!" When Addy shook her head, Nick's hand went to his brow. "We're running out of pilots."

"Yeah. Did things fall apart after I arrived, or has it always been this way?"

Nick smiled. "Hey, all this stuff doesn't have anything to do with you. It's just the way the cards fell." His hands went to his hips, resting on his tooled leather belt. "You're not leaving, too, are you?"

If she'd had the answer to that question, she would have gladly shared it with Nick, but the truth was, the answer was as elusive to her as it was to him.

~

ALONE IN HER APARTMENT, ADDY STOOD AT THE living room window overlooking the treed hills and dialed her friend Lindsey.

"Hey, Lins! How's California treating you?"

"Addy, it's so good to hear from you! Are you flying for that millionaire guy?"

"Billionaire," Addy corrected with a laugh. "And yes."

"You're lucky. I still haven't landed a job, and Mom's couch isn't as comfortable as I thought it would be."

"Actually, that's why I'm calling."

"You want to sleep on Mom's couch?"

"Not hardly." They both laughed. "But I have an apartment with an okay couch, and you're welcome to stay with me as long as you'd like."

"Hey, thanks. I really appreciate it, but if I can't get a job in Los Angeles, it's not likely that I can get a job in small-town America."

"It might be more possible than you think."

Silence. Then, "Okay, what do you know that I don't know?"

"I want you to come back to Texas and fly with me as F/O for Fray Transport."

"I thought you were first officer?"

"I was, but I got promoted to captain. Temporarily, at least."

"No way!" Lindsey nearly screamed the words.

Addy had been working toward a pilot-in-command position for over three years, and although Fray Transport wasn't the *majors*, she felt good about finally adding an extra bar to her epaulets. And if she left this job—if she left Jack—the position would look good on a résumé.

"Incredible, right?"

"I'm not surprised, Addy. You're an amazing pilot. Congrats on the promotion."

"Thanks, Lins. So are you interested? If you are, I'll ask Thabo to call you tonight, and you two can make the arrangements."

"Are you kidding me? I'm already packing! How long until Janet comes back?"

"She's not coming back, Lins."

"What? Why? You two would be an amazing team."

"She and Tom are moving to California to be nearer to his family and to live in the wine country that he loves so much."

"So, are you saying this would be a permanent position?"

"Yes, if you want it to be." Addy hesitated. "But is anything ever really *permanent*? I mean, I haven't given up on returning to the airlines. My contract with Fray Enterprises expires in June. By then, I may decide to return to Dallas, and you might be promoted to captain here."

"Yeah, right." Lindsey laughed.

"Actually, I'm serious. I told Thabo that you're qualified for either position."

Lindsey hesitated, taking a silent moment before saying, "Yeah, but Addy, you know I've never actually held a captain's position."

"I know. But between now and June, you'll get all the experience you need. If I return to the airlines when the furlough ends, you'll have a good shot at some captain's bars if you want them. This is a great opportunity, Lins. It seems to be a solid, respectable company, and Thabo Fray is a great boss."

After the call ended, Addy took a deep breath, exhaling the doubt and inhaling a breath of possibilities.

CHAPTER 33

Nick drove the Fray Enterprises King Ranch truck toward the San Antonio International Airport with Addy as his copilot.

The highway split sections of the limestone escarpment, so indicative of the Edwards Plateau—its land ranging from gently rolling hills to rugged bluffs, many endowed with winding rivers and streams etched deep into the rocky upland, often only visible for a moment at nature's whim. Its gentle jade-green waters reflected the surrounding landscape, often pooling in quiet picture-perfect swimming holes—their trails rarely seen and probably barely known to anyone but the elusive landowners.

Red-shouldered hawks, turkey vultures, and the massive black vultures with white-tipped wings soared in autumn's pastel-blue sky while the Hill Country wildlife—white-tailed deer and spotted Axis, opossum, armadillos, rabbits, red fox, and raccoons made well-camouflaged homes in the rocky terrain. Along the highway, headed southeast, exotic game ranches in multiacre parcels cleared of cedar and sparse with oak were protected by gated entrances with predator-proof high fencing where Arabian oryx, blackbuck, and gemsbok roamed.

"So, tell me about this friend of yours," Nick asked Addy as they drove.

"Well, first," Addy said in all sincerity, "she's beautiful." When Nick shot her a glance, she said, "Truly drop-dead gorgeous, but Lindsey is really smart too. Sometimes people don't see it because they're too busy fawning over her."

Nick adjusted in his seat. "No kidding?" He looked at Addy again, searching her honesty.

"Not kidding," she said with a knowing smile. "But look, Nick, Lins hates it when guys fall all over themselves when they meet her, so just be yourself, okay? She doesn't like being treated like a Barbie doll."

He grinned at Addy. "Got it." Then a moment later, he said, "Has she got a boyfriend?"

"See? That, right there, is what I mean!" Addy glared at him. "Stop thinking about dating her. You're coworkers. She's a professional pilot. A really good and competent one. She's well respected in the industry. That should earn her high marks all by itself."

"Okay, yeah, you're right. Sorry."

The slower Hill Country pace disappeared shortly after leaving the city limits of Boerne. San Antonio traffic was similar to rush-hour traffic in Dallas, with lots of stop-and-go, bumper-to-bumper travel with vehicles merging from every lane.

When Dallas-Fort Worth International had been home base for Addy, she had regularly flown routes to

Houston Hobby or George Bush International, but she was unfamiliar with San Antonio, except for what she'd read about it. The large metropolitan airport was located about eight miles north of the downtown area and had three major runways servicing commercial air carriers, air cargo, business, and general aviation. It also had an area for military operations, but from her own research, she also knew that fifteen miles north-west, high-intensity glider activity could be found— another item on her bucket list.

As Nick took the turn to the lower level of Terminal B, Addy studied the stone veneer exterior and eight exit doors in the arrivals area.

While waiting in the passenger pick up zone with the truck idling, Addy's phone rang. She looked at the caller ID and told Nick, "It's her." She answered, "Hey, Lins! We're outside waiting. Nick's driving a white pickup truck with Fray Enterprises printed on the doors. Just come out the exit marked Gate B3, and we'll be about two vehicles down on your left."

Ten minutes later, Addy pointed to the automatic doors. "There she is!" Addy jumped out of the truck and hurried to help her friend with the luggage.

Lindsey Wright was supermodel quality. Her mermaid-long, matte-black hair hung freely down her back in stark contrast to her peach-colored tank and near-matching Capri jeans. Her stride in high-heeled shoes brought Nick outside the truck, engine still idling, to grab a suitcase and heave it into the back.

"Hi," he said, hand out. "I'm Nick, airport manager for Fray Transport."

"Lindsey," she said with a smile for him. "Lins, actually."

"Hi, Lins." Nick returned the smile, still holding her hand.

"Hey," Addy said. "Some help over here, please?" She had another suitcase on its way up over the side of the truck bed when Nick grabbed it, hefted it over, and then lowered it inside.

"Sorry," he whispered. "I should have been paying attention."

Addy rolled her eyes in a private look at him, then turned to her friend with a hug. "I am so glad you're here, Lins."

While Nick slowly maneuvered the airport exit lanes, Lindsey leaned forward from the back seat of the King Ranch and said, "Mr. Fray asked me to come by and meet him as soon as I arrived. Did he talk to you guys about that?"

Nick glanced in his rearview mirror to see her, staying his gaze a little too long. "That's where we're headed unless you want to go change clothes first or something?"

"Change clothes?" Lindsey grabbed Addy's seat-back. "Should I change before meeting him? He told me casual was okay."

"Lins, you're fine. You look great," Addy said. "Thabo told me it was casual too. 'Brief and casual' is exactly what he said."

"I didn't mean you *needed* to change clothes," Nick fumbled with his words, "or *should* change. Addy's right, you *do* look great. *Really* great."

Addy glanced back, grinning at Lindsey, and then turned to Nick with a laugh. "Thanks for that clarification."

Nick gave a flushed-face nod, then glanced in his

rearview again. "I should have you there in about forty minutes."

"YES, A DOZEN ROSES," JACK SAID OVER THE PHONE to the florist. "No, not red." Thinking better of it, he asked her, "Do you think an apology should be in red?"

Red roses were reserved for an admission of love, weren't they? He just wanted to say he was sorry. Ask for another chance. He wanted to rekindle the fire, not set it ablaze. But he knew flowers—wildflowers anyway—and colors had meanings.

"What other colors do you have?" he asked.

The florist's grandmotherly voice patiently recited the variety of colors: red, peach, white, yellow, lavender, coral, burgundy, deep pink, pale pink, orange, green, and multicolored.

"One of each," Jack said. He took out the paper with Addy's apartment address written on it and placed the delivery order.

Seeking the solace of isolation, Jack walked to the flower fields. Migrating season was in full swing and his crops were drawing monarchs, swallowtails, the yellow sulphur, snouts, and his childhood favorite, the common buckeye, a yellowish-brown butterfly with intricately colored eyespots.

Jack didn't just love this place; he loved the creatures who lived on it and the memories within it. His grandparents had been kids when their parents had homesteaded it, making him a fourth-generation owner. Land was the only thing he completely trusted. It was the one thing that had never let him down, and it was always there for him when he needed grounding. He reached for a handful of soil, working the grains through his fingers, letting it fall like seeds onto the land beneath his feet, farmable after decades of tilling and conditioning. His grandfather had willed the property to Jack and only him, leaving the stocks, bonds, and money to Nick. The inheritance had changed them, each in their own way.

He leaned against the corner fence post where Addy had first kissed him. New memories were converging with the old. She had touched his soul and he'd felt her spirit. The woman had emblazoned herself on his heart—here on this land that meant so much. Would he ever be able to stand here again without the memory of her?

His muscles tensed, sending an ache to his heart. He wanted her to stay. He wanted *this* again—he wanted this a thousand times! If she decided to merely honor her contract, he'd have until June. Maybe by then, she would decide to stay permanently.

But if in the end, she couldn't love the land, this place, *them* enough, he would have to find a way to let her go. Until then, he wanted a chance to prove that he was the man she thought he was.

ADDY AND NICK WAITED IN THE FOYER OF THE FRAY residence for Lindsey's prearranged meeting with Thabo. Technically, he had hired her over the phone, so today was simply protocol. He would have her sign a short-term contract and tend to a few other formalities, and then they'd be free for days. If the meeting went well, their upcoming flight to Seattle, still tentative until Thabo approved, wasn't scheduled until Thursday.

Nick stood at an oversized mirror that hung near the entrance doors and gently dabbed his split lip. Without turning around, he said to Addy, "Still looks bad, doesn't it?"

"It looks much better than it did. Besides, it gives you kind of a macho look."

He turned. "It does?"

"Sure. Like an action movie hero."

"Yeah, one that got beat up."

When the study door opened, Lindsey and Thabo came out together.

Thabo walked straight to where Addy stood. "I can't tell you how relieved I am to have Lindsey onboard with us." He flashed a file folder. "Her credentials and background checks are impeccable." Then to Nick, he said, "Give Lindsey a day or two to breathe and get settled in, and then I'm counting on you and Addy to orient her to the transport property and the aircraft. I want her comfortable and up to speed on things before Thursday."

Nick nodded. "Good as done."

"So, Thursday's flight to Seattle is confirmed?" Addy asked him.

"Yes, Portland too. I'll have Noah send you the itinerary."

The three drove back to the Fray Transport office and parked alongside the Miata.

Nick reached for the handle of Lindsey's largest suitcase, which had slid to the tailgate on their drive. He pulled it upright, standing the hard-sided case on its swivel wheels in the bed of the truck before giving a glance to Addy's snowflake-white sports car.

"Uh-oh," he said. "Hey, Addy, remember that ironing board problem you had?"

She clamped her hand over her mouth.

"Yeah, so..." he said. "Want me to just follow you home again? This luggage is never going to fit." He looked at Lindsey. "You are staying at Addy's place for a while, aren't you?"

"Yes, I am," Lindsey said with a glance at Addy. "If she can tolerate me for a few weeks until I can find a place of my own."

"There's no rush," Addy told her. It would be nice to have one of her friends back, if for no other reason than to remind her why she loved the life she'd left.

After parking near the outside stairs leading up to Addy's unit, each of the three carried a piece of luggage but they stopped on the landing to an exterior hallway when they saw a delivery boy tagging her door with a notice—a vase of colorful roses at his feet.

"Hi," Addy said as she approached him. "Can I help you?"

"Depends. Is this your apartment? Are you—" he glanced at the delivery order, "Addy Piper?"

"Yes. To both questions."

He bent to pick up the vase and then handed it to her. "I was about to take these to the leasing office and leave them there for you since you weren't home."

"For me? Are you sure? Who are they from?"

The boy pointed to an envelope with her name on it. "There's a card." Then he took the stairs down.

Addy smelled the roses, then handed the vase to Lindsey. "Hold onto these for me while I unlock my door."

"Roses, huh? They're beautiful, Addy." Lindsey put her nose to the flowers and inhaled the fragrance. "Did you forget to tell me something? Like you've found an amazing man who sends you flowers?"

Addy stepped inside and then held the door open for Lindsey and Nick. She took the vase of many-colored roses from her friend and set them on the dinette table, pulling the card from its envelope as they wheeled the luggage into the apartment and then stopped and waited, watching her. Silently, she read:

Addy —

> *Life has too many unexpected goodbyes.*
> *Unexpected hellos are better.*
> *Can we start over?*
> *Jack*

"Well?" Lindsey asked, impatient. "Who sent them?"

Addy glanced at Nick, then back to her friend. "The greatest guy I've ever met, but he's in love with another woman."

Nick shut his eyes and lowered his head, silent.

Lindsey glanced from Nick to Addy. "Is he married or something? What's the story?" She waited. "I mean, come on, the guy sent these beautiful roses to *you!*"

"No, he isn't married," Addy told her. "And I'd never date a married guy, Lins, you know that." She set the florist card on the table. "But I can't compete with the woman he's in love with. Let's just drop it, okay?"

Nick looked up with the spark of an idea, offering a change of subject. "Hey, it's four o'clock, and it's Saturday. I can almost smell Dad's brisket from here. Why don't I call and let them know I'm bringing you two home with me for supper tonight?"

The last time Addy had gone with Nick, it'd felt good to be in Jack's childhood home. To be included in his family, even when his parents didn't know she'd

fallen in love with their lost son. Doug and Rebecca
Brown had been warm and welcoming, but most of all,
she just loved being there—imagining Jack as a boy in
their home. Seeing photos of him at every age on their
walls. She was grateful they'd never talked about him
while she was there, or she might have confessed to
loving him.

"Well, I'm starved," Lindsey told Nick, then she
leaned into Addy and whispered, "and I'd kind of like
to get to know Nick better." She raised a brow at Addy,
then aloud she said, "Want to go?"

The glances between the two made Addy laugh.
"Sure. It'd be hard to turn down Doug's brisket any
day of the week."

"Good," Nick said. "I'll call Dad." He pulled out his
cell phone and turned, walking into Addy's small hall-
way-like kitchen. "Hi, Dad. I was wondering..."

Lindsey grabbed hold of Addy's arm, pulling her
out of Nick's view. She whispered, "The man is
gorgeous! Are you sure you're not interested? If he's
hands-off, just say so."

"No," Addy said. "Nick's a great guy. You should
definitely give him a chance."

Nick walked back into the living room, slipping his
phone into his jeans pocket. "Folks are thrilled. Mom's
out shucking extra corn on the cob for us."

"I'm going to freshen up. Just give me a few
minutes." Lindsey dashed off to Addy's bathroom with
her carry-on bag.

Nick walked to the dinette and picked up the florist
card. He fingered it without reading. "You should call
him." He turned to her. "Ask him to come with you
tonight. Mom and Dad would bust with joy to see him.
Maybe he could bring Juli too."

Tender, she said, "He won't come, Nick." She lowered her eyes. "And I'm not sure I can put myself in that place again."

He nodded, then said, "I get it, Addy, but how will you ever know if you don't try?"

CHAPTER 34

When Jack's cell phone jangled in his pocket, he pulled it out, checked the number, and when he recognized it as Addy's, he answered.

"Addy—hello."

Quietly, she said, "Hello. Thank you for the roses. They're really beautiful."

Although he was alone in his home, he spoke in a hushed tone too. "Every time I see a flower, I think of you, and you know how many flowers I have."

Out on her balcony, Addy stood head down with her back to the glass door. "I miss you." She'd failed miserably at pretending she didn't still love him. "Everything seems wrong without you, Jack. But I'm so afraid to open myself up to you again."

"I know." He hesitated. "*I know*. I've been wrong about so many things. Addy, I need to see you."

Nick's words stumbled through her thoughts. "Tonight?" Was it fair? She didn't know.

"Yes," he said. "Dinner?"

"Yes, but I already have plans. You're welcome to meet me there, though."

"Name the time and place. I'll be there. I promise." Jack paced, waiting for her reply.

"My friend Lindsey arrived today. We've been invited to your parent's house with Nick for your dad's weekend brisket." Addy held her breath, listening for him to disconnect the call, but all she heard was silence. "Jack, I want you to come. I want Juli to come too."

"Addy, I can't do that." His whisper was torn. Head down, he paced, anger battling love.

"Jack, the thing is, I love you so much that sometimes I can't even breathe—but there's too many bruised and broken pieces inside of us to stay together. Pieces that need to be mended or neither of us will be whole ever again. Please don't ask me to live the rest of my life broken."

The quiet between them felt as strong as their passion. Neither spoke, just listening to the other breathe. For the moment, the world stopped.

Then quiet but clearly, Jack said, "I don't need anyone but you and Juli."

Addy hesitated. "But I need you to have more than me and Juli."

With the phone to his ear in his bedroom, he weighed her words, then he pulled open the drawer to his nightstand and fingered Kaitlin's letter. *Find another who loves you as much as I do.*

Barely audible, tears threatening his strength, Jack said, "What if I can't do it?"

It was hard to distinguish whose voice he heard—was it Addy, or was it Kaitlin?

"Oh, but Jack, what if you can?"

Addy swept her hand through her blonde pixie, fisting her long side-swept bangs. "I don't know, Nick," she said, the phone still gripped tight in her other hand. "I tried. I asked."

Fixated on the glistening in her eyes, Nick pulled her to him. He held her, tears wetting his shirt. "Hey, it'll be okay." He rubbed her back.

Lindsey came from the bathroom, her makeup freshened, and her long, silky black hair brushed. "Hey," she said, staring at the two of them. "I wasn't gone that long. What did I miss?"

Addy pulled away from Nick but stopped to kiss his cheek. "Thanks," she whispered to him. Then to Lindsey, she said, "It was just a *moment*." She tried to laugh to lessen the tension but couldn't pull it off. "Just give me a minute to clean myself up, and then we can go."

Though Lindsey had a natural glamour, Addy accepted her own everyday-girl look with no apologies. She wore light makeup, minimal jewelry, and her ombré-colored rough-cut pixie, light blonde with dark brown undertones, barely required a brush. She glanced at herself in the mirror, realizing her blouse was wrinkled after the long San Antonio drive. She called out, "Hang on, guys. I want to change shirts."

Addy put on a V-neck feather-patterned white, brown, and blue chiffon with cap sleeves, keeping on her dark rinse jeans and flat-white sneakers. She washed her face, ran a comb through her hair, and then dabbed concealer on her nose freckles before grabbing her mini travel wallet and cell phone. She pushed them into her pants pocket, rejoining Nick and Lindsey.

"New blouse?" Lindsey asked Addy, fingering its light material. "I love it."

Nick scanned Addy's attire but then shifted his gaze to the floor. "You look amazing."

"Good," Addy said, shunning more talk. "Let's get out of here."

The yellow farmhouse-style home was set a half mile back off River Creek Road. Its wraparound porch and antique-white trim created a stunning backdrop for the wildflower yard, bursting with sunflowers.

Nick pulled onto the gravel drive, advancing slowly, urging flight to a flock of Inca doves calmly pecking the ground for seeds. In the west field, behind a fence, were six horses, wild in nature, thundering across the cleared hills, but the herd of Axis is what drew the newcomer's attention.

"Look at all the deer!" Lindsey pointed to the rust-colored deer with white spots grazing alongside the roadway. As the truck slowly approached, she opened her window for a better look at the herd. The herd bolted when they drove too close, jumping the fence in graceful leaps.

"They're everywhere," Addy told her. "I still can't believe there's so many."

"Dad owns a hundred acres now, but he used to have over a thousand. We used to be able to ride all the way to the river, following a herd of one kind or another."

Nick pulled around back to the home's backyard entrance. The smoky scent of beef brisket wafted through the truck's open window. When Nick shut off the engine, his parents came outside to greet them.

Doug pulled Addy's door open, offered a helping

hand, and then held Lindsey's open door, reaching for her hand next.

"By golly," Doug said, "you two are the prettiest girls we've had here for a while." Then he glanced at his wife, "Except for Rebecca, of course."

"Anyone for a glass of sweet tea?" Rebecca gave a pleased smile at seeing hands raised.

The dark soot-black half-barrel smoker stood ten feet off the back porch on cut limestone laid in a circular pattern, and then a few feet from the smoker was an aboveground steel fire pit, its natural rust patina finished with Texas star cutout designs. Adirondack wood chairs, painted in different colors, encircled the fire pit.

With the late afternoon sun giving its last burst of daylight, they all gathered at the patio table beneath the porch roof.

"So, Lindsey," Doug said, "you work with Addy on the airplane, do you?"

"I do, but we don't usually fly together on the same flights. Until now, we've both been first officers, so we've always had to work different flights."

"Dad, Addy just got promoted to captain," Nick explained, "so Lins hired on as first officer, taking Addy's old position. These two will be flying the Gulfstream together."

"Flying? You're pilots?" Doug pulled back in his chair, brows raised. He looked at Addy. "I thought you were the girl who served drinks and peanuts."

Addy forced a smile. "Common mistake. It's okay."

Doug sat forward in his chair, calling loudly to his wife, "Rebecca?" When she came out the back door with a tray of sweet tea, he said, "Did you know these girls are pilots?"

Rebecca set the tray on the patio table. "I had no idea," she said, distributing the glasses. Then she touched Addy's shoulder. "Hon, I'm so sorry. I think I called you a stewardess before, didn't I?"

"Flight attendant," Addy corrected. "But it's okay. It happens all the time."

When the attention and conversation turned to Lindsey, Addy took her glass of iced tea and slipped away, wandering out to the chairs around the fire pit. Swallowtails, attracted to a tree-like shrub with violet lance-shaped flowers, drew her to it. She couldn't get her mind off Jack. How could she have thought inviting him was a good idea? She knew how he felt about his family. What right did she have to put pressure on him to fix a relationship that wasn't hers? It was unfair, and she knew it.

JACK FOUND HIS DAUGHTER IN THE BACKYARD, playing with her dolls in the playhouse. He knelt in the drying autumn grass at the pink-trimmed window.

"Hi, Daddy," Juli said. "Want some tea?" She held up a toy teapot. "It's really just water. I'm just pretending."

Jack's memories were fighting with his heart. He rubbed his forehead, then ran his hand back through his brown hair.

"Listen, my girl. I've been thinking."

"About what, Daddy?" Juli cocked her head, her blonde hair falling over one shoulder.

"About you. And about me. And about—"

"Miss Addy?" she asked.

Jack smiled at her. She was intuitive, like her mother. "Yes. How did you know?"

Juli shrugged but then said, "The painted bunting told me."

"The bird?"

"Uh-huh." She glanced up, but then she looked back down at the teacups. "Remember when I wanted to talk to it?"

Jack nodded; his brows scrunched into well-worn creases. "Yes."

"Well, I got to, but it didn't answer me until after I went to sleep and had a dream." She glanced at him again. "That counts, doesn't it?"

"Sure. Yeah." He nodded. "At least, I think so."

"Me too," she agreed. Then, "Daddy, do you like Miss Addy?"

"Yeah." He answered, cautious about her feelings. "Do you?"

"Yes." Juli pretended to pour tea. "I like it when she's here."

Addy hadn't just affected him, she had affected his daughter, too. Juli was only six years old, but Jack needed to tell her. "I miss your mom. I am always going to miss her." A single deep breath paused him, drawing Juli closer to the window of the little playhouse. She studied him for a moment, but then she reached through the window opening and softly touched his face, giving him strength. He looked down at the ground, not wanting her to see the glisten he felt in his eyes. "My heart was broken for a long, long time—"

"But then Miss Addy came."

Jack looked up at her. "Yes. Then Miss Addy came."

"I know, Daddy." Juli brushed the length of his face with her small hand.

He nodded at her, knowing that she somehow understood. He'd tried to hide it from her, but she had felt his emptiness. "I need to go and get her, Juli. Will you come with me?"

It'd been a long time since Jack had driven the road home. When the yellow farmhouse with the big wraparound porch came into view, he pulled off onto the shoulder of the road and stopped. His thoughts were on the remembered faces of the people and the life inside. Holiday dinners. Birthdays. Summers of friends and family gathering at the fire pit, pecan wood scenting the air. Everything had changed except the look of the place. It was still home.

"Whose house is that?" Juli asked. "I like yellow houses." She stretched for a better view and then pointed. "And look, Daddy. They have flowers, like us."

Jack glanced in the rearview mirror at her. "That's the house I grew up in."

Her eyes widened. "It is? Do my grandma and grandpa live there?"

"Yes."

"Can we go see them, Daddy? Please, please, *please*?"

Jack took a deep breath and then pulled out onto the road again, driving the last quarter mile before making the final decision to turn into the driveway leading to the front of the house. He and Juli got out of the truck and then walked the meandering path through the wildflowers. They climbed the stone steps together, and then, just as he had always done, he opened the front door and stepped inside.

Sounds came from the kitchen—his mother, his

father, Nick's laugh, then Addy. His boot steps echoed on the oak hardwood floor, silencing the voices.

Into the kitchen, Jack walked with Juli, curious eyes focused on the doorway, waiting for the unexpected visitor.

At the sight of him, Rebecca dropped a tray of silverware and napkins. "Jack..." was all she said.

"Hi, Mom," he said softly, then glancing at Doug, he nodded. "Dad."

Rebecca flew to him, grabbing Jack in a hug. She was crying.

Nick stood back against the long kitchen counter, his eyes on his father, who had stepped in to hug the son Nick had almost lost for him.

Then Jack's searching gaze found Addy. Silently, he crossed the room to her, took her in his arms, and kissed her.

"Hey!" Juli said, pointing at Nick. "I know who you are! You're the man that was at Miss Addy's airplane."

Nick grinned and knelt where he was—his focus on the blonde girl. Delicate in his tone, he said, "I'm your uncle, Juli. It's nice to see you again."

"*You're* my uncle Nick?"

When he nodded, Juli ran to him with a hug.

In the corner of the kitchen, with her arms around him, Addy whispered to Jack, "Thank you for coming."

OUTSIDE, IN THE DWINDLING LIGHT OF DAY, JACK slowly opened up, talking about his business, Juli and her school, and Addy to his parents. Not a lot at first, but it was a start.

Addy stayed at his side, adding a lighter tone when subjects became awkward.

"Rebecca," Addy said. "Juli is the little girl I was talking about at the rodeo when I saw the Kindergarten Kowgirls. I didn't know she was your granddaughter at the time."

Rebecca turned to Juli. "Juli, do you like horses?"

"Uh-huh." Juli nodded. "Miss Paige is teaching me how to ride. She bought me a pink helmet, and next time, I get to ride Bitsy all by myself!"

Rebecca clapped her hands, then she leaned closer to Juli. "If your daddy says it's okay, I'd like for you to come out and ride Butterscotch sometime too."

"You have horses?" Juli asked.

"Yes. One very special horse that we bought a long time ago. She's been waiting and hoping that a little girl would want to ride her someday."

"Daddy!" Juli turned to Jack. "They have a special horse! Can I ride it?"

Jack smiled like he always did when Juli was happy. He curled her blonde hair behind her ear. "Maybe," he said.

Doug served platefuls of his weekend brisket with potato salad to everyone at the dining table. Conversations were polite but subdued, with no subject pushed too far, everyone seeming to understand that Jack needed time to ease back into a family that included more than just him and Juli.

Afterward, Jack held Juli's hand, just the two of them walking about the home, quietly discussing each of the childhood photographs displayed.

Addy stood back and watched. Lightly, Jack brushed his fingers against the photographs and gently touched the belongings that decorated the side tables and the credenza. His memories had to be strong.

Was he aware of the immeasurable love that existed here? She could feel it, but could he?

Rebecca came from the back porch, standing inside near Addy for a moment, watching too.

When Juli saw her, she asked, "Is the game ready, Grandma?"

Rebecca smiled and said, "Yes, it's all ready."

Jack released his daughter and watched her hurry to her grandmother, taking hold of her gentle reach.

"I like having a grandma!" Juli said to Rebecca.

"And I like having a granddaughter."

On the back porch near a big pot of mums, Juli sat with Doug and Rebecca, each with a glass of sweet tea. Patiently, they taught her the game of Parcheesi while she talked almost nonstop about all the things she wanted to do now that she had grandparents.

"I can't wait to tell Allison!" Juli giggled.

Out at the fire pit, Nick and Lindsey sat in Adirondack chairs, absorbed in the other's presence, talking and intermittently laughing together. A few times, Nick glanced back at the others, once catching Addy's attention with a smile, but otherwise, he kept a respectful distance so as not to disrupt the long-awaited reunion.

When the sun dipped below the horizon, leaving a painted sky behind, Jack took Addy's hand. In silence, they walked past Lindsey and Nick as they stacked wood inside the rust-colored steel pit.

Sounds of a healing family drifted, reaching into the distance, as Nick lit a fire, sending pecan-scented smoke into the air.

At the very back of the fenced acre, Jack stopped and looked upward into the night sky. He had loved

Kaitlin. He still loved Kaitlin. But Addy was a once-in-a-lifetime woman too.

Though the night was holding tight to its last glimmer of twilight, the moon rose above the housetop.

Jack stood, staring up at it, his arm around Addy. The spark, uniquely hers, settled within him. He pointed skyward. "Do you know what that is?"

"Pretty sure that's the moon," she teased.

"But it's not just any moon. It's a blue moon tonight." Jack stood steady, his arm around her. "It's a rarity. Like you." He glanced at her, catching a glimmer in her soulful hazel-green eyes. "Most years have twelve full moons—one for each calendar month. But every so often, a second full moon comes along in the same month."

Addy gazed at the luminescence of the crystalline orb, so bright. "Tonight is special," she said. "The heavens know." She leaned into Jack, inhaling the scent of him.

"Yes." Jack took Addy in a heart-to-heart embrace, whispering to her, "Once in a blue moon, true love comes along twice. Thank you for finding me."

AUTHOR'S NOTE:
OFFICIAL STATE FLOWER OF TEXAS:
BLUEBONNETS

BLUEBONNET, LUPINUS TEXENSIS AND
ANY OTHER VARIETY OF BLUEBONNET
(Supplementing LUPINUS SUBCARNOSUS
designated by Senate Concurrent Resolution No. 10,
27th Legislature, Regular Session (1901)

—House Concurrent Resolution No. 44,
62nd Legislature, Regular Session (1971)

The bluebonnet, a species of lupine, is the official state
flower of Texas as adopted by the Texas state legislature in 1901. Its sapphire blue petals are said to
resemble the sunbonnets worn by the pioneer women.

In March 1901, *Lupinus subcarnosus* became one of
the first state symbols. This variety is a smaller flower
that grows mainly in southern Texas, but over the
years, a movement formed, petitioning legislators to
change the official species to that of the *Lupinus texensis*,

which is a heartier blue and a showier flower, mainly found growing naturally in the Edwards Plateau and Blackland Prairie regions of Texas. Finally, in 1971, the state legislature agreed to revise the designation to "Lupinus Texensis and any Other Variety of Bluebonnet."

In Texas, *Lupinus texensis* is planted extensively along roadsides throughout the state but also thrives in open fields, prairies, and in home gardens.

The bluebonnet is said to be the most photographed flower in Texas.

A LOOK AT BOOK THREE:
LONE HEARTS OF TOPAZ

Award-winning author K.S. Jones brings to life another sweet, heartfelt contemporary western romance in the fan favorite *True Hearts of Texas* series!

Kelsey-Rose Flowers and Shane Delany were once the fairytale couple in the small town of Topaz, Texas. When Shane dies in an accident caused by Kelsey-Rose, her final gift to him is her promise to never love another. In the aftermath, she walks away from The Forty Flowers Ranch—her family's homestead and her inheritance. She turns to flowers instead of Texas Longhorns, opening a floral shop as a balm against the hurt she feels.

Colton Wilde, former Managing Editor of a Dallas area newspaper, buys *The Blue Topaz Times* and moves to Central Texas to begin a new life. The last thing he expects is to fall in love with the local florist…

In a parallel twist of fate, simultaneous tragedies force Colton to leave town, while Kelsey-Rose must return home to fulfill her ranching obligations—the last thing in the world she wants.

When the two are reunited, everything has changed—even her unbroken promise.

AVAILABLE MAY 2023

ABOUT THE AUTHOR

Karen (K.S.) Jones comes to us from the beautiful Texas Hill Country where she writes Historical Fiction and Contemporary Western Romance. In 2014, *Southern Writers* magazine awarded Karen their grand prize for "Best Short Fiction" of the year, and soon after, her first two novels, *Shadow of the Hawk*, Historical Fiction, and *Black Lightning*, a middle-grade sci-fi/fantasy, saw publication. Her work has garnered numerous literary awards, including the coveted WILLA Award from Women Writing the West in 2016, as well as the 2015 and 2017 Literary Classics International Book Award, the 2015 Chaucer Award, and the 2016 RONE Award. Her newest novel, CHANGE OF FORTUNE, was released this past February and within hours it rose to #30 on Amazon's list of top 100 in American Historical Romances. The novel is already in its third printing.

Made in the USA
Coppell, TX
07 November 2023

23911642R00184